Praise for Moira Rogers's
Deadlock

"The heat generated each time Carmen and Alec get together is nothing short of volcanic."
~ *Long and Short Reviews*

"...a great story which is capable of standing alone while still staying true to the other tales in the series. Both Alec and Carmen are well drawn characters, as each goes through their own growth and change."
~ *RT Book Reviews*

"Everything about this book, and series, is fantastic and will leave readers anxious for the next story."
~ *The Romance Studio*

"To say I enjoyed this book would be an understatement. I loved it! The suspense in DEADLOCK is off the charts with many unexpected twists that kept me guessing. And the heat! Oh, the heat."
~ *RR@H Novel Thoughts & Book Talk*

"The Southern Arcana series is one of my all time favorites. Anyone that enjoys novels featuring domineering Alpha wolves and the sassy women determined to show them the error of their ways will love Deadlock."
~ *Joyfully Reviewed*

"I lost myself within the story, completely enthralled, and experiencing it vicariously through the characters, totally forgetting that I was actually reading about it."
~ *Escape Between the Pages*

Look for these titles by
Moira Rogers

Now Available:

Southern Arcana Series
Crux
Crossroads
Deadlock
Cipher

Red Rock Pass Series
Cry Sanctuary
Sanctuary Lost
Sanctuary's Price
Sanctuary Unbound

Building Sanctuary Series
A Safe Harbor
Undertow

Bloodhound Series
Wilder's Mate

And the Beast Series
Sabine
Kisri

Children of the Undying Series
Demon Bait

Print Book Collections
Sanctuary
Sanctuary Redeemed
Building Sanctuary

Deadlock

Moira Rogers

SAMHAIN
PUBLISHING

Samhain Publishing, Ltd.
11821 Mason Montgomery Road, 4B
Cincinnati, OH 45249
www.samhainpublishing.com

Editing by Anne Scott
Cover by Kendra Egert

First Samhain Publishing, Ltd. electronic publication: January 2011
First Samhain Publishing, Ltd. print publication: December 2011

Dedication

This is dedicated to all of our Twitter peeps, who get us through the day with name suggestions, informal polls and laughter. And to all of Alec's fans, who've waited so patiently for his well-deserved happily-ever-after.

Chapter One

Alec wrenched himself out of the path of a flying fist and acknowledged, for the first time in his increasingly long life, that he might be getting old.

It didn't help that his opponent was a young, strong wolf. Andrew might still be adjusting to the new power inside him, but Alec had no doubts where the man would stand once he'd acclimated to life as a shapeshifter. Age would give the boy experience. Training would give him confidence.

Alec's days as the strongest wolf in New Orleans were numbered.

Instinct rebelled at the treacherous thought, and Alec threw a little something extra into his next swing, catching Andrew with a fast, brutal jab that landed on the younger man's chin and snapped his head around. Alec pressed the advantage out of habit, spilling his opponent to the thick mats lining the dojo floor.

All right, maybe his *years* were numbered.

Andrew lay on his back and blew out a long breath before rolling to his knees. "That won't happen again." It sounded more like a promise than a boast or threat.

That won't happen again. It was a promise Alec had heard plenty of times over the last six months, quiet and focused and always accomplished. He'd been told that surviving the transformation from human to wolf was like being born again, forced to navigate a body beyond one's control and instincts that were anything but human. In his lifetime Alec had mentored a dozen transformed wolves, but none of them had been like Andrew.

He held out his hand. "You're doing fine."

The third person in the room laughed, her rich voice echoing off the mirrored walls. Zola was dark, dark skin and dark hair and gorgeous chocolate eyes, a dangerous woman who moved with a grace that never failed to put Alec's instincts on high alert.

She prowled toward the center of the room as if she owned the place—which Alec supposed she did. The dojo was her home and her life, and though the rare shapeshifting cats in the area tended to be uninterested in the strict hierarchy under which the wolves thrived, she never passed up an opportunity to remind Alec that him being the top wolf in town didn't mean much to a lion.

Like now. "You are not doing fine like you could be," she declared. "Not if you are letting an old man like Alec beat you. You watch with your mind still, thinking too much. With humans, with other wolves like you, you can waste time thinking. Not with shapeshifters born. Alec does not think. Alec does not need to think, and so Alec wins."

Andrew smiled a little. "Then I guess I need to learn how not to think."

"Yes." After a moment, Zola unbent enough to return Andrew's smile. "You are good at learning. Alec can teach you to be a wolf, but soon he will be done. You will come to me, three days a week. My mate and I will teach you to fight like a lion."

She didn't wait for a response, as if she couldn't imagine a person turning down an offer of private lessons. Instead she pivoted and deigned to catch Alec's gaze. "I will be having a lesson in this room in one hour. You may stay until that time."

Alec nodded his thanks and waited until she strode past him and reached the stairs before turning his attention back to Andrew. "I'd think pretty seriously about taking her up on those lessons. She doesn't offer them often, and her man might be the only person in New Orleans more scary than she is."

"I know. I've asked...before." His eyes clouded for a moment, then he shook his head. "She turned me down flat. Guess I'm more interesting now."

"Times are more interesting now." Alec stretched slowly and could console himself, at least, with a lack of nagging aches. Damn impressive for a forty-four-year-old man who'd spent the last hour sparring with a man nearly two decades his junior. "If it helps, I don't think it's being a shifter that made the difference. Plenty of those get turned down too."

"So I've heard."

Not surprising. As far as Alec knew there was only one other person receiving Zola's exclusive, private tutelage at the moment, and he was too old and too jaded to believe it was a coincidence that Zola had offered the same to Andrew. Not considering who that other student was.

Following that train of thought would lead to a headache and an emotional quagmire Alec had no intention of stepping into this afternoon. Instead he gestured to the middle of the floor. "Ready for another go?"

Andrew answered with a quick right and left. Neither punch landed, but too late Alec realized they were meant to distract him. The other man came in low, hit him in the solar plexus, and knocked him onto the edge of the mat. "Yep. Ready."

Zola had one thing right—Andrew learned fast.

By the end of their practice, Andrew had dumped Alec on the floor twice, something that would have bruised Alec's ego a little more if he hadn't set the boy on his ass a round dozen times. He was extending his hand to help Andrew up from the latest fall when a creak on the stairs reminded him that he had very good reason to hustle them out of the room before Zola's other private student showed up—the one person Andrew didn't need to see.

Of course, the soft footsteps meant it was already too late. Even if he hadn't recognized that too-familiar tread, he couldn't miss the distinctive scent: hazelnut, vanilla and cinnamon, a combination that made his secretary—and therefore his office—smell like a bakery more often than not.

Alec dragged Andrew to his feet and turned in time to see Kat pause on the landing, her blue eyes widening a fraction before she hastily schooled her features. She lifted a hand and ran it through her hair in a newly acquired nervous gesture; the shorter, spiky haircut was just as recent, as were the wild streaks of color that made her look like she'd barely survived a fight with a set of finger-paints.

A lot had changed about Kat in the past year, but her gaze

still snapped straight to Andrew whenever she walked into a room, even though nothing lay between them anymore but bruised feelings and broken hearts. Kat stared at him for one painful second and looked away. Andrew went tense, his usual unflappable reserve shaken.

It hurt, watching them hurt, so Alec cleared his throat and broke the tense silence. "Hey, Kat, you here for your lesson?"

"Yeah." She stepped into the room and sidled to one side, keeping close to the mirrors, as if she needed the walls at her back. "Zola bumped me up from three to five times a week. Lucky me."

"We'll get out of your way." Andrew tossed a towel over his shoulder and lifted his gym bag, pausing only to flash Kat a tight smile before heading down the stairs.

Her face closed off, and Alec hated it. Even more, he hated that some predatory instinct inside him whispered a warning every time her eyes went cold. Six months ago, he'd seen the proof of how dangerous Kat could be. He'd had to deal with the two mindless, drooling husks that had remained after she'd focused her rage and pain as a weapon and used her empathic gifts like a scythe.

She'd destroyed two powerful shapeshifters with a thought, and only knowing it had killed something inside her made it possible for Alec to check his wariness and treat her the same way he always had—like a hapless young woman too sweet for the big, bad supernatural world.

The fierce look in Kat's eyes softened, leaving him wondering how much of his inner turmoil she could sense. She didn't enlighten him, just smiled wearily and shrugged one shoulder. "It's okay. He and Anna have been fucking like rabbits for months now, and I'm dating. I've got a date tonight. A hot, hot date, and if I go on enough of them I'm going to find someone else. Who the hell ends up with the first person they ever fell in love with, anyway?"

He had—for a while—and look how well it had gone. "Who's your date with?"

"None of your business."

"Jesus. You're touchy."

Kat dropped her gym bag and bent over to retrieve a handful of hair clips from it. "Yeah, because the overprotective assholes I work with keep abusing their private-investigator skills to terrorize my dates."

Alec grinned, pleased to see some of her humor returning. "Everyone's gotta have a hobby."

"What the hell ever, Alec. Get lost. I don't like getting humiliated in front of an audience."

He obeyed, still smiling. Downstairs, he found Andrew talking quietly with Zola as she flipped through a leather-bound schedule.

The blond man's tension hadn't faded. If anything, he looked like he wanted to bolt from the building. "Mornings would be best, honestly."

Mornings, which would presumably eliminate any chance of him running into Kat.

If Zola had drawn the same conclusion, she gave no indication. "For mornings, you will have to be arriving early. Before my beginners. Seven?"

"That's fine. I'll come in before work."

"Mondays, Wednesdays and Fridays."

"Got it. Thanks, Zola." Andrew tugged on a T-shirt and avoided Alec's gaze. "How's Kat?"

"Got a hot date tonight."

Alec had expected some sort of reaction, but clearly Andrew's momentary lapse was past. He showed no emotion as he replied, "That's nice."

"Yeah." *Don't poke him, don't fucking do it.* "She told me no one ends up with the first person they fall in love with."

Andrew hesitated, then exhaled on a quiet sigh. "I know you think I'm doing the wrong thing by Kat, and I don't blame you. But don't you think you've smacked me around enough for one day?"

Guilt and annoyance and frustration formed a sickening knot in Alec's gut, reminding him of all the reasons he did his best to avoid thinking overly long about Andrew and Kat. His instincts didn't know which way to jump, who to blame and who to protect—probably because there *was* no answer.

Except Andrew had no one else who could understand, so Alec made an effort. "I know you're doing your best, but I know the truth too. I saw you the day you rose from the ground as a new wolf, and you only needed one thing. You needed her, and needing her that hard, in the shape you were in...you had to let her go. One slip and she'd be dead, or you would be, because she'd turned your brain to pulp, and she'd never survive that." He dragged in a breath. "I know all of it, Andrew, and I still want to kill you some days because you made that girl cry until her heart broke, and I couldn't do a damn thing to stop it."

Andrew stared at him for a long moment and nodded. He hefted his bag again and patted the counter in front of Zola. "I'll see you Monday."

Then he walked out.

Zola tilted her head to the side and regarded Alec from those darkly exotic eyes. "My English has been learned many places, from many people. It is not always...precise. But when I am arriving in New Orleans, I have heard one thing again and again, until I finally asked what these words mean."

"Don't suppose it was *Mind your own business*?"

"Alec Jacobson is a jackass."

Imprecise though her English might be, Zola had no trouble landing a verbal blow. Alec refused to give her the satisfaction of a reaction. "Nice to be popular."

Zola shook her head. "Wolves have no subtlety. Why speak words that hurt without purpose?"

"He needed to know."

"Even I am seeing that he knows. Only a fool would be thinking he doesn't know."

The woman was starting to get on his nerves. "Fine. I'm a fool."

Zola smiled and walked from behind the counter. "No, you are maybe something else, something you want no one to make comments about. I am thinking you are a romantic. You want a happy ending for Andrew and Katherine?"

Once upon a time, it wouldn't have been an insult. Once upon a time, he'd been young and stupid, had told his rich, snotty family to go fuck themselves and had married his one true love, a no-name human who had roused everything good and protective inside him. She'd made him a man, made him a lover, made him whole.

In return, his family had made her disappear. One night, one bullet...

Once upon a time, he'd thought the pain would fade with the passage of years and the comfort of his vicious revenge. He *was* a fool.

Andrew wasn't, so he would do the one thing Alec hadn't. He'd keep the woman he loved alive. Kat would heal from a broken heart, but she'd never survive a life chained to the violence of Andrew's new world.

Zola had paused at the foot of the stairs, her eyebrows pulled together and an uncertain frown curving her lips. "Alec?"

The press of her sudden sympathy was unbearable. Alec snatched up his bag and strode toward the door. "I'm not interested in happy endings." A lie, but only a little one. After all, his happy ending had died and forgotten to take him with it.

Chapter Two

Carmen picked up the last chart and rubbed her eyes. "I haven't gotten used to Franklin's handwriting yet."

Tara, the clinic's senior nurse, snorted. "Yours isn't much better. You came from a hospital with electronic charting." It wasn't a question.

"Busted. Vanderbilt's ER even has a computerized whiteboard."

"You're from Nashville?" Tara leaned one hip on the desk and eyed Carmen. "How do you like the Big Easy so far?"

"I love the city. I always have." She was no stranger to New Orleans. Her best friend had already moved to Louisiana, and it was her recommendation that had led to Carmen's decision to join Franklin Sinclaire's small clinic.

Lily's recommendation, and Carmen's own heritage. The clinic served the public as well as the underground supernatural population of New Orleans, witches and shapeshifters and psychics who had no other place to turn to for help with their unique medical problems.

It was outside the realm of what she'd learned officially, but Franklin had proven a skilled teacher. After four short months, he apparently felt comfortable enough with her performance to leave her in charge of some of the day-to-day operations at the clinic.

A wave of intense and foreign curiosity washed over her. Carmen took a deep breath, methodically built the mental walls necessary to block out Tara's emotions and smiled. "You were either a cat in a past life, or you have more questions for me."

The woman blushed. "Is it that obvious?"

"Only to an empath." Carmen's phone chimed, and she checked the display to find a text message from her brother Miguel. *See you @ 8.* "Is it always this dead on Friday nights?"

"Don't say that," the younger woman warned as she gathered the completed charts and turned toward the tiny filing room behind the desk. "It draws them in like flies."

And I thought people in the ER were superstitious. "My kid brother's meeting me here in an hour. We're having dinner."

The petite blonde stuck her head out of the filing room. "Is he cute?"

"He's young," Carmen answered automatically. "Only twenty-one."

"When you say 'kid', you're not joking."

"I was twelve when he was born." Her phone chirped again, this time indicating an incoming call. "Speaking of brothers, there's my other one."

"Older?"

"Younger." She grinned. "But only by a couple of years. He's a firefighter in Charleston."

Tara laughed. "Come to mama."

The lobby door buzzed, and Carmen hit the button to ignore the call on her cell phone. If it was important, Julio would keep trying until she finally answered. For now, she had work to do.

That work happened to be a stuffy nose soon treated and dispatched. It was a far cry from the busy hustle to which Carmen was accustomed, but that was nice in its own way.

Tara winked as she handed Carmen a can of soda. "Calm before the storm. It'll pick up later, but that's the night shift's problem." The door buzzed again, and she snorted. "On the other hand, maybe people got a head start on the night."

It was only Miguel. "Almost ready to go?"

Carmen couldn't leave until her shift replacement showed up, ready to work, but she was more interested in the wave of nervous energy that had accompanied Miguel into the lobby. "Are you all right?"

"Sure." He smiled, bright and brittle.

He was the worst liar she'd ever met. She didn't bother to shield the thought from him, and his sudden look of guilty discomfort told her he'd caught it, loud and clear. Carmen let it drop. "Where are we going to eat?"

"I'm in the mood for steak. How about Besh?"

"That place in Harrah's?" Carmen groaned. "I'm not dressed for it, and I don't want to go all the way over there either. Can we pick up a pizza and take it to my place instead?"

The discomfort sharpened, and she realized she could not only see it on her brother's face, but feel it as well. He looked away. "Car..."

If he didn't want to alter his plans, it could only mean one thing. Carmen shivered. "Harrah's. Who's here, Dad or Uncle Cesar?"

He rubbed his face and leaned on the counter. "Both."

"Both? That's new." They couldn't be there for a visit, because neither of them gave a damn about her. "What do they want?"

"You didn't answer their calls or letters, and they—"

"That's why they're here, not what they want." She fought to keep her tone even. It wasn't Miguel's fault their father and uncle could still manipulate him, and did so at every opportunity.

"I don't—" The denial rose but, to Miguel's credit, he choked it back. "Shit, okay. They want to introduce you to some guy."

A politically advantageous marriage, no doubt. "Tell them no, but thank you."

"Carmen, just come to dinner. Then say no, if you want."

Someone entered the lobby with enough roiling emotion to hit Carmen like a blow, and she bit her lip to hold back a pained moan. "Go sit, Miguel. I'll be a while."

He started to argue, then caught sight of the young woman who'd walked into the clinic. She was almost as tall as Carmen, with spiky short hair that bore nearly every color in the rainbow.

Her wide blue gaze darted around the room, skipping over Tara and only lingering for a heartbeat on Miguel before fixing on Carmen. "Franklin's not here?"

"No, I'm sorry." She eased around the counter, taking care not to move too quickly. The girl had a swollen lip, and one eye was red and puffy, like she'd been hit. "I'm Carmen. Come in the back and sit down."

"It's bad. It's *bad*." The girl tightened her grip on the strap of her bag until her knuckles turned white. "There's a body. I mean, he's not dead, but I didn't know how long my stun gun could keep a shapeshifter down and I panicked and called Alec, and if Franklin's not here to calm him down it's going to be so bad. I should—I should go before he sees me..."

Tara held the cordless phone in her hand. "Should I call someone?"

The police or Franklin, the nurse could mean either—or both. "Not yet." Carmen touched the girl's shoulder and braced herself against the immediate jolt of emotion that ripped through her. "We can deal with your friend when he gets here. If not, I'll page Franklin. He'll hustle right over."

The girl laughed, and it sounded hysterical. "No one can deal with Alec Jacobson when someone he cares about just got punched in the face."

Carmen recognized the name. She was confident in her ability to handle almost anything, but a black-sheep alpha wolf with a questionable reputation might be beyond her. "All right. Tara, call Franklin. We'll be in room three."

The girl let Carmen lead her down the hall to the last examination room on the right. Franklin had laid out a lot of money to have the room warded specifically for psychic magic, and that could be important once the girl's shock began to wear off. "What's your name, honey?"

"Kat. Katherine. Katherine Gabriel. I—I have a file, I think. I need to go to the..." She trailed off as they stopped in front of the room, which she clearly recognized. "Yes. This one. You can tell I'm psychic?"

"So am I." Carmen started to reach for a gown, but thought better of it. "I can't tell what kind, but I can sense it."

The confession seemed to settle her a little. "Empath. Me, I mean." Her lips tugged down into a frown. "You are too, aren't you? You feel...feely."

"I guess I must." She helped Kat onto the table and reached for the ophthalmoscope hanging on the wall. "I'm going to use a light to look in your eyes. It might be a little uncomfortable."

"I'm okay. I got punched in the face a couple times. It's all uphill from there, I guess."

"That's one way to look at it." She started examining Kat,

quickly but carefully, checking for lingering signs of trauma. "What happened?"

"I'm not sure. I—I was on a date. We walked out to where he'd parked his car, but I guess he'd locked his keys in it? So I was going to call someone I knew who could spring the lock, but then..." Her voice trailed off into uncertainty. "It happened so fast."

"Someone attacked you?" Carmen prompted.

"Him. They attacked him first. My date." Another pause. "I think. He turned his back on me and I got out my stun gun, but shifters move fast. He knocked me back into the car..." Kat lifted a hand and rubbed at the back of her head. "I don't think it's bleeding."

"You hit your head?" The girl's pupils were even and reacted well to light, but head injuries could be tricky. "What else do you remember?"

"I don't remember where my date ended up." Her fingers curled around the edge of the exam table. "I think he ran while I was trying to get the shapeshifter off me."

She sounded so lost. Carmen spent a moment shoring up her mental defenses. "Kat, do you think there's a chance that—"

Noise and voices in the hallway distracted her from her question. One belonged to Tara, raised and pitched in distress. "Look, you can't go back there. You have to—"

The door slammed open.

Alec Jacobson—because it *had* to be him—was tall, solid and angry as hell. Not that Carmen could feel his emotions, not with the shielding on the room, but it didn't take an empath to see the man was pissed. Dark eyes fixed on Kat as his jaw clenched under his neatly trimmed beard. "Katherine LeBlanc Gabriel, tell me the bastard's name *right now*."

Kat heaved a tortured sigh and gave Carmen a look that clearly said, *I told you so.*

Tara skidded to a halt behind him. "I tried to stop him."

"It's okay. I've got it." Carmen rose to stand between the man and Kat, careful to keep her gaze steady but not challenging. "Out."

"No." He didn't raise his voice. He didn't have to, not when he could convey so much arrogant confidence in one word. "Katherine? The name."

"Damn it, Alec, it wasn't my date. And I didn't ask the mugger for an introduction while I was tasering his ass, okay?"

Carmen took a deep breath. "You're upsetting my patient. Please step out into the hallway. I'm not going to ask again."

For the first time, the man looked away from Kat and fixed that piercing stare on Carmen. His gaze traced her face, as if he was looking for something in particular, and he frowned. "You're the Mendoza girl."

It wasn't a question, but he seemed to be waiting for some sort of response regardless. "Dr. Mendoza. I notice you're not moving yet."

Kat's voice came from behind her. "You're wasting your time. He's not going to—"

Alec took a step backwards, then a second, until he stood squarely in the hall.

"—whoa."

Carmen turned to Kat. "Sit tight. I'll be right back." She could calm the man down, or at the very least distract him until Franklin arrived.

Except that, once she'd closed the door, she wasn't quite sure what to do or say. She shoved her hands into the back pockets of her jeans and tried to smile. "Thank you. She's had a rough night."

Worry tightened his expression. "What happened?"

"She and her date were attacked. She's shaken up, has some minor injuries and might have hit her head. But she's mostly scared of what you might do."

"No she's not," Alec replied, voice steady. "She's scared I'm going to call her cousin, her cousin's oh-so-scary little wife, my partner, my partner's pissy alpha bitch girlfriend, and we're going to form a posse and kill some folk. And to be fair, she should be."

"All right," Carmen conceded. "But that's a hard thing to have on your conscience, so cut her some slack and hold off on calling together the mob, okay?"

Alec raised one eyebrow. "How much do you know about your family's political activities?"

"About *my* family?" The question was so unexpected that all she could do for a moment was gape at him. "What could that possibly have to do with anything?"

"I didn't mean—" He rubbed at his beard. "Shapeshifter politics, then. Wolves. Franklin told me you don't get tangled up in the politics, but he never said if you knew the first thing about them."

She wanted to ask him what the hell he'd been doing, talking to Franklin about her. Instead, she shrugged and tried not to get defensive. "Enough to recognize that there's a big damn difference between shapeshifters and shapeshifter politics. What do you really want to know?"

"Do you know who John Wesley Peyton is?"

"He's the Alpha. Has been for years."

"Yeah." Alec pointed at the room where Kat sat. "That girl's overprotective cousin just married Peyton's daughter. Unless you're a witch who's gonna magic those bruises off her face, the only way to stop mob action is for me to take care of it now. Fast."

"Right. Where is her cousin?"

"Wyoming."

"Then you've got a few hours." Arguing was getting them nowhere. "Look, my priority is making sure Kat's all right. Give me ten minutes to check her out, and I'll ask her to talk to you. I promise."

"Fine." The corner of his mouth tugged up. "Better go let your nurse yell at me. Sinclaire gets pissy when I rile up his employees."

The smile transformed his forbiddingly handsome face, and Carmen had to remind herself not to stare. "With good reason." God, she sounded breathless. "Your reputation precedes you, Alec Jacobson."

For some reason the words made him flinch. "So I've heard."

She hadn't meant it as an insult, but trying to explain would only make it worse. "I'm sorry."

He waved it away. "Not your fault. I am a raging jackass. Comes with the gig."

The casual words disguised real pain, and she had to take a step back before she reached out to comfort him. "Wait in the lobby. I'll let you know how Kat is once I finish her exam."

Alec pulled a battered cell phone from his pocket and turned away. "I've got a few calls to make anyway, but tell Kat

I'm not going to call her cousin. Yet."

"Sure." His back was broad under the tight black T-shirt he wore, and his jeans were just worn enough to—

Carmen dragged her gaze away from his receding form. She was trembling a little from the effort of keeping up her emotional shields, so she turned and ducked quickly back into the room.

Kat was eyeing the door with obvious worry, and Carmen smiled. "Alec's going to hold off on calling your cousin, but you'll have to talk to him when we're done here."

Some of the tension bled out of her. "I don't want them to worry. My cousin and his wife, I mean. His sister-in-law just had a baby, and they need to be up there with her, not down here pulling muggers apart."

"I got the feeling there wouldn't be much left by the time your cousin arrived."

The girl's lips pressed together. "Yes, Alec is good at cleaning up my messes. You'd think they'd stop acting like I'm helpless, though, since I'm the one who keeps leaving bodies on the ground."

There was something hopeless and chilling in the words, and Carmen fought a shiver as she pulled on a pair of gloves. "I'm most worried about your head. If you smacked it on the car like you said, I mean."

"It hurts." Her fingers drifted up to her head again. "It aches. I think I smacked it pretty good."

"If that's true, you might need to go to the hospital, get a head CT."

"No. *No.*" Both of Kat's hands dropped to the edge of the exam table, as if she was expecting Carmen to pry her off and throw her out. "I have to stay in this room, especially if I have something wrong with my head. I can't be outside the shields."

Even if Carmen kept her at the clinic for observation, watching for complications to arise, there wasn't much she'd be able to do about them. A hemorrhage would probably require surgical intervention, something beyond her capabilities on the best of days. Franklin might be able to handle it in a pinch, but not with the clinic facilities. "We can't fix a brain bleed in this room, Kat."

Kat's stony expression didn't waver. "The last time I got

scared and lost control, I killed someone. I'm not going to a hospital full of people. If something happened, I wouldn't care if I lived or not."

She could have understood depression or hopelessness, but the sheer, steely resolve of the girl's words scared the hell out of Carmen. "What if I knew someone—a psychic? A telepath who could come in here, peek in your head and tell me if anything seemed off?"

Silence, as Kat's eyes narrowed. "What's their name?"

Clearly, she didn't trust that anyone Carmen could suggest would be someone she didn't already know. "It's my brother, Miguel. The guy in the lobby."

Kat tilted her head, her icy chill thawing to curious interest. "So you're an empath and he's a telepath? It must have been strong in your family, for both of you to be psychic."

She helped Kat peel her brightly colored cardigan down off her shoulders. "Think that's impressive? My other brother, Julio? He's the overachiever of the family. A precognitive *and* a shapeshifter."

"Really? Is it reliable? Strong?"

"There aren't many guys in his fire house who'll—" Carmen sucked in a sharp breath as she caught sight of numerous contusions marring Kat's arms. Only a few were fresh, and most carried the sickly yellow tinge of at least a week's age. "How did you get these bruises?"

Kat blinked and looked down. "Oh, fuck. That's why I wore the sweater. I swear, it's not what it looks like."

If she had a dollar for every time she'd heard that, she wouldn't have to work. "Has someone been hurting you, Kat?" Carmen looked her dead in the eye as she asked. Not many people could prevaricate without hesitation.

"Well, yeah. But I'm paying her to." Kat held up both arms and studied the bruises with something approaching pride. "Self-defense lessons. Have you ever heard of Zola? She's a shapeshifter. A lion. And she can set Alec on his ass, though he won't ever fight with her in front of anyone else. I think it stings his manly ego to get schooled by a girl."

Carmen didn't need empathy to see the truth in the girl's words. "Okay. How many fingers am I holding up?"

"Uh, three? Are you going to have your brother look at my

head?"

"It's either that or a trip to the hospital for that CT we talked about." Carmen eased up to sit beside Kat on the exam table. "Does it bother you, the thought of having someone you don't know poking around in your head?"

"Not really. A lot less than the thought of having someone I do know poking around in there." Kat smiled wanly. "It's been a long year. I've had a few uncharitable thoughts, and I wouldn't want to hurt anyone's feelings. I know they're doing their best."

"It'd be reasonable, you know, if it bothered you. It would me, and most everyone else too."

"That would make me a little bit of a hypocrite, wouldn't it? I'm strong. Too strong to block out everything, unless I want to give myself a permanent migraine. People don't get much privacy from me."

She sounded sad, and Carmen didn't blame her. Outside the warded confines of this room, she had to be beset on all sides by other people's emotions. Everything they felt, Kat felt. It was a surprisingly lonely way to live, enough to drive a person insane. "I'm lucky. My abilities are low, midlevel at most, and I've had a lot of training. I can block pretty much anything, if I concentrate."

"Yeah. I can't." Kat dropped her hands back to her lap, her fingers toying with the loose, flowing fabric of her long dress. "With great power comes a great need for jumbo bottles of Advil."

"Then maybe you and Miguel have more in common than I thought." Carmen peeled off her gloves as she slid off the table. "I'll go get him, and maybe hold off your glowering friend for a few more minutes, hmm?"

"Thanks. I didn't mean to cause so much trouble, but I panicked. I'm feeling better now, I swear."

"You're probably going to be fine. Humor me for a little while longer."

Kat wrinkled her nose. "Humoring people is my part-time job."

Halfway down the hall toward the lobby, Carmen heard Miguel laugh. "No, see... To hear my grandmother tell it, she never actually married Primo Ochoa before she ran off with my grandfather. And really, who can blame her for it? The Mendoza charm is legendary."

"Uh-huh. Well, the current crop of Ochoa boys are famous for being the least charming bastards of their generation." Alec sounded amused, as well. "Meanwhile, I hear your big brother just about caused a riot by laying a little Mendoza charm on the oldest Reed girl. Didn't he get challenged over it?"

"Twice," Carmen answered. "Set her brother *and* her cousin on their asses. Miguel, can you help me out for a minute?"

"Sure." He shoved his cell phone in his pocket. "What is it?"

"Kat whacked her head, but she wants to avoid the hospital. She's willing to let you take a look, make sure nothing's scrambled."

Alec frowned. "Does she need to go? If so, she's going. Over my shoulder, if necessary."

Deadly handsome or not, the man was *infuriating*. "Sit down, for Christ's sake. No one's going anywhere over anyone's shoulder."

His gaze tracked along as Miguel made his way down the hallway, but Alec gave in and dropped into a chair. "What's he going to do?"

For a moment, she debated following her brother to make sure Kat was at ease while he did what he needed to do. But what she'd told the girl was true—she and Miguel probably had plenty in common, and not many people felt ill-at-ease with him.

She settled into a chair across from Alec's. "He's a telepath. It's hard to explain exactly how he reads thoughts, but...suffice it to say, if she has head trauma from the attack, he'll know."

"Ah, yeah." He inclined his head. "I forgot about the Mendoza psychics. Stupid of me."

The words held recrimination, but it was directed at himself, and Carmen got the distinct impression that he prided himself on knowing all the facts of a situation, on exhaustively examining a situation for every possible outcome.

Except that wasn't it, not exactly. It wasn't a matter of taking pride in his own preparedness—it was a matter of necessity. "It bothers you when you think you've dropped the ball."

His face closed off and his eyes narrowed. "Obviously I get that empaths can't help picking shit up, but it's rude to rub it in our faces."

Something about the man turned her into a complete ass. "Psych rotation, not empathy, but you're right. It was impolite. I'm sorry."

Alec just shook his head and rubbed at his jaw. "Me too. I'm pissy. Shouldn't be taking it out on you, but I'm at my wit's end with that girl."

Franklin had explained to her the unique nature of some of their cases, and how they couldn't always be handled the way she was used to. Sometimes patient confidentiality had to be set aside.

Still, some things had been ingrained in Carmen, and she debated how much to share with Alec. Finally, she said, "Kat told me why she needs to stay in the warded room. About what happened the last time she had a meltdown."

"She did, huh?" The words were flat, but a sliver of surprise wiggled past her shields. "She doesn't talk about that much."

Carmen braced her elbows on her knees and folded her hands together. "I got the feeling she doesn't know many other empaths."

"A few, but she's..." He shrugged. "Have you ever heard of Callum Tyler? The British empath?"

"I have." The man was highly gifted, highly trained—and very much in demand.

"He owed a friend of ours a favor, so he came here over the winter. Helped get her grounded, shielded, whatever psychics do." His dry tone made it clear he hadn't inquired too closely.

Tyler had a reputation for being effective in all but the worst of cases. "So why does she seem to think none of that matters, and more people are going to wind up dead if she steps out of that room?"

Alec looked away, presenting her with his hard profile. "He wasn't impressed with her level of training, and he was *too* impressed with how strong she is. Guess that's a dangerous combination. He's coming back this summer for another round of lessons."

So the man had chastised Kat's friends and family, and Alec resented it. Carmen knew from experience how unhelpful blatant criticism could be, even when it was deserved. "I don't have any answers. I wish I did."

"I think she's got control, but I don't know how it works. Could a concussion make her lose it?"

"Maybe," she admitted. "Can you stay with her tonight? Someone should."

That earned her a snort of laughter. "Already called a friend. I can stick around until she shows up, but Kat's better off with someone a little more...comforting."

"Okay." Carmen stood. "I'm going to go check on things. Miguel might need my help."

"Can I come? I'll keep my mouth shut."

She figured that was as good as it got. "Sure."

The door was slightly ajar, and Carmen knocked before pushing it open to find Kat and Miguel standing by the exam table. Kat had a pen in hand and was writing on Miguel's outstretched palm, her lips curved up in a smile. "I'm pretty much done with my grad work for the semester. I took a term off from teaching labs, so I finished all my projects early."

"Yeah? Great. I've got a couple of classes to finish up this spring, and then I'm done."

Carmen cleared her throat. "How is she?"

"Fine, just fine. Jacobson can relax." Miguel didn't look away from Kat as he smiled and took the pen from her. "Give me a call."

"I will. Or you call me when you've got some time. I know finals are coming up."

"See you around, Kat." He eased past Carmen and Alec and out the door.

The faintest hint of pink rose in Kat's cheeks, and she studiously avoided Alec as she fiddled with the strap on her bag. "It's not a thing. He just...gets it. Not being able to shut the psychic stuff off, I mean."

Lying was useless, but Carmen managed to keep the censure out of her voice. "I admit I would have preferred he wait to ask you out until we were sure you weren't suffering from an altered mental state."

"He didn't ask me out. I asked him for his number." She shot Alec a defiant look. "If I wake up tomorrow and decide I'm not interested, I'll screen my calls. I'm a big girl."

Alec looked like he wanted to retort, but when he finally spoke, his voice came out mild. "I'm glad you're feeling steadier, kiddo. I called Jackson and Mac. Mackenzie will be around to pick you up and take you back to their place as soon as the good doctor here's ready to let you go. Hold off going out on any more dates until you get some sleep, would you?"

She could have sent Kat on right then, but Carmen laid a hand on her shoulder instead. "I'll get you a cold pack for that eye, and I have a few more questions for you."

Kat nodded. "You can go, Alec. I'm okay. Just promise me you and Jackson aren't going to go track down my date and eat him."

"Not going to track him down."

"Or eat him."

The corner of Alec's mouth twitched. "Or eat him."

Kat narrowed her eyes. "Fuck if I can tell if you're telling the truth while I'm in this room. So go before I change my mind."

"Will do." Alec looked to Carmen. "You can keep her company until Mackenzie gets here?"

She was past due to leave. The night-shift doctor had probably already arrived and was hiding out in the lounge, drinking coffee. "I'll stay with her until then."

"Thanks. And I'll see you"—he pointed at Kat, adopting a mock scowl—"no earlier than noon tomorrow. Take the morning off."

Kat gave him a sloppy salute. "Yes, sir. Call me if you forget how to log into your email."

With another of those odd, short laughs, Alec turned, his eyes catching Carmen's for one moment. His stare was deep, intense, full of quick flashes of emotion she couldn't begin to read, especially within the shields of the room. Though it was impossible to tell what prompted the odd darkness, he looked almost frustrated.

Almost.

There was a strange heat lurking in that inscrutable stare, one that left her fighting a hot blush. She opened and closed her mouth, suddenly unsure of what to say. "Good night."

"Good night, Dr. Mendoza." Then, with a small, enigmatic smile, he left, pulling the door closed behind him.

"Well," Kat said without preamble. "He thinks you're hot."

The proclamation made Carmen's stomach twist with

nerves and something undeniably like anticipation. She ignored the words as well as the emotions and pulled an instant cold pack from the cabinet, activating it with a snap. "If the swelling in your eye doesn't go down in a day or so, you'll need to see an ophthalmologist."

"An eye doctor, I'm guessing?"

"Right." Carmen wrapped the pack and handed it to Kat. "You should be feeling more in control by the time that's an issue. If it's an issue."

"Hey." Kat closed her hand on Carmen's before she could pull away. "I'm sorry. I've blurted out enough dumb crap by now to know when I crossed a line. I just thought... Well, you know. Women seem to think Alec's hot shit. I didn't think you'd be upset."

Carmen couldn't stop the laugh that bubbled up. "He *is* hot shit. And I'm not upset." Not like Kat thought, not at all, but her past romantic entanglements were hardly an appropriate topic of conversation. "It's fine."

"Okay." She looked a little dubious, but she released Carmen's hand. "And don't give your brother a hard time. I really did ask for his number. He was...refreshing. He was in here five whole minutes and didn't once promise to find the asshole who'd punched me and kill him. Shapeshifter guys can be kinda exhausting."

"Yeah, tell me about it." Carmen was attracted to strong, dominant men. Shifters tended to fit the bill, but her relationships with them had a tendency to fail spectacularly, so she'd sworn off them entirely. That way, she didn't have to spend weeks after every bad breakup cursing her own bad judgment, and she didn't have to risk the sorts of matches her family might try to force her into.

She glanced at the door. She didn't have a clue how Uncle Cesar felt about the Jacobson family, but if there was the slightest advantage to be gained, he'd probably jump at the chance to throw her at Alec.

Which only reinforced the fact that she had to stay far, far away from him.

Chapter Three

Alec didn't bother looking for Jackson as he eased his truck into the small parking lot in front of Kat's apartment. No doubt his partner had hidden himself behind his favorite spell as soon as his girlfriend had dropped him off, which meant Alec's best bet was to park his truck and wait for Jackson to make his presence known.

He chose a space a few doors down from Kat's, a spot next to a compact import that gave him a fair amount of coverage without sacrificing line-of-sight on Kat's door.

There was a sudden thump on the passenger door of his truck, and Jackson stood there. Instead of motioning for Alec to open the door, he grinned and passed his hand over it. The lock disengaged with a dull snap.

"Got you a soda." Jackson tossed a can at Alec as he climbed up into the truck.

Alec barely managed to catch the damn thing before it smashed into his face. "While you were invisible? If Kat hears rumors about a haunted snack machine, she's gonna yell at us both."

"Nah, I delurked long enough to hit the vending machines over by the laundry room."

He didn't have the faintest idea where the laundry room was, since his experience with Kat's apartment building began and ended with the parking lot in front of it and a nagging concern that security there wasn't nearly tight enough now that Kat's cousin had married into the most important shapeshifting family in the country.

A worry for another time. Alec cracked open the soda and watched two teenagers stroll down the sidewalk in front of them. "I left Kat with the doctor at the clinic. The new one Franklin hired a few months back."

"I remember." Jackson snorted. "You've already bitched my ear off about how Franklin's compromising his clinic's neutrality by hiring on a member of the Mendoza clan."

Alec fought a flinch. "It's a valid concern. Her uncle's spent the last six months putting his ducks in a row so he can get his hands on that empty Conclave seat. For all I knew, she was one of his ducks."

"For all you *knew*, past tense?" He squinted at Alec and chuckled. "She's cute, isn't she?"

Smooth dark hair, smoky brown eyes, curves to make a pin-up jealous... *Cute* was puppies and kids. Carmen Mendoza was a guilty fantasy come to life. "Sure. Sending hot women to spy is pretty much an institution, isn't it? Or is that just in movies? I can't remember."

"Oh yeah. I'm sure, between the sprained ankles and the nasal allergies, she's gathering some *fierce* intel over there."

Appearing casual was vital, since Alec had given Jackson hell over the man's descent into idiocy whenever Mackenzie Brooks blinked those big blue eyes at him. Unfortunately, appearing casual had never been his specialty. "Fuck off, Holt."

"Jesus, have a sense of humor." Jackson stretched his legs out as much as the cab of the truck would allow. "Mackenzie said Kat liked her a lot. The doctor, I mean."

It figured that Jackson's girlfriend had already retrieved Kat. For all the complaints Alec got about his lead foot, everyone knew Mackenzie was the one who drove like she was looking to run the NASCAR circuit. "Not surprising. Doctor's an empath. Low level, I think, but still." He hesitated, but setting Jackson on the case of future trouble might mean he wouldn't have to deal with it. "She also has a smarmy telepathic brother who's already wheedled Kat's phone number out of her."

"Smarmy?" Jackson considered that for a moment. "From what I've heard, that's par for the Mendoza course."

"You mean the shit with the oldest one? Julio?" Alec couldn't help but laugh, though he didn't feel particularly amused. "Gotta give the Mendoza propaganda machine their due. Only Cesar Mendoza could spin the fact that his little brother snuck off and played house with a psychic for over a decade. Talk to the man for more than ten minutes, and he'll find a way to let you know the Mendozas are so badass that they father shapeshifting sons on human women. Asshole."

"It is quite the manly feat, if you overlook the part where Diego dumped his wife as soon as his big brother told him to."

Alec knew Jackson hadn't meant anything by it, but he still tensed. Some things he'd never forget—his cousin, telling him that the family wouldn't stand for the embarrassment of Alexander Jacobson the Third being married to a human. That night, he'd found his wife on the kitchen floor, surrounded by half-thawed bits of broccoli.

A few years ago, the memory would have paralyzed him. Liquor would have been the only cure. Now he took refuge in temper. "Because we all know staying is a brilliant fucking plan."

Jackson stared at him for a moment and turned his attention to the building in front of them. "Best description Mac was able to get out of Kat was that the attacker was tall and blond. Her date, on the other hand, was shorter, with dark hair. If either shows up, it shouldn't be hard to tell them apart."

There was no question Jackson was pissed, but Alec didn't have the emotional reserves to navigate an apology or—worse— a conversation about Heidi and the past that felt too raw today. Instead he accepted the tacit change of subject and tried to turn it into a peace offering. "Kat did real good. Zola says she's been working hard, and obviously she has. She held off the guy with her stun gun."

"Yeah." Jackson pulled out his phone, punched a few keys and held it out. "That's the date. I ran a check on him already. Nothing in the NCIC database, but that doesn't mean he's clean."

Alec took the phone gingerly. It was the exact same model Kat had purchased for him at the beginning of the year, after she'd proclaimed them both woefully out of date and behind the times. Jackson had adapted to his just fine. Alec had gotten a week's worth of silent treatment from Kat for trading his back in for a phone that didn't try to load up the internet or play music every time he wanted to make a call.

He'd hated the thing, but he had to admit it had its uses as he studied the picture. A young man, probably midtwenties, smiled back at him. Dark hair, dark eyes, nothing remarkable about his face aside from a tiny bump in his nose. Probably a

shapeshifter, unless Kat had broken her habit from the last five
dates. If he was a shapeshifter, he didn't come from any of the
prominent families. "What's his name?"

"Christopher Gilbert." Jackson hesitated. "Maybe."

"Maybe?"

"Everything I could dig up on him is too neat. There aren't
any holes. Like someone sat down and came up with his story
all at once."

"Kat would have run his info..." Alec sighed. "But she
wouldn't notice that. Damn. You should be the one to tell her."

Jackson tapped his knuckles against the passenger
window. "Yeah, I'll handle it."

Still pissy. Alec scrubbed his hand against the side of his
face and forced himself to apologize. Kind of. "Sorry, man. It's
been a shit day. Kat showed up while me'n Andrew were still at
the dojo."

"That couldn't have been pleasant."

"I keep hoping I'll turn around and she'll be over it. So
far..."

"She's doing the best she can." Jackson flashed him a
knowing look. "And, from the looks of it, so is Andrew."

Great. The supernatural gossip mill was operating at full
speed. The fact that Andrew's best friend was married to
Jackson's best friend didn't help matters. "You got an earful
from Nicole on the subject, I'm guessing?"

"She says you're being insufferable again, and someone
should smack you for it."

"According to half the town, that's pretty much business as
usual."

"You could try to—" Jackson's words cut off as magic
shuddered through the truck. "Someone just set off the wards I
laid around Kat's balcony doors."

Alec popped his door open. "Take the front. I'll circle
around to the balcony."

Jackson grinned. "He shouldn't be too hard to run down."
With those cryptic words, he slid out of the truck and
disappeared.

Once Alec rounded the side of the building and got a good
look at the courtyard under Kat's window, he figured out what
Jackson had meant. A tall blond man lay huddled on the grass

a few feet away from one of the downstairs neighbor's plastic chairs. Whatever spell Jackson had twisted into the wards had clearly triggered as soon as the man had gotten his hands on the railing.

Fear spell. Alec had seen it enough times to recognize the aftermath, and it made it easy to drag the man to his feet. He stumbled as if drunk, which would hopefully explain to any onlookers why Alec was dragging him bodily around the yard. It wasn't late enough for Kat's apartment complex to be quiet for the night—not on a Friday—so Alec hauled his captive around to the parking lot to meet Jackson. "Upstairs or into the truck?"

"Depends. Are you going to knock him around?"

"He punched Kat in the fucking face."

"Point taken." Jackson reached for the stumbling man. "Load him up in the cab, and we'll head to your place. I can keep him unconscious until we get there."

At least there wouldn't be any argument about whether or not the man deserved a good punch or two. Maybe it would teach him to keep his fists off of women.

And if it didn't, he wouldn't get a second chance to hurt any of Alec's people.

Carmen managed not to drop her dinner as she wrestled her keys from her pocket and got the correct one in the lock on the front door. As soon as she did, the door swung open, and Lily reached for the tipping pizza box. "I heard there was trouble at the clinic. How bad?"

"Bad enough to call Franklin." She dropped her keys and bag on the polished table in the entryway. "Did he come by?"

"After you called him off, yeah. He's in the kitchen, making margaritas." As if on cue, the soft whir of the blender drifted from the other room. "What happened?"

"A girl and her date were attacked and roughed up a little. Franklin knows her, apparently. Kat Gabriel?"

The blender stopped. A moment later Franklin appeared in the doorway, his usually mild expression exchanged for a frown. "You didn't tell me it was Kat. Is everyone all right?"

"She's fine." But that wasn't what Franklin was asking. "So are Tara and I."

His steely grip on the doorframe eased somewhat. "If Katherine Gabriel comes in, you should always call me. And get her into a shielded room as fast as you can."

"I know. She gave me her history." *History.* The word seemed too innocuous to refer to the sort of death and psychic destruction Kat had mentioned.

Franklin seemed to echo her thought. "Words don't quite do it justice. I was there, in the aftermath. A Conclave strike team tore open a man's abdomen, and she attacked them. They were catatonic when I arrived."

Carmen dropped to the sofa. It was an extreme response, one born of fear, and that's exactly what Kat would have conveyed to the attackers—fear. Gut-wrenching, mind-numbing *terror.* "She said she killed them."

"No. Someone else did that, once we realized what we were dealing with. I saw it happen once before, in the eighties..." He shuddered. "They made the mistake of keeping the guy alive. Trying to heal him. Three weeks later a psychic finally broke through and figured out he'd been reliving that one moment of terror on an endless loop. There's no coming back from it."

Lily touched his arm on her way into the kitchen. "Shouldn't she be getting help or training or something?"

Carmen frowned at the toes of her sneakers. "Alec said she had. Callum Tyler, the hotshot English empath, took on her case."

Both of Franklin's eyebrows climbed toward his hairline. "Alec Jacobson stopped to chat? Did you have to tranq him?"

"Come on, Franklin. Give me a little credit." She fixed him with her best stern glare. "That reminds me, why were you talking to him about me?"

"Because working with him helps me keep the clinic neutral. I can't do it by ignoring all of the politics, no matter how much I want to."

It was such a sensible reason that Carmen felt terrible for overreacting. "Sorry. I just got the feeling he thought I shouldn't be there."

"It's not entirely personal. We had a little scuffle a few months ago when some lions immigrated here and brought a mercenary hit squad with them. The Conclave's feeling defensive, and... Well, trust me when I say that's not a good thing for anyone."

"Because of my family." *And the empty Conclave seat.*

"Because of your family," Franklin agreed. "But that doesn't mean Jake's got a problem with you. He knows a little something about having family members trying to claw their way into power."

The name made her sit straighter. "Jake? Alec Jacobson is the army buddy you talk about?"

"I never told you that?"

"No." Though there was no reason he should have. Carmen wasn't interested in wolf politics, and she wouldn't be interested in Alec if they'd met under more mundane circumstances.

Yeah, tell yourself that, honey. She'd be interested, if only because he was attractive and commanding. It was a deadly combination, one that had never failed to ignite an intense, primal reaction inside her, no matter how much she tried to deny it.

Lily walked out of the kitchen with a plate of pizza and an open bottle of beer. She put both on the coffee table in front of Carmen and stared at her.

Carmen took a gulp of her beer, then another. Finally, she sighed. "What?"

"Nothing." Lily's gaze shifted to Franklin in a barely perceptible glance. "Is the girl all right? What happened to her attacker?"

"Kat will be okay. And I guess Jacobson was going after the guy who did it."

Franklin hooked his arm over Lily's shoulders and tugged her against his side. "Jake'll take care of it, but we should follow up with Katherine. Just to make sure she's doing okay mentally *and* physically."

It was community medicine at its finest, and exactly why she'd chosen to work with him. Carmen nodded. "I've got it covered, unless you'd rather take it."

"Better if you do. There's a lot she might not tell me." Franklin hesitated, and tense pain spiked strongly enough for Carmen to sense it from across the room as he continued in a quieter voice. "Kat and Sera were close."

Carmen ached for him. His daughter was barely twenty-one, right around Miguel's age, but she'd dropped out of high school and run off just before her eighteenth birthday to marry another coyote, an older man. Franklin had to physically restrain himself from hauling her back home, maintaining a fragile sort of peace, but at least this garnered him monthly phone calls about her well-being.

The pain rolling off Franklin didn't subside, and Carmen closed her eyes against it, drawing slow, even breaths as she blocked it. "Kat was comfortable with me. She seems like a nice kid."

"Kid," Franklin agreed quietly. "She used to be a nice kid. Even though she was older than Sera, she was always...young. But shit, she grew up fast this year. Life made her grow up."

He still missed Sera. Lily closed her hand around Franklin's in quiet comfort, and Carmen looked away.

After a minute of silence, Lily spoke. "Your dad called again, Carmen. From a local number, not his cell. Is he in town?"

"He and Uncle Cesar both," she confirmed. "That's why I skipped dinner with Miguel. He wanted to go meet them, and I don't have the energy for it tonight."

Her friend's blue eyes clouded with sympathy. "If he calls back, I'll tell him to go fu—"

Carmen cut in. "If he calls back, I'll talk to him." She tilted her beer bottle from side to side, swirling the amber liquid. "Maybe this time, I can make him understand."

And then he could go home, and she could stop wondering if every innocuous dinner invitation from her baby brother wasn't so innocuous, after all.

Jackson hurried through the revolving door and skidded to a stop on the polished marble floor before turning to hold up both hands. "Are you sure you want to do this?"

Alec stopped, more so he wouldn't have to run Jackson over than out of any desire to discuss his plan. "No, I'm pretty damn sure I don't, but it has to be done."

"Okay, shit." Jackson glanced around. "Wait here. I'll go find out which room we're hitting."

Jackson sauntered off toward the front desk, his best lady-killing grin fixed firmly in place, and Alec tried not to look too closely at his surroundings. Harrah's wasn't his sort of place—this kind of opulence tended to give him unpleasant flashbacks to childhood and his mother's rigid expectations of class and style. Heidi hadn't cared for blind consumerism either—given two quarters, she'd donate one to charity.

But he'd brought her here. Once, just after she'd made her first major art sale to a private collector. The suite had cost more than she'd been paid, but Alec took the money from his inheritance and considered it well spent. They'd still been dating then, and he'd been in town looking to buy some land in the one city that ignored wolf politics. He'd been thinking about marrying her.

It had taken another year to convince her marriage didn't have to mean giving in to society's institutionalization of love. She'd gotten her hippie barefoot wedding, and he'd gotten tangible proof of what instinct had already decided—that she should be his.

And she was. For four years.

There should have been ghosts here, but instead it was gilded and shiny and so bright and cheerful it set his teeth on edge. He wanted to be gone, not chasing down leads that would bring him face-to-face with the sort of man who valued bloodlines and legacy and all the broken shit in their godawful world.

You wanted to be the boss. Suck it up.

Alec turned to check on Jackson's progress with the girl behind the counter. He couldn't quite make out the words they exchanged, but Jackson's easy smile never slipped, even when she picked up the phone and dialed.

After a moment, she dropped the receiver and nodded, and Jackson blew out a deep breath as he motioned for Alec to join him. "No luck getting the room number until I dropped your name. She called up, and lo and behold—Cesar Mendoza wants to see you."

That was about as surprising as ice in the arctic. "Great." *Now he knows we're coming.*

"Sorry, man. The charm usually works, but the woman was stone cold."

"Charm's never going to work again, Holt. Women can tell you're a tamed man."

"Then I need to either get smarter or find another line of work."

"You'll manage." Alec jabbed the call button on the elevator and the doors slid open. "You sure you want to come up with me? They may not be friendly."

Jackson stepped in, pressed the button for the top floor and shoved his hands in his pockets as he leaned against one side of the car. "All the more reason for you not to go alone. If that kid was telling the truth about the Mendozas' involvement, there'll be hell to pay. They might try to shut you up."

They'd argued about it for most of the drive. Once he'd gotten good and scared, their prisoner had been all too happy to start pointing fingers. *Too happy* being the key words—anyone betraying the Mendozas should have been pissing himself at the thought of the retribution sure to follow. "I still don't buy it, unless Kat is mixed up in some seriously questionable shit we don't know about. I can't think what could be worth that risk."

Jackson nodded his agreement. "True, but if there's one thing I've learned in this business, it's that sometimes people do ragingly stupid things. I wouldn't rule it out just yet."

It would be a waste of breath to try to convince Jackson that Cesar Mendoza wasn't *people*. He was a ruthless, cold bastard who didn't make impulsive decisions, or any decision at all, without considering a thousand possible consequences. Alec couldn't imagine a scenario where hurting Kat could gain Mendoza anything—

Except an in for his niece. A darkly suspicious thought, but one that held Alec for a split second before he discarded it as nothing but his own paranoia surfacing. A hot Mendoza girl with just enough wolf blood to stir his instincts was the last thing he wanted to deal with right now, but only a fool would trust in the precarious series of events that had led to Alec fighting down an uncomfortable attraction to Carmen Mendoza.

Her uncle was many things, but not a fool.

The elevator doors slid open, and Jackson nodded to the end of the hall. "That's the suite number. What's your approach?"

Alec stepped from the elevator and considered the door. "The one thing they'll never see coming. The truth."

Jackson raised both eyebrows. "And if they deny it, but they're lying?"

"You asking how I'm going to tell, or what I'm going to do?"

"Telling's the easy part. The hard part is explaining to the hotel manager why you slammed the lid of a baby grand on his guest's head."

"I did the piano thing once, Holt. Let it go."

"Hey, it was quite the memorable performance." Jackson lifted a fist and pounded on the door.

A man built like an NFL offensive lineman opened the door. "Jacobson?"

"And Holt," Jackson added genially. "Your boss around?"

The man nodded once and stepped back. "He's expecting you."

The suite was as lavish as he remembered, and Cesar Mendoza met them with a smile and an outstretched hand. "Alexander." He was dressed in dark pants and a white Oxford shirt, and he looked as though he'd just discarded a tie. "How have you been?"

Alec ignored the outstretched hand and hooked his thumbs in his belt. "Been better. Got a wolf in my basement babbling that he mugged our secretary on your orders."

Cesar looked genuinely taken aback. "I can assure you that I've done no such thing. My brother and I are in town to visit his children." He gestured to the sofa and sat in an adjacent chair. "Diego's younger son has been attending Tulane for several years now, and his daughter recently moved here."

"I know." They could take that however they wanted, though they'd probably view it as tacit acknowledgement of the rumor that Alec kept tabs on every supernatural in the city of New Orleans. He waited for Jackson to sit, then leaned against the arm of the couch and raised an eyebrow. "So who'd you piss off so bad they're trying to use me to break your face?"

"Could have been any number of people." Cesar signaled the guard by the door. The man nodded and stepped into the other room. "My presence in New Orleans may simply make me a convenient scapegoat."

"Mm-hmm. I assume you know who my secretary is?"

Cesar smiled again. "I make it my business to know. I think you understand that."

"Yes, I do. So you know that this little attack on her isn't going to end up swept under the rug. What pisses off her cousin pisses off the Alpha's daughter, and John Wesley Peyton's already been contacted. An extraction team will be here to take the kid into custody tomorrow."

He held up his hands. "It's in my best interests for him to be questioned by the Conclave. Surely that would clear me of involvement."

Not a flicker, not even a hint of worry. Alec trusted his instincts, and his instincts said Cesar Mendoza was telling the truth. "I didn't think it was your sort of deal," he acknowledged. "You wouldn't have left any witnesses."

"And I would have used my own men," he added. "But you're right. It's not the sort of thing I'd do. I prefer more directness in my dealings."

Alec didn't care that his amused snort was a blatant insult. "I hope you don't have any dealings in New Orleans that don't involve visiting your brother's kids. We don't want your politics or your messes here."

Cesar's smile turned cold. Calculating. "New Orleans falls under the purview of the Southeast council, and I am a member. Who denies my right to be here? You?"

It was a trap, but Alec had been playing his game too long to walk into it. "No one's denying you anything. Just expressing a lack of interest."

"And how far does that lack of interest extend?"

"Miguel's a kid at college. Your niece is working on neutral ground. They're not here to bring trouble."

"Of course they're not." Cesar rose and walked to the small bar in the corner, flashing Jackson a meaningful look as he passed. "I thought we might be able to talk in private, Alexander."

It fell just short of being a rude command for Jackson to leave, but his partner stood anyway. "I'll wait outside."

Alec straightened as the door swung shut behind Jackson. "If this is about the empty Conclave seat, you're wasting your time."

He shook his head. "This is something of a more personal nature. Drink?"

Warning bells went off. "No thanks."

Cesar poured a scant amount of whiskey and raised the glass to his lips. "I'd like to introduce you to my niece."

Oh yeah, this was headed nowhere good. Alec crushed down every hint of interest he might have felt for that oh-so-dangerous little bit of temptation and made his voice as flat and bored as possible. "We've met."

Cesar studied him over the rim of the glass. "You sound somewhat less than charmed."

At least he'd managed that much. "Your niece was even less charmed, so if you're about to suggest a dynastic alliance, maybe you should talk to her first."

The older man waved the suggestion away. "Carmen is stubborn. If left to her own devices, she'll continue to deny her nature. She says she's not a wolf, but she isn't human either. Of course, some might say that means she has the best of both worlds."

Even if he hadn't met the girl, such blatant disregard of her right to choose her own life would have raised Alec's ire. "Maybe you haven't been doing your research, Cesar. I'm not a big supporter of the shapeshifter custom of selling off our unwilling daughters to the highest bidder."

Cesar shook his head and laughed. "Forget I asked. There are others vying for her hand. I thought it might be to our mutual advantage to ally our families, but if you're not interested, you're not."

Protectiveness stirred inside Alec. "Not if she's not willing."

Something sharpened in the other man's eyes, though his expression didn't change. "Sometimes all it takes to change that is a little romance."

"Uh-huh. Might want to warn her more aggressive suitors that pushing a lady is a dangerous game in New Orleans. We play for keeps."

Cesar's glass hit the bar with a thump. "I owe your father a favor. See your way out now, Jacobson, and I'll forget that insult."

"Don't bother." Alec pushed off the couch and started for the door. "My father needs all the favors he can get." Behind him, he heard Cesar pick up the phone and ask for security.

Jackson opened the door before he reached it. "I was listening," he explained. "Just in case."

In case I got us thrown out of the hotel? Alec couldn't even pretend it wasn't exactly the sort of reaction he'd wanted. The more the upper crust of wolf society loathed him, the more they avoided him. "We better move. Cesar's pissed."

"I can't imagine why." Jackson closed the door and fixed him with a stern look. "Admit it, man. You just like making them mad."

"More fun than kicking a hornets' nest." Only this time he had the sinking feeling he might have miscalculated. Carmen wasn't the usual shifter daughter, with the strength and magic to defend herself. If she was the one who ended up stung... *Shit.*

"He had a point."

Alec jabbed the elevator call button more roughly than he meant to, and the plastic casing cracked under his finger. "What point?"

Jackson snorted. "A couple of times in there, I don't think anyone would have blamed him for calling you out. But you like to dance around those challenges, huh?"

"You think I'm afraid I can't win a challenge?"

The elevator arrived, and Jackson walked inside before answering. "Hell, Alec, you know you'll win. That's why you won't fight."

Alec settled for a noncommittal noise, because there was no answer. Jackson was right and he knew it. They all knew it. He'd protect his rag-tag circle of friends through whatever means necessary, but he wouldn't validate the corrupt values the wolves worshiped. He wouldn't join their fucked-up game.

But he *would* keep an eye on Carmen, just in case he'd sent trouble her way. It was the responsible thing to do.

And if that wouldn't have Jackson rolling on the floor of the elevator in a fit of helpless laughter, nothing would.

Chapter Four

Alec jerked awake to the sound of his front door crashing in off its hinges.

It could have been any of a dozen threats—someone come to rescue the prisoner still in his basement, someone he'd pissed off recently, even a pointed message from Cesar Mendoza—but as Alec rolled from the bed a familiar voice sounded from the entryway, the words a rage-filled roar. "*Where is he?*"

Oh shit.

Alec had fallen into his bed too tired to take off his jeans, and he didn't waste time with a shirt. By the time he got down the hallway, Andrew had already torn the basement door from its hinges. It crashed to the floor as Andrew disappeared down the stairs, his nose leading him unerringly to the one person Alec had to keep him from killing.

When he found out who'd spilled their guts to Andrew, he might do some killing of his own.

Hopping the last three steps got him to the basement in time to see Andrew lunge against the side of the cage, one strong arm sweeping between the bars. The man inside cringed against the opposite side, but Andrew only stalked around and snatched him by the hair.

At least the guy had his priorities in order, and an apparently functional sense of self-preservation. He scrambled away again, even though doing so left a handful of his hair still clutched in Andrew's fist. "Get him off me!"

"Callaghan!" Alec planted his feet and put the full thrust of his power behind the words. "Back the fuck down."

Andrew wrapped both hands around the bars and snarled

through a vicious smile. "Not this time."

Someone had blabbed. Someone who believed Andrew's calm facade was the truth, who thought his apparent lack of interest in Kat's day-to-day life signaled actual detachment. A foolish mistake that might get someone killed. "At least tell me what you've heard. I know you haven't seen Kat."

"Wrong." He tilted his head, still studying his quarry with that terrifying smile on his face. "I stopped by this morning to talk to Mackenzie about a renovation project at her dance studio. Ran into Kat there."

Jesus Christ. "And did you ask any questions? At all?"

"Mac talked at me, tried to tell me how it was all under control."

"It is." Alec nodded to the cage, where Kat's attacker huddled cowering in the corner. "The Conclave's coming to get him."

"Yeah?" Andrew's arms flexed as he pulled at the bars. They creaked but held—for the time being. "Open the cage, Alec."

"So you can do what? Rip the guy's guts out? You gonna put his death on Kat's shoulders?"

"He's already dead." The man in the cage blanched at the flat words. "He just hasn't figured it out yet."

A chill gripped Alec as he took one careful step forward. The magical wards layered into the bars of the cage would probably keep Andrew out, but now they were balanced on a far more dangerous precipice. "You can't do this, Callaghan. You can't kill every person who touches her."

Andrew eased away a little, as if in capitulation, then dove against the bars. This time, they bent enough to activate the wards, and the snap of energy drove the young wolf back. He snarled again and paced, all his attention focused on the cowering man's face.

Finally, he released a deep breath. "Have it your way, Alec." To the man in the cage, he flashed another feral grin. "I won't forget your face. Remember that when you try to sleep at night."

Alec didn't look away, in case Andrew decided to push a challenge. "If you want to talk, you can wait for me upstairs."

"I'm sick of talking." Andrew turned from the cage and glowered at him. "I'll come back later and fix your door. Doors, whatever."

Alec nodded. "For what it's worth, Kat dropped him. By herself. The idiot underestimated her."

Andrew paused. "I heard. I'm still going to kill him one day." He ducked through the open doorway and hurried up the stairs.

The sound of his footsteps faded, and Alec turned to his captive and tilted his head. "He's going to kill you one day."

The guy didn't stand, and it took Alec a moment to realize he was shaking so badly he probably couldn't. "He won't find me."

"Don't make any bets on it. You punched the wrong girl in the face."

His prisoner didn't speak again, maybe because there was nothing to say, or maybe for fear of pissing Alec off badly enough to call Andrew back. Alec scrubbed a hand over his chin and slogged up the stairs, pausing at the top to haul the door up and lean it against the wall.

The front door was in slightly better condition. Andrew had pulled it shut, but the frame was shattered where he'd smashed open the deadbolt. He shouldn't have been able to do it at all, but Alec had gotten lazy and complacent, secure because no one in the city would dare challenge him in his own house. Not after what had happened the last time.

Not after Heidi.

The biblical-style vengeance he'd delivered to those responsible for his wife's death was the stuff of supernatural legend, but maybe he'd been riding on his reputation for too long.

Better safe than sorry. Repairing the damage was beyond him, but he could at least get Mariko out to make sure the magic in the cage wasn't compromised by the bent bars...and to renew the wards on his doors. After that...

Well, he might have to pay Carmen a visit after all. Someone had to warn Miguel Mendoza that getting too friendly with Kat could get him killed.

When Kat found out, she'd probably take her stun gun to Andrew's face. *And won't that be fun?*

Alec fought a groan as he returned to his bedroom to get ready for work. The sun was barely up and the day was already shittier than yesterday. At this rate, tomorrow was likely to be hell.

It was almost eighty degrees already, a little warm for early April, even in New Orleans. Carmen locked the front door behind her and dialed her cell phone as she stepped off the porch.

Kat answered on the second ring, sounding slightly out of breath. "Dr. Mendoza?"

"Carmen," she corrected. "Call me Carmen, remember?"

"Carmen." The faint strains of music in the background cut off. "Hey, listen, I appreciate this, but you don't have to come take me to lunch. I'm fine. You have to have better things to do."

"Too late. I'm already on my way." She squinted against the midday sun and slid on her sunglasses. "I just need directions to your office."

Kat gave her quick, concise directions to a side street in the Central Business District. "If you hurry, you'll get here before Alec comes back from bugging whoever he's bugging. He's been even crabbier than usual today."

All she had to do was hit St. Charles, and it would be a nearly straight shot. "I can be there in—" Her phone beeped. "I've got to go. Someone's on the other line. Give me ten minutes, tops."

"See you then."

Once she looked at the caller ID, Carmen stopped in her tracks and hesitated before flashing to the other line. "Hi, Dad."

"Honey." He sounded almost relieved. "I thought you might not answer."

"I considered it."

"Don't hang up," he said quickly. "You didn't come to dinner last night with your brother."

She'd parked on the opposite side of the street, so she crossed carefully and leaned to sit on the hood of her car. "I didn't feel like having to defend myself."

"I would have liked to have seen you."

He sounded sincere. As a child, Carmen would have given anything to hear him say those words and mean them, but it hadn't happened. Not after she'd watched him look her mother in the eye and tell her that he loved her, but he still had to go. "Miguel told me why you're here, and you should know I have no intention of meeting this guy you've picked out for me."

"That's a shame. Richard is a very solid young man. He's successful, and he's looking forward to meeting you."

He spoke as if it were a foregone conclusion, and Carmen's temper spiked. "How much are you and Uncle Cesar paying him?"

"Excuse me?"

"To take a human as a wife," she clarified.

He hesitated just a little too long before stammering out a denial, and a piece of Carmen's heart she hadn't realized was still whole shattered. Her eyes stung, and she clenched one hand around the edge of the hood. "Never mind. He'd just leave one day anyway, wouldn't he?"

"That's not fair," he objected, his voice showing the first tinges of anger. "You were barely twelve, Carmen. A child. Things were more complicated—"

"I know." And she did, that was the hell of it. She'd rather be back in that childish ignorance, believing that her father had left them, left her pregnant mother, because he no longer cared.

Now she knew that he cared, had always cared, just not enough to stand up to the rest of his family.

"Will you meet Richard? He's in Memphis on business. He could fly down this weekend."

She eased her sunglasses up and rubbed her eyes. "No, and you need to stop asking. We're not talking about political alliances, Dad. We're talking about the rest of my life, and I'm not for sale."

His silence now was heavy, almost sad. "I'm sorry to hear you say that, honey."

Fear shivered up Carmen's spine. "Dad?"

"I have to go now, but I'll see you soon." With that, he hung up.

She sat there for a moment, staring at her phone. Every not-quite-human instinct in her screamed danger, and she dialed Julio's number almost without thinking.

It routed directly to his voicemail, and she tried to think of something reasonable to say as she half-listened to his greeting.

I'm afraid of our family was alarmist, and she'd be hard pressed to explain exactly why she was scared. What could they do?

What *would* they do?

A shrill beep interrupted her thoughts, and Carmen swallowed hard. "Hey, Julio. It's me. Look, I don't—I don't know what's going on, but I'm a little worried. If something happens to me—"

A white van screeched to a stop beside her car. The door slid open, and two men dressed in dark clothes reached for her.

Carmen ran. She almost tripped over the curb, but recovered enough to keep going. Halfway across a neighbor's tiny postage-stamp-sized lawn, strong hands wound in the back of her shirt.

She screamed, but a hand clapped over her mouth a second later, muffling the sound. "There's a witch in the van. If you don't cooperate, she'll make you cooperate."

Her odds weren't good if they managed to get her into the van. She kicked wildly, more in hopes of attracting attention than hurting the man. All it earned her was a tiny, frustrated sigh, and then she couldn't move at all.

Sheer animal panic gripped her. Being restrained was one thing, but literally having no control over her body was another. Hot tears streamed out of her eyes, and she tried to scream again.

Nothing.

The other man helped lift her into the van like a doll. A woman sat in the back, and she tilted her head, sending the wild cascade of beads woven into her hair clinking against each other. "Be calm, child. Your family has decided to give you the ultimate gift."

No. No, please. She had no idea what the witch meant, but her family had never wanted what was best for her. Only what was best for them. *No.*

The engine rumbled beneath them as the van squealed away from the curb. The hulking man beside her steadied her with a gentle but impersonal hand on her shoulder. The witch waved a hand, and the paralysis gripping her vanished.

If she fought or made too much noise, they'd do it all over again. So Carmen pushed her hair back with shaking hands and tried to still her trembling lips. "My father. Call—call my father. Please." She'd dropped her phone, but they could find the number.

Something almost like sympathy filled the woman's eyes. "Where do you think we're taking you?"

Alec took one step into his office and knew his day was about to go from worse to catastrophic.

Kat sat at her desk, her fingers flying over the keys even though she was looking at Jackson. "—been here an hour ago. I'd just talked to her but now her phone keeps going to voicemail." She glanced back at the screen, but her gaze shot straight to Alec. "Hey, Carmen's missing."

"Missing?" Alec glanced at Jackson. "How missing?"

"Pretty damn missing." Jackson shoved his wallet and keys into his pocket. "No one's heard from her, there are no major traffic snarls between her house and here...and I've got a real uneasy feeling."

Protective anger twisted inside Alec too fast to be anything but bad news, and guilt followed hard on its heels. He'd provoked Cesar the previous night and hadn't bothered to warn Carmen. "What exactly happened, Kat?"

"She called to say she was on her way over, and then she had another call to take. I thought it might be the clinic, an emergency or something..." Kat trailed off and returned her attention to the computer. "She's not there. She's not anywhere."

"What are you looking up?"

"Her cell records." A frustrated noise escaped her. "I'm trying, but I've still got a headache and this is a carrier I've never had to hack before."

"It makes a difference?" He regretted asking when Kat paused long enough to level a scathing glare at him. "Never mind. Do you know where she was when she called?"

"Leaving her house maybe? Jackson's got the address."

His partner held up a small square of paper. "Uptown. You coming with me?"

"Yeah. But someone needs to stay—"

Kat made an annoyed noise. "If you say *with Kat*, I'm going to taser your balls."

The stun gun sitting next to her made it no idle threat, even if it wasn't an accurate one. Worry for Carmen made him choke back his knee-jerk reminder that Kat didn't own a taser. "Fine, lock the door behind us, at least."

Jackson held the door, his usual easy grin conspicuously absent. "How loose do you think old Cesar's definition of the word suitor is?"

"The usual." Which should be enough to impress upon Jackson how dangerous their situation might be. "Kidnapping a mate isn't standard operating procedure, but that doesn't mean it doesn't happen."

"How in demand would a woman like Carmen Mendoza be?"

"Hard to say." Which was a lie. Plenty of wolves would be willing to marry a halfbreed to get a chance at the Mendoza fortune—or a little influence with a council member—but Cesar hadn't spent decades building the mystique of his psychic niece and nephews just to throw it away on a nobody.

"Maybe something came up and she's just busy at home."

It took a few seconds for Alec to figure out why that felt wrong, to put words to what instinct had already decided. "She didn't seem thoughtless. If you were an empath, would you stand Kat up right now?"

"No, I wouldn't," Jackson admitted as he unlocked the car, "but I'm working up to the worst-case scenario."

"This is shapeshifter politics, Holt. Start at the worst-case scenario, and you'll already be pretty damn close." *Unless it gets worse.*

It got worse.

Alec crouched on the tiny scrap of grass across the street from Carmen's house and picked up a cell phone with a cracked casing. "Has her scent on it."

"Skid marks on the street." Jackson bent and retrieved a set of keys from beneath the front bumper of a late-model navy-blue Camry. A key ring jingled, and he held it up. "Kappa Kappa Gamma. Think our girl's the sorority type?"

He didn't have a clue. "Do they go with the Camry?"

When Jackson depressed a button on the black key fob, the

car's locks disengaged. "Yeah, worst-case scenario."

Tension twisted into anger, and Alec fought a brief, dirty battle with his instincts to keep from stalking to his truck. Cesar Mendoza wasn't stupid enough to haul a kidnapping victim into the front lobby of Harrah's, and they didn't even know if it *had* been Cesar. Alec straightened and held up the phone. "Between this and the keys, think you have enough to track her?"

"Yeah. I learned a new one. Won't take a minute." He didn't bother with the phone, just walked to the passenger side of the truck and opened the door. He unfolded a map of the city on the seat and clutched the keys in one hand. "Just need to concentrate..."

As Alec watched, Jackson's hand began to shake and glow slightly. Another hint of light swirled over the paper, growing tighter and brighter until it condensed on a single spot on the map.

The phone in Alec's hand started to ring.

He flipped open the phone and saw the name *Julio Mendoza* flash across the screen. Shit. "You found where she is?"

Jackson shook his head. "Somewhere in Algiers, near the ferry. I've got to keep trying to pin it down."

"Get in the truck." He started toward the driver's side as he hit the talk button on Carmen's phone. "Julio Mendoza?"

Silence greeted him, and then a voice growled, "Who the fuck is this, and where's my sister?"

"Alec Jacobson, and that's what I'm trying to find out. You know anything about why your father and uncle are in town?"

"In New Orleans?"

"Yeah." Alec climbed into his truck and shoved the keys into the ignition hard enough to make the dashboard tremble, a clear sign his temper was starting to slip. "I don't know how fast you can get here, and I might just be riling you up for nothing, but I'm pretty damn sure someone snatched her off the side of the street."

Julio swore. "I'm already on my way to the airport. She left me a message, said there was something going on and she was worried. Then I heard a scuffle, and the call cut out."

Dread fisted in Alec's gut as he pulled away from the curb.

"Did she say why she was worried?"

"She didn't get to that part." A car door slammed. "Look, if you're asking about my dad and uncle, then you're not a cop. I know that much. But who *are* you?"

It was oddly refreshing to talk to someone who didn't have a clue who he was. "I'm the unofficial alpha of New Orleans."

"Okay. Okay." Julio seemed to be talking to himself. "I have to connect in Charlotte, but I should be down there by five. If you don't find her before then, I can take over."

Alec cut a glance at Jackson, who was still concentrating on the glowing map in his lap. "We'll have her back safe by five, kid. You need to be here for whatever comes next, since I'd wager you're the only one your uncle gives two shits about pissing off."

"Yeah, I get it." He swallowed. "If anything happens..."

The steering wheel creaked under Alec's hand. "Nothing's going to happen."

Julio didn't argue. "I'll call when I land. If you find Carmen, tell her I'm on my way."

"Got it." Alec ended the call and pressed his foot a little more firmly against the accelerator. "Her brother's already on his way to the airport. She got snatched leaving him a message. I just need to figure out how to make this phone pull up the incoming calls..."

No more than a few city blocks now glowed on the map, and Jackson blinked and shook his head. "Give it to me." He thumbed the buttons quickly, scanning the phone's small screen. "Lily, Lily, Miguel, Julio... The last one's just after noon. Diego Mendoza."

Alec thought his blood couldn't chill any further. "Her father. Fuck."

"It could be unrelated," Jackson reminded him. "Plenty of reasons her father would call while he was in town."

"Can you find out how long she waited between that call and calling her brother?"

He skipped to another screen. "She called Kat, received the call from her father and then called her brother, all in the span of a few minutes."

"Mendoza said she called him because she was worried. Either her father said something that reminded her, or he said something that scared her. Otherwise why would she have wasted time calling Kat first?"

"She also could have noticed something fishy on the street during the call." Jackson laid the cell phone on the console. "I know you're predisposed to suspect her family of being involved, Alec, but don't let it blind you. Remember there are other possibilities."

Jackson was right, and Alec hated it. Cool detachment wasn't usually a problem, but they didn't usually work cases with guilt riding him, either. Not since their first, when Jackson had used magic and logic to help him track down the men responsible for Heidi's death.

Christ, the comparison scared him.

At the speed he was driving, he couldn't chance a look at the map. "You pinpointed a location yet?"

"Within a few blocks. Can you handle the rest?"

Unless they'd let Carmen out long enough for her scent to linger, it would mean searching block by block. "We could call Andrew. He wants blood today, and this could give him a fight, at least. Is it secluded enough for me to shift without attracting notice?"

Jackson made a skeptical noise. "Better if you didn't, on both counts. This is a residential area."

Which was going to make possible witnesses a real danger. "So if this turns violent, we could have witnesses calling the cops down on us?"

"Better give McNeely the heads-up, just in case. He'd want to know anyway."

Alec's own phone was still clipped to his belt, and McNeely's number was—through sad necessity—on speed dial. The wolf answered on the second ring, and Alec didn't waste words. "Me'n Jackson might be about to cause a stink over in Algiers."

"Shit, Jacobson." He slurred the words, and Alec could picture the burly man chewing on a toothpick or a pen, anything to distract himself from his nicotine addiction. "It's been so damn quiet lately. What you stirring up?"

"Not me, McNeely. Southeast council's come to town and one of Sinclaire's doctors has gone missing. We're tracking her now."

"Yeah, I got a guy over in the Fourth. You want some backup, or some room to breathe?"

"Room to breathe. No clue what we're walking into, but it's safe to assume a whole mess of pissed-off shapeshifters."

"I'll send word, but he won't be able to hold them off if all hell breaks loose. Keep it quiet and, for Christ's sake, keep it contained."

"Got it. If it gets bad, I'll try to warn you."

Jackson grabbed the phone. "McNeely, tell your contact we'll be starting our search on Lavergne, near the river." He flipped the phone closed and folded the map, careful not to disturb the swirl of magic that dotted it. "If you were going to snatch someone, what? Large car, SUV? Van? Should narrow it down."

Deadpan sarcasm was the only thing holding panic at bay. "Derek's truck worked surprisingly well last time I kidnapped somebody."

"Hey." Jackson waited until he glanced over. "We're going to find this lady, okay? No sweat. It's what we do."

Because it was Jackson, and Alec trusted him, he gave voice to the nagging fear inside him. "I shouldn't have poked at Cesar. I knew better."

His partner snorted. "You didn't *do* anything, Alec. Unless you think you should have agreed to marry her to keep her family from forcing the issue with someone else, I don't get how you could possibly blame this on yourself."

"This is my town."

"And you're taking care of it."

"Things are gonna get worse, Holt. The Southeast council can only stay deadlocked for so long. Eventually one of them'll get an advantage, and who knows if they'll be as willing to leave us in peace as Coleman was."

"Why haven't they gotten off their asses and picked someone already?"

"What Derek did when he beat Coleman was unheard of. By our law, Derek could have taken possession of everything Coleman owned. Accounts, investments, property. That's what happens when you lose a challenge. The Southeast council is too evenly matched. No one wants to be the first one to move and risk losing a battle—or being weakened enough that someone else can challenge them right after they win."

Jackson studied the road ahead of them with a grimace. "What are you going to do if this eventual council leader causes problems for New Orleans?"

Same thing he always did. "Figure out what his weaknesses are and find a way to use them."

"A solid plan." Jackson glanced at the clock in the dash as Alec turned toward the expressway. "We've got a jump on this one. Fast response, that's a good thing."

It would have been more comforting if Alec hadn't been aware of just how many things could have gone wrong in the time it had taken Kat to realize Carmen was missing.

On the second street they checked, Jackson spotted a windowless white van parked in front of a house that still had a *For Rent* sign tilted precariously in front of it. None of the houses on the block had driveways, so Alec rolled down his window and inched past the vehicle, all of his concentration on trying to pick up any lingering scents.

If Carmen had been in the van he couldn't tell, not without getting inside the damn thing, but the exterior carried the scent of unfamiliar wolves too strongly to be coincidence. "This is it."

"Yeah, it is." There was a tangible heat wafting off the map now, and Jackson whispered a few words that dissolved the magic entirely. "Want me to create a distraction?"

"Can you feel anything off about the house? Magically speaking?"

"No, nothing. I—" He paused, his eyes narrowing. "Shit, it's shielded. There's a barrier, something meant to block magic."

Alec pulled the truck up to the curb and threw it into park. "How strong?"

"Big time. Serious magic."

"Fuck. Chances of sneaking in?"

"Slim to nonexistent. It's bizarre, though."

Alec paused with his hand curled around the door handle. "Bizarre how?"

Jackson hesitated. "The shield didn't stop us from finding her, so it's—it's almost as if it's not meant to keep magic out. More like...it's meant to keep it in. Like they're doing something in there they need to hide."

The handle of his door, which had withstood years of abuse, bent under his fingers. "I need to get in there. *Now.* What sort of magical protection can you give me?"

"Make you quicker, harder to hit. The usual." Jackson opened his door as well. "Let's go, and any casters in there, you leave to me."

The house was situated in a quiet neighborhood, one where any sort of loud, protracted fight would be sure to garner police response. They'd have to hit fast and hard, and keep the carnage to a minimum. If things escalated beyond that, it would be ugly—or one more favor Alec owed McNeely.

His partner slowed as he approached the side of the house and held out one hand, as if testing the air. "Here. Past this point, there's no hiding us." He closed his eyes and whispered. Alec couldn't understand the words, but he recognized them.

With the last syllable, power coursed through him, smashing into the magic that made him a shapeshifter. For one tense moment energy buzzed through him, raising the hair on the back of his neck. It settled with a snap, flooding his limbs with lazy strength. The duration of the spell always varied, but the results were the same. As a shapeshifter, he was fast. Enhanced by magic, he was untouchable.

Now all they had to do was get in. "Around back?"

Jackson nodded and hurried through the invisible barrier toward the back door.

It slammed open to reveal two large men in quiet discussion. One shouted a warning and swung at Jackson, while the other lunged for Alec.

With magic curled around him, the rest of the world moved in slow motion. He pivoted before the meaty fist could connect with his jaw and used the shifter's own momentum to help him through the still-open door.

Jackson landed two good punches on the other, then shoved him at Alec. "Don't dawdle," he called back as he ran through the open doorway and down the long hallway.

A hard slug across the jaw dropped the second man, but by the time he hit the floor the first was back, pissier than before. Alec dispatched him in the same manner, wincing slightly when his knuckles split against a jawbone harder than a slab of marble.

Crashing sounds from deeper within the house led him to a narrow hallway where Jackson was bent over a man on the floor, punching him between terse words. "Don't—get—back—up."

The man had been guarding a door, so Alec kicked it in. The shattered wood rebounded against the unfinished wall and smashed into his shoulder as he shoved into the room.

He caught a glimpse of a startled woman with gray hair woven into beaded braids, and then she literally vanished in a pulse of magic that shook the room.

Someone whimpered, and he caught movement out of the corner of his eye.

Carmen. She was huddled in on herself, shaking with terror...and something else. Power.

To his heightened senses, Carmen felt like a wolf. Weak, traumatized, but a shapeshifter, not a human.

She sensed him or smelled him or *something*. Her body went stiff for a moment, and she scrambled to hide behind a freestanding shelving unit loaded with paint cans.

Jackson stomped in. "The magic's dissipated, but there's a hell of an echo in—" He stopped and stared at Carmen's balled-up form. "Shit, is that her?"

"Yes." Her fear scraped Alec's nerves as he concentrated on pushing out a wave of comforting energy. "What the fuck was going on here, Holt?"

"I don't know. Until a minute ago, this room was shielded more than the whole rest of the house."

She still hadn't moved. Alec waved Jackson back and sank into a crouch. "Carmen, sweetheart. You're all right."

She looked at him and away, a quick glance with no eye contact, making sure he kept his distance. The only visible effect his words had was a slight crinkling between her eyebrows, as if she was trying to discern his meaning.

Jackson leaned down slowly, just enough to speak low words to Alec. "Unless you want to have to kill those guys out there, we've got to book. Grab her and let's go."

If he did, she was likely to fight him the whole way and hurt herself. "Can you put her to sleep? Like you did for Mac when her instincts went crazy?"

Jackson looked like he was fighting a battle within himself. "I don't know what they did to her. More magic could hurt, and bad."

"Fuck." With no other choice, Alec rose and closed the distance between them, concentrating on maintaining that steady, soothing aura of shapeshifter power. "I'm not going to hurt you, but I need to take you out of here."

She shifted her weight suddenly and fell over backwards, landing hard on the floor. She still didn't speak, but she made a terrified noise and swung when he reached for her.

Alec had seen newly changed wolves react the same way. Steeling his heart, he knocked her flailing limbs aside and curled his hand around the back of her neck with just enough pressure to be a warning. "Stop."

She struck him on the shoulder and shoved at his chest. When he didn't yield, she wound her hands in his shirt and met his eyes. After a few hitching breaths that finally caught on a sob, she whispered, "Please. Help me."

Terror could break her mind. It happened in more infected wolves than not, driving them so mad they had to be put down. His instincts rebelled, and he'd swung Carmen up into his arms before he realized it, cradling her feverish body against his chest. "Now, Jackson, or there won't be enough of her left to save."

Judging from the hard set of the man's jaw, Jackson recognized the truth of his words. But when he reached for Carmen, she snapped at him, her teeth closing viciously only inches from his fingers. "Jesus Christ." He tried again, and this time he managed to press his hand to her cheek.

One low word, and she sagged in Alec's arms, still whimpering and fitful. "The rest can't be helped," Jackson said. "We need time to figure out what happened."

Alec could only hope it was time she had.

Chapter Five

They were talking about her. Arguing, judging by their harsh tones, even if they fought to keep their voices lowered.

She curled tighter on the narrow backseat and pressed her hands over her ears. Everything was loud, too loud, and she couldn't stand it.

Fight. She wanted to, except that she didn't know where the hell to start. The sandy-haired man in the front seat, the one who seethed with the same sort of magic the witch had carried inside her? She couldn't very well battle the glare of the sun or the ear-splitting rumble of the engine.

Or the chaos inside her. Half of her wanted to fight, but the other half wanted to run, to kick through the back window if she had to. *Fight or flight.* Instinctive reactions, and they left little space for anything else. Still, some tiny part of her...

It remembered the dark, scared man behind the wheel.

He'd glowered at her before, though Carmen couldn't quite place where it might have been. She vaguely recalled heat, as well, the sort that warmed her blood and made her shake with longing.

She could test him, stand still and see if he approached, if he liked her scent. She liked his. It clung to her clothes, her skin. Leather and sweat, strong and earthy.

Strong. She closed her eyes and reached inside for some semblance of lucidity. It made no sense that she could feel that, the magic that dwelled in him and matched her own.

"—heard rumors, but they're just that. They're rumors. You can't make a wolf, not like this."

"But she's not human. Hell, she's not even your usual

brand of halfbreed. Remember, one of the brothers turned up shifter."

"I don't care if one of her brothers is a little gray man from outer space, Jacobson, you can't do it. It's exactly because she's not your average human that you'd have to be insane to try." He sounded upset, almost sick. "The usual way will turn a halfbreed plumb crazy in about two minutes. Too much *wolf.*"

Wolf. Yes, that felt right. Carmen moved her hands, just a little, and tried to concentrate on the conversation.

"A council member would never use the regular way anyway. They can't have dirty infected wolves in their family. Being a halfbreed may not be much, but it's still better than that."

"Like I said, there are rumors of old ways, but it's beyond me. I wouldn't know where to begin."

The witch. Carmen struggled to remember, but a terrifying blankness formed where her memories should have been.

She snarled.

Warmth surrounded her at once, a comforting pressure born of magic, almost tangible. "You're okay, Carmen," the darker man murmured, his voice a soft rumble. "We're taking you somewhere safe."

She opened her mouth to tell him she wasn't okay, but all that came was a low moan. If she could order her thoughts, she could talk to them, ask what the hell was going on.

The other man cursed. "I can't repeat the spell, Alec."

"Doesn't matter. When we get to my place, I'll let her run a bit. Burn off some energy."

"Will that work?"

"Probably won't hurt."

The dark man was driving, and the other turned to peer over the seat at her. He had kind blue eyes, filled with a calm, soft sympathy that scared the hell out of her. How many times had she looked at someone like that, someone with injuries or illnesses so severe they wouldn't live to see another sunrise?

He spoke. "Hey, don't freak out. You're all right. You're going to be all right."

Carmen laughed. She couldn't help it.

A soft curse from the front, and the engine roared under them. "Leave her be, Jackson. We don't need her coming over the seat at you if she gets spooked."

He sputtered something, but she didn't listen. She clamped her hands over her ears again and rolled face down on the seat. Every instinct screamed for her to turn over, not to leave her back unprotected, but she ignored the urge. Instead, she began to meditate.

She'd never been so strong that she couldn't control her empathy, not even from her earliest memories. Unless under duress, she had always been able to close herself off, in a box if necessary, until she was ready to come out. It was only as she grew older and began training that she learned how to do it no matter what was going on around her—or in her head.

Walls. Usually she preferred clean ones, but these she envisioned as a faded red. Plenty of buildings in the Quarter were made of rough bricks just that shade. In her mind, she traced every chalky white line of mortar, until she'd built up five walls—four all around her, and one to close the box.

Nothing penetrated, not until a warm, gentle hand dropped on her shoulder.

She stiffened, but managed not to jerk away as she sat up and looked around. The truck was parked in front of a white house with a large front porch, and a soft breeze carried the scents of grass, earth and water into the cab.

The man stepped back, leaving her a clear path to the door.

Outside, pine trees and live oaks rustled in the breeze. Suddenly, the thought of walking into another closed-off space was unthinkable. Unbearable.

Carmen shoved past him and hit the ground at a run.

It took a minute to recognize the light feeling singing through her as relief. She ran every day, but this was different. No mp3 players or cross trainers, and she didn't run out of concern for her cardiovascular health. Running meant *freedom*.

Trees flashed by—magnolia, cypress, more oaks heavy with Spanish moss. She only stumbled to a halt when she hit the edge of a marshy pond and almost fell into the water. Her legs shook, and she clutched one hand to the painful stitch in her side.

"Better?"

He wasn't even winded, but the observation melted into a realization that he'd followed her. Logically, she knew he'd had to; she was out of her head, high on magic and probably crazy.

Instinct told her he would have chased her anyway.

She was too exhausted to begin the complicated dance that came next, the give and take of wary attraction, so she shook herself and answered his question. "I don't know. Nothing fits, but I'm so tired." The thick sound of tears in her voice embarrassed her.

"I know." His tone was quiet. Gentle. "I don't know what happened to you, but we're going to find out. Make it better."

This time, the reassurance didn't make her want to laugh. "I remember you. Kat's boss. Franklin's friend from the army."

He nodded. "Alec. Or Jake, if Franklin's been telling stories."

"Alec Jacobson." With the nervous magic quieted, her mind cleared a little. "Where are we?"

"My house." The corner of his mouth kicked up. "Actually, my lake. A little swampy, but not so bad."

"It's lovely." Carmen took a step and groaned when her legs almost gave out. She had no idea how long she'd run, but the house had to be over a mile back. "I'm an idiot."

"Nah. Seems like you got a pretty big dose of magic." He took a careful step forward, his gaze locked on her face. "Feeling okay?"

Pride almost made her lie. "No."

"Tired?"

"I think I need to rest before we go back."

Alec nodded toward a patch of grass a few yards away. "Wanna sit? Fresh air can't hurt."

She didn't sit so much as crumple to the ground, and only sheer willpower stopped her from stretching out on the grass. "My father. I talked to my father, and then the van came—"

"Shh." He sank down a few feet away. "It'll keep. Tell me how you feel."

"Confused. Wary." She sighed. "Confused."

"Wish I could say that'll go away. Just try to remember I'm not going to hurt you."

"I remember." What he had to know already was that it didn't matter if she recognized intellectually that he wasn't a threat. What mattered were the tense, heart-stopping moments where primal instinct took over.

"Good." He leaned forward and braced both elbows on his knees. "Don't worry if you get angry and try to rip my head off, either. I won't take it personal."

"Ha. Franklin tells stories, *Jake.*" She gave up and lay back, closing her eyes against the afternoon sun. "I'd never get my hands on you."

His low chuckle vibrated deliciously over her nerve endings, and she relaxed a bit. "I dunno, I'm slowing down a bit. A new wolf landed a few punches on me yesterday."

"You don't say."

"Mmm. Then, this morning, he kicked my door in. Still working on his temper."

Carmen considered laughing, but all she managed was a soft smile. "Lucky for you, I don't have a temper."

"We'll find out. I have it on good authority I can piss off just about anyone."

I think you probably could. After her exertions, just lying there felt like floating, and she fell asleep.

Alec paced by the closed guest-room door for the third time in under twenty minutes and wondered—also for the third time—if opening the door to check on her would make him a creep.

Only a little creepier than prowling in front of her door. That the thought came to him in Kat's voice had to be a sign that his mind was slipping. Or his sense of humor was returning. He could only imagine the look Kat would give him if he admitted instinct demanded he shove open the door and count every damn breath Carmen took.

Not that he couldn't hear her from the hallway. Adrenaline had brought every sense on high alert. If he stood outside the door, he could number the beats of her heart, slow and steady in a sleep so deep it might have been unconsciousness.

She'd slept through the arrival of a Conclave team, and he'd fought himself to allow them inside at all. Only the knowledge that they were going to leave—and take Kat's attacker with them—let him grit his teeth through the invasion. Once they were gone, he'd begun pacing.

He reached the end of the hallway and kept going this time,

refusing to allow himself to make another pass by her door. Instead he moved into the kitchen to check the time.

Five minutes after the last time he'd looked.

Another circuit, first to the table and his cell phone to see if he'd missed any calls, then to the guest room door to make sure Carmen still slept. He'd been doing the same thing over and over in the hour since Jackson had called to say he was on his way with Carmen's brother. Not the young one, who was inconsequential, but Julio.

Another wolf.

His own wolf snarled softly, and Alec ignored the inner urging toward violence. Carmen might not have changed, but his instincts were so confused by the magic pulsing inside her that it didn't matter. For primal urges nothing mattered but perception, and every sense told him Carmen Mendoza was another shapeshifter.

A beautiful, vibrant, hungry shapeshifter whose out-of-control power all but demanded his strength in return.

"Fuck." He bit off the word and stalked away from the door, bypassing the clock completely this time as he moved toward the kitchen table. Two weeks' worth of mail sat awaiting his attention, most of it catalogs stacked on top of the latest issue of *Guns & Ammo.* The catalogs were addressed to Heidi—proof that neither magic nor a psycho-shapeshifter reputation could convince a company to take a client off its damn mailing list.

Rifling through them gave him something to do other than check Carmen's breathing for the seventeenth time that hour. He discarded sleek advertisements entreating him to buy beads, clay, fabric, power tools and yarn. Then he browsed through his magazine and pondered buying a new shotgun until the distant purr of an engine tickled at the edge of his senses.

The sound drew closer, turned into a too-familiar rattle. Jackson had reclaimed his rust-bucket truck from Mackenzie at some point, and the distinctive engine was impossible to mistake for any other vehicle.

Julio Mendoza was about to invade his territory.

Visit his sister, he corrected viciously. The man had every right to be worried about his sister. Hell, Alec would have thought less of him if he hadn't been ready to kill anyone who stood in his path.

It didn't make it any easier to have another young, cocky interloper shoving his way into Alec's battered territory, even if Andrew had apologized and already fixed his front door.

The rattle of Jackson's truck became a rumble, and that inner uneasiness prodded Alec out to meet his guests on the porch.

Both men looked like hell. Of course, Julio had been traveling all day, and Jackson had been hitting every one of their contacts and resources hard, trying to figure out what the hell that witch had done to Carmen.

He waved a hand in Alec's direction. "There he is. Alec Jacobson. Knock yourself out."

Julio Mendoza studied Alec as he approached the porch steps. "Is she inside?"

"Yes." Sizing him up as an opponent was inevitable. Julio wasn't tall, but he was the sort of solid that came from adding muscles to an already strong frame. He wouldn't be fast in a fight, but he'd be a wall you could pound yourself against without knocking him over. Youth and stamina would make him a frustrating—and dangerous—enemy.

He had power too, but the magic was more like Derek Gabriel's. Dominant strength directed inward, a strong wolf with strong instincts, but not someone who felt like a threat. Julio Mendoza could rule if he had to, but he lacked the fire that made Andrew so deadly.

That changed in an instant as his dark eyes heated. "Stop looking at me like that. It makes me think you might be a threat."

"That just makes you smart."

"Smart, maybe," he allowed, "but a lot less inclined to believe your friend there when he says Carmen would be better off staying here."

Alec brought his aggressive instincts under control by willpower alone. "She's better off staying here because I *am* a threat. I can keep her from hurting herself, and no one in this city can get past me to lay a finger on her."

The kid didn't guard his thoughts well. Alec could almost see him running through the possibilities and questions, analyzing his own resources in comparison. Finally, he nodded. "If she wants to stay, all right. All I can do is find someplace to hole up here or take her back to Charleston."

It was a concession, and Alec accepted it. "Why don't you come inside and check on her?"

"Thanks." He headed through the open door.

Jackson drove his fingers through his hair and pitched his voice low. "I got nothing on the witch, even after calling everyone I know all afternoon, which is damn strange."

It was damn *scary*. Alec stepped back into the house and gestured for Jackson to follow him. "What about Mahalia? Is she still in New York?"

Something odd flashed in Jackson's eyes. "Actually, she's out at Luciano's ranch."

John Peyton was in Wyoming too, celebrating the birth of his grandson. "With the Alpha? Or visiting Nicole and Michelle?"

"Not sure," Jackson hedged. "Peyton could have asked her to be there in case Michelle's magic went wonky during the delivery."

It was a fair enough reason. "I suppose Michelle's the first Seer to give birth since... Hell, probably since Zola was born."

"Probably." Jackson eased onto a stool at the kitchen island and braced his elbows on the counter. "Anyway, I called her. She's looking into it."

Mahalia had more magical connections than Jackson—as she should, since she'd been the one to train him—but it could take days for her to reach out. Days Carmen would be suffering. "I don't know what the fuck is going on. She's acting like a new wolf. Exactly like a new wolf—except she should have changed by now."

"Magic's a tricky thing."

"Ain't it just?" Alec leaned back against the sink and tilted his head toward Carmen's room. "The brother gonna be trouble?"

Jackson shrugged. "I don't think so. He hasn't been bringing the alpha bullshit. He's been pretty reasonable, considering the circumstances."

Alec had already thumbed through his mental file on the man, sparse though it was. Most of the gossip surrounding Julio seemed to involve one of two things—the scandal his father had caused by bedding a psychic, or the scandals Julio had caused by bedding the daughters of far too many important men.

None of it hinted as to how he might react now, when the situation was serious. Frustrated, Alec changed the subject. "The Conclave sent a few men to pick up the bastard who attacked Kat. One headache gone, at least."

"We've still got enough to go around."

"Seems to be the way of things. Trouble follows supernaturals."

"It follows us or we make it or something. All I know is—"

"She'll barely wake up." Julio stood in the doorway, his hands clenched into fists. "What did they do to her?"

The wrong word or move could trigger a fight. Alec eased upright, but kept his voice level. "We're trying to figure that out. Maybe now that you're here, we can divide and conquer."

Jackson stayed perfectly still. "Could your family do something like this? Try to turn your sister into a wolf?"

It took the kid a moment to speak. "My uncle doesn't trust spell casters, but he wouldn't hesitate to use one."

He hadn't answered the question, and Alec felt the first tug of sympathy. It was hard to admit your family capable of evil, especially for a shapeshifter. Pack was supposed to matter. *Family* was supposed to matter.

Not for humans and halfbreeds, apparently. "I can't take care of your sister and shake down your family for info."

"Shakedowns don't work on Cesar Mendoza." Julio's eyes glinted with anger and a hint of satisfaction. "But I know what will."

Carmen woke in a bed, fully clothed, with only moonlight shining through the blinds. The bed creaked as she sat up and swung her bare feet over the edge of the mattress.

Her stomach growled angrily, and she bit her tongue to keep from echoing the sound as she rose and crept across the floor. Alec was probably sleeping, but she could rummage in the refrigerator and find something.

Except when she opened the door and stepped into the hallway, Alec stood at the end of it wearing a pair of beat-up jeans and nothing else. "Heard you moving around. Need some food?"

"I, uh..." Carmen shook herself and focused her eyes on his chin instead of his bare chest. "Food. I can get it."

He studied her, then gestured toward the other end of the hall. "Kitchen's down there. I'll be right out."

She walked to the kitchen, her face flaming. After the way she'd stared, he was undoubtedly going to put on a shirt to spare himself her drooling. Which was ridiculous, because she'd seen plenty of hot, naked men in her time.

Okay, she'd seen a few.

His voice came from behind her before she realized he'd returned, soft and amused. "I'm not much of a cook, unless you want me to fire up the grill, which I will. It's never too late for steak."

What he'd put on didn't qualify as a shirt. A thin white cotton undershirt stretched across his chest and left his shoulders bare. "I can handle it, if you don't mind me messing around in your kitchen."

"You feel up to that? Your aura's still..." He cleared his throat. "Fuck, I don't know. You feel like a new wolf, but a new wolf as wound up as you were earlier would have shifted."

"I feel all right." Embarrassed and worried that she'd practically fallen asleep in his lap. Mortified that, even now, with her stomach rumbling and a million questions whirling in her mind, she couldn't stop her gaze from tracing the lines of his body.

"It's natural." He caught her eyes and held them, an oddly compelling power in his gaze. "All of it. Whatever you're feeling. New wolves sleep a lot, and when they're not sleeping it's pretty much an even split between food, fighting and fu—" His gaze jumped away, and flustered discomfort tickled over her skin. "Sex," he said, voice a little choked. "The basic three."

Oh God. "I don't feel different, not like I did earlier," she explained, trying desperately to keep her carnal interest hidden. "The world's not as loud or bright, just..." Smaller. It had shrunk to the size of his kitchen, to the scant space between them, and she had to distract herself. "What should I cook? What do you like?"

"Food." He took a cautious step forward, as if she was a wild creature he was trying not to startle. "I'm not picky. Make something you like."

His proximity made her want to run—not out of fear, but in anticipation of another chase. She turned abruptly and opened the refrigerator. "Maybe just sandwiches or something." The sooner she got away from him, the better.

"I think I've got some bread. Want something to drink?"

"Please." It came out huskier than she intended, almost suggestive.

The heavy anticipation in the kitchen sharpened. "Beer?"

It was the only beverage in the refrigerator besides an empty plastic jug that had once held milk. "I've got it." She lifted two bottles and held them out.

He accepted them both, but tilted his head. "I think I have some Coke in the garage, if you want that instead. And a few cases of the shit Kat likes to drink that looks like antifreeze."

Whatever that was, it didn't sound appetizing. "Beer's fine."

Alec nodded and shifted both bottles to his left hand, holding them by the neck, then twisted off the tops without bothering to find a bottle opener. "Feel like talking, or does it make you nervous?"

Carmen blinked, taken aback by his words. She *should* have felt nervous around him. Instead, she found herself not wanting to lose his company. "I don't mind."

"Good." He held out one of the beers. "Can I ask you some questions about what happened, or do you need some more time?"

Her mind shied away from the subject, and she focused on the bottle in his hand. "When I try to think of what happened...it's like I can't, but not because I don't remember."

"You might have a compulsion. Or the magic might have just shorted out your brain. Jackson may be able to help." His voice was gentle. "We'll figure it out. We always do."

"Yeah." She dropped cold cuts on the island and squeezed her eyes shut as a flash of memory assailed her. "My brother. I remember calling Julio, and I must have scared the hell out of him. I have to—"

Alec's hand landed on her shoulder. "He's been here. While you were sleeping. Jackson brought him so he could check on you, and we explained what we know."

She stiffened under his touch, unsure if she wanted to shrug off the contact or invite something more intimate. "He could have driven me home. I can call him now, or Lily..."

"No." His thumb slipped beneath the fall of her hair to brush along the back of her neck in a slow, soothing stroke. "You're safe here. You need to be somewhere safe until we know for sure that you're not going to change."

The strange confusion clouding her mind gave way to lust. She twisted toward him, past the soft caress, until the back of her neck rested in his hand, testing its careful strength. The same tangled magic that had left her shaking and scared earlier now had her trembling in another way entirely. "You're touching me like you own me."

His body tensed, though his hand remained gentle. "I don't own you. But you're mine to take care of. Not the same thing."

"Yours to take care of?" She leaned closer, inhaling his scent on a deep breath. "What does that mean?"

"No, Carmen." Fingers tightened around the back of her neck in a warning pressure. "This isn't you. It's just instinct telling you I'm the strongest wolf in the room."

"You're the *only* wolf in the room." Except that wasn't quite right, not entirely. "You can let me go. I'm not going to climb you."

He didn't, not right away, and a sudden surge of empathy drowned her in a tightly leashed attraction that managed to be predatory and proprietary at once. The rough tips of his fingers dragged across the back of her neck as he pulled slowly away. "Don't worry. I won't let you, sweetheart."

But he wanted to. "You couldn't stop me." Her own reaction to his emotions drove the words, challenging and seductive. "Not because I'd take you anyway, but because you'd want me to."

Alec laughed, low and hoarse, and leaned down until his lips were just over hers. "You underestimate my capacity for masochism. I'd let you ride me into the sunset if you were thinking straight, but you're not. And I'll stop you."

A long chase, then, full of feints and strategy. It pleased her, even though it meant she'd end up spending the rest of the night alone and aching. "I'm going back to bed," she whispered. "Not that hungry, after all. But I'll cook breakfast in the morning."

He straightened abruptly and took a step back. "Your

brother had your roommate pack a bag for you. It's by the front door. I got the feeling he'd be back for breakfast, so you might want to plan for that."

"Consider me warned." It was easier than she expected to move. The wild *something* simmering inside her had come to a conclusion, and Carmen had no choice but to reasonably agree.

If they wanted Alec, it would take time.

Chapter Six

Alec only realized he'd finally fallen asleep when the smell of breakfast cooking woke him.

The blurry numbers on the clock next to his bed told him it was six in the fucking morning, barely past dawn. Too early to crawl out of bed, but he couldn't leave Carmen in the kitchen. Literally couldn't, not with instinct riding him, demanding he check to make sure she was safe.

He jerked open drawers until he found fresh clothes. He got into the jeans and pulled on the T-shirt as he walked down the hall toward the kitchen, where he found Carmen standing in front of the open refrigerator, two eggs in one hand.

She looked up and smiled, a hint of a blush coloring her cheeks. "Scrambled, fried or other?"

Her little spaghetti-strap top bared miles of skin that made it hard to focus on the question. "Eggs? Cooked."

"Obviously. Salmonella isn't pretty." She ducked back into the fridge and came up with a jar of salsa and an onion. "How about something vaguely resembling an omelet?"

The faintest twinge of embarrassment struck without warning. He should have asked Jackson to bring him groceries, something to put in the fucking fridge that made it look like he actually lived in the place. "Sounds good, but you don't have to cook. I can—" *What? Grill steaks at six in the morning?*

She ignored him in favor of stacking things in her arms. "I told you last night I'd make breakfast."

Which just went to show how badly she'd scrambled his brain. "You must be starving. I'll make sure we have some decent food here later."

Carmen only laughed. "You only say that because you don't know what I can do with a skillet. Sit and watch."

She seemed in her element, so Alec obeyed with an amused smile, sliding onto one of the stools at the counter. "So you're a doctor, a psychic, *and* you can cook."

"Running down the list of things you know about me?"

If she had any idea just how much he knew about her, she'd go for the closest weapon. "Just noting that you're multitalented."

"I can also roller skate." She nudged the frying bacon with a spatula and began to peel and slice the onion. "I'm a Leo, and no one's ever beaten me at five-card draw. What about you? All I know is that you were in the army with Franklin, and you apparently have a thing for damsels in distress."

The damn woman was flirting with him.

He liked it.

They were so far past screwed that he gave in and laughed. "Yeah, you could say that. Or you could say I have a thing for trouble, because you're sure as hell that, sweetheart."

"Me? I'm harmless. At least..." Her smile faded a little. "Until I start howling at the moon, I guess."

He moved before he realized it, making it halfway across the kitchen before pulling himself up short. His fingers itched with the need to touch her, soft or soothing or anything that would head off the fear gathering inside her. "It'll be all right. Either way, it will."

She went rigid. "I'm making breakfast. I don't feel that different. If I'd changed that much, would I be this calm already? It doesn't make sense."

It had always been different for everyone...but he'd never felt feral power curled inside someone when the change hadn't taken. "Not a lot of it makes sense, but your brother's going to find out what happened and then Jackson will figure out how to fix it."

"Okay." Her hand trembled, and she set the knife on the cutting board. "Salsa in the omelets and bacon on the side. How does that sound?"

Her fear sliced at his nerves. Stepping up behind her, he slid one arm around her waist and pressed his lips to her hair. "Sounds perfect."

Carmen shuddered and gripped his arm, her nails digging into his skin. "You may be a masochist, but I'm not. If I'm not allowed to climb you, then you shouldn't hold me like this."

A dangerous line to walk. He had to be strong enough to reassure the beast inside her without being forceful enough to terrify the woman. "Is that what your instincts are telling you to do? Fuck me?"

She stomped on his foot, which would have hurt if she'd been wearing shoes. "Maybe it has nothing to do with instinct. Maybe I just want to fuck you."

Instinct or not, his dick hardened at the words, and he slid his hand up to curl in her hair, fisting his fingers in the disheveled strands just hard enough to let her feel it. "You telling me this isn't the magic? That a sweet little empath like you wants to get rough before she gets down and dirty?"

Her back arched. The movement rubbed her ass against him—and pulled her hair even more. Carmen hissed in a breath. "Is that what's tripping you up? Wolves aren't the only ones who like it hard."

Sweet Jesus.

Alec steeled his voice, made it a command wreathed in a growl. "You can fuck us both into next month with whips and chains, if that gets you hot. After I know you're the only one driving."

She growled right back. "Then why are you still *on* me?"

Because he couldn't stop himself. Alec swore and released her abruptly, reeling back until he bumped into the counter behind him. "Better?"

"No." The bacon had started to smoke. She moved the skillet off the eye and turned to him, her jaw set in anger. "If you don't want me getting turned on or thinking about sex, don't put your arms around me and talk about magic and rough, dirty fucking."

Alec closed his eyes. "Wasn't planning on it. Things sure do seem to spiral into depravity when we start talking."

"Then maybe I shouldn't be here."

Maybe she shouldn't. Except she could sprout fur in the next moment and tear up a crowded New Orleans street. "Franklin could keep an eye on you. Or your brother. Or I'll sit over here and talk about the weather while you make eggs."

After a moment, she retrieved an egg and cracked it into a bowl. "If you value your virtue," she warned, but a little of the sparkle had returned to her eyes.

That's it. Nice and easy. "Awful warm for April, lately."

"You don't actually have to limit yourself to discussions of seasonal temperatures, Alec."

He cast about for another safe topic. "Do you like working with Franklin?"

"Very much." She lifted one shoulder in a tiny shrug. "I believe in what he's doing. People should always have a safe place."

"I agree. I keep hoping that's what we can make New Orleans, but so far no one has the power to keep all the potential threats at bay."

Carmen tilted her head and studied him. "Franklin said the Southeast council doesn't have much to do with things here."

Interesting that her information came from Franklin even though her uncle was on the damn council. "Not usually, but that doesn't mean they're not quick enough to step in if they feel like it."

"And you resent that." It wasn't a question, and he wasn't sure he felt comfortable with how easily she'd fallen into reading him. Not that he wasn't used to it—Kat usually didn't even realize she was picking up stray emotions and asking too-pointed questions—but it was different when those questions came from a wide-eyed kid.

There was nothing wide-eyed or kid-like about the woman standing in his kitchen, and her understanding tread dangerously close to intimacy. It made it hard to keep his voice level, caught as he was between the urge to claim and the urge to run like hell. "I guess."

"I don't blame you." She fell silent, focusing on the task at hand.

The urge to screw was nothing new. He liked sex and didn't see any need to go without when plenty of women were willing to take him home. Casual fucking with no messy complications and no one to be left at home, cranky that he was too damn busy to give a woman the attention she deserved.

No one to make breakfast out of the dismal wasteland of his abandoned fridge.

"There we go. Just like...that," Carmen murmured as she prodded the eggs. She lifted them as she tilted the pan, and a triumphant smile curved her lips. "This is going to be the perfect omelet."

It had been a depressingly long time since he'd had a home-cooked breakfast, perfect or not. "Even though you made it with salsa?"

"Are you kidding? I make them with salsa all the time. It's already seasoned, and it beats the hell out of chopping a bunch of tomatoes." She folded the omelet and slid it onto a plate, then added a few slices of bacon and a fork. "Here. Eat."

"Bossy little thing, aren't you?" Not that he had any intention of disobeying. It smelled damn good, and he was always hungry.

She laughed and cracked another egg. "I'm assertive. You're bossy."

"Yeah, women always have a different word for everything. You remind and we nag."

"Hmm, you must have me confused with someone else. I definitely nag."

He might even put up with it from her. "Good to know."

She eyed his untouched plate. "If you want to do something, you could make coffee. I couldn't find it."

"Because I'm probably out again." But he rose and circled the counter, easing past her without touching her, as tempting as it was to rub against her back.

This time, she didn't lean into him, and she didn't pull away. "I could have asked Julio to bring some."

"I'll add it to the grocery list." He dragged open the cupboard and dug around, past enough canned soup to make him wonder where it had all come from, and finally found a shiny, vacuum-packed block. "Here, this is coffee...I think."

She whistled. "Your tastes are a little more expensive than mine."

Alec laughed and headed for the coffee pot. "Not my taste. Nicole Peyton. She likes to buy everyone Christmas presents."

"Right, you hang out with the Alpha's daughter."

His arm brushed hers as he reached for the filters, and he tensed, waiting for her reaction. But she only straightened his sleeve carefully and handed him the package of filters.

A sweet gesture. A tiny intimacy.

He wanted to tear off her clothes and bend her over the counter.

Jesus Christ, get your head in the game. She was an empath. A magic-riddled empath who would *let* him bend her over the counter if he wanted it badly enough, regardless of her own desires.

He couldn't drag in a deep breath, not with her standing there smelling sweeter than sunshine, but he managed a shallow one and a gruff "Thanks."

"You're welcome."

An engine rumbled outside, unfamiliar and well tuned, and tension shot through him before he remembered that her brother was returning for breakfast. "Think your brother's back."

She exhaled shakily. "He's got great timing, as usual."

More than one way to interpret that. Alec chose the innocent one. "Always shows up when there's food around?"

"Something like that." Carmen ran her hands through her hair, leaving it even more tousled than before. "I'm not looking forward to this."

Neither was he. He wanted to tell her to put another shirt on—one that covered all that gorgeous damn skin—but it felt too much like admitting he couldn't control his own reactions. "I'll deal with your brother. You're okay, honey."

"Quit babying me. I'm not going to fall apart." She grabbed a dishtowel and swatted him lightly.

Catching the towel was instinct. Jerking it hard enough to send her stumbling against him was outright insanity. "Maybe I'm going to fall apart," he murmured. "Be nice."

Something dark and hungry flashed in her eyes. "You're impossible." Not exasperated condemnation, but a soft, almost wondering confusion.

A car door slammed outside, and Alec cursed life and fate and the wolf who'd be bounding up the steps any second. Curling both hands around Carmen's shoulders, he leaned down and kissed her forehead softly. A gentle, soothing touch, and all he'd allow himself before he stepped back. "I'll answer the door."

The mental and emotional whiplash was going to kill her.

Carmen hurriedly finished cooking the second omelet and started a third, using the rote task to focus her mind. Her skin still tingled where Alec had touched her, and she whispered a few blistering curses.

"That bad, huh?"

Julio. Something inside her eased, a tiny part of her that had been convinced her brothers had been under attack, as well. "You have no idea."

He stepped away from the door and met her halfway across the kitchen with open arms and a sigh of relief. "You scared the hell out of me."

"Gives me something to do." Even as she pulled free of his hug, she was looking him over, making sure he was unhurt. "Are you all right?"

"Only you would ask me something like that at a time like this, Carmen."

"I'm taking care of her." Alec sounded a little defensive.

Julio didn't react visibly, but Carmen felt the spike of disappointed anger that lurked behind his smile. "Yeah, I know."

She probably smelled like Alec, and Julio's first ridiculous assumption would be that she'd been taken advantage of. "Sit down, Julio. I made you an omelet."

"Carmen—"

"Sit." She moved without thinking, putting herself between her brother and Alec.

He didn't argue further, probably because he was afraid she'd take the plate away. "You got the stuff I left, I guess."

"Yes, thank you." She bumped into Alec, and she had to stop herself from twining her fingers with his. Further proof she'd gone insane—he'd spent the last twelve hours confusing the hell out of her, and she still wanted to hold his hand.

Alec shifted his weight, and his fingertips brushed her lower back in a barely-there touch as he addressed Julio. "Did you find anything out about what they did to her? Or the witch who did it?"

Julio eyed them and shook his head. "There's a little problem. Uncle Cesar doesn't know anything about it."

Alec didn't ask if he was sure, just bit off a curse and fisted his hand against her back for a brief moment. "What about your father?"

"I think you missed the memo. Our dad doesn't shit without permission."

"You sure?"

Julio shoved a forkful of eggs into his mouth and chewed. "I'll keep working on it." He arched one eyebrow. "How're things going here?"

"Fine," Carmen answered. Standing two inches away from Alec wasn't going to ease the tension in the room, so she walked to the counter and busied herself with starting the coffee.

As it turned out, nothing would ease the tension. They ate breakfast in near silence, with Carmen trying unsuccessfully to lure Alec and Julio into conversation. Instead, they stared each other down, her brother versus the man who'd touched her like a lover.

She wanted to hit them both.

When Julio had gone, Carmen dressed and tried to settle in to read a book Lily had packed for her. It turned out to be a Regency romance with a tall, dark hero the author described as stern and commanding, and the only thing Carmen could say was that at least the effort it took not to picture Alec in the scenes kept her occupied.

She set it aside before the hero got naked, just in case.

Sitting in the guest room wasn't an option, so she wandered into the living room just before lunch. She found Alec stretched out on the couch, his bare feet propped up on the coffee table. He held a banged-up legal pad in one hand and a pen in the other.

He looked up as soon as she cleared the hallway and smiled. "Feeling okay, still?"

Her heart skipped, and she had to admit the dashing Regency-hero fantasy might have been safer than actually being near Alec. "Yeah, sure. I feel good."

"Wanna sit?" He nodded to the oversized chair across the table from him. "Kinda boring out here, I guess. Don't watch a lot of TV and I don't have internet."

She sank into the chair. "So what do you do when you have

downtime?"

For a second, he almost looked uncomfortable. "Uh, doesn't happen that much."

From some of the things she'd heard, he probably spent more nights in women's beds than he did at home, alone. "It's good to stay busy."

His eyes narrowed. "Uh-huh."

Nervousness clashed with the urge to flirt, and she laughed, unable to help herself. "I think we should change the subject."

He snorted and looked away. "I can only imagine the stories they tell about me."

"Franklin mostly talks about the old days, when you served together."

"Long time ago." He tossed the legal pad aside. "Joining the army isn't the smartest way for a shapeshifter to run away from home, but you'd be surprised how many of us seem to do it."

"My brother almost did. Julio?"

"Not surprised. He had more reason than most."

"Maybe." Instead, he'd dropped out of college and run off to Charleston to become a firefighter. "We all run away from home somehow."

"Ain't that the truth." Alec stretched, straining the fabric of his T-shirt as the strong muscles of his arms and shoulders flexed. "So how'd you run away?"

It took effort, but she managed to quell her shudder of arousal. "Uh, I said 'thanks, but no thanks' to the nice young shapeshifter they'd picked out for me, and I moved to Nashville. Medical school."

"Good for you." He sounded like he meant it. "Maybe if enough of us keep doing that, the old guard will die out in a few generations."

"I doubt it. There are some who say yes, right? Enough to keep it going."

He eased his feet from the coffee table and leaned forward, bracing his elbows on his knees. "Probably. If there's a way to change it, though, it's gonna take a smarter brain than mine."

"Or mine." She couldn't help matching his pose. "So you ran away and joined the army. What did you do after that?"

"This and that. A few of us who met in the military went

freelance. Franklin. A wizard named Nelson who'd been a pilot. A couple of shifters—Ollie was in intelligence and Karl was a sniper. Did okay for ourselves."

"Freelance? As in mercenary?"

He studied her, his face giving no indication of the thread of uneasiness working through him. "Does that bother you?"

"No, not in the least." If he'd been human, perhaps, but the supernatural world existed mostly outside the law, which meant it had to police itself.

Alec nodded, almost as if he'd sensed the path of her thoughts. "We did that for a few years. Then we lost Ollie and Karl in the same month."

The timbre of his voice lacked the sadness she would have expected if something terrible had happened to his friends. "They retired?"

"They got domesticated." His lips curved in a wicked smile. "Ollie fell for a pretty little psychic socialite in Atlanta. Karl got dumb over a cowgirl from South Dakota."

Carmen laughed. "A classic tale. How did you survive without them?"

"Got dumb myself." Pain sliced through the room, twisted into guilt and dissipated so fast it could only have been through a conscious effort to guard his emotions. The words that followed were glib, almost practiced. "Then I got a job. Harassing deadbeat dads gives me something to do when I'm not saving pretty ladies."

Her own pain surprised her. There was no reason for him to be open with her, to share himself, and she had to remember that.

She *had* to.

She changed the subject to distract herself. "Do you play cards?"

"Not so much." He leaned down and tugged out a plain wooden box from underneath the coffee table. "Don't even think I have a deck of cards, but I've got these."

It was an ancient set of dominoes. "I don't know how to play."

Alec slid the wooden cover back and spilled out an array of tiles that looked hand-carved, with dots burned into the faces. "Got the concentration to learn some rules?"

"I told you, I feel sharp as ever. And no smart comments about that," she added with another laugh.

"I don't make smart comments," he replied, voice and expression deadpan serious. "Ask anyone. I'm dumb as a post."

"People don't really believe that, do they?"

"You'd have to ask them." He started flipping the dominoes over, until they were all face up. "Mostly they just think I'm a scary asshole."

"Yeah? I think you're sneaky."

One eyebrow popped up. "That's a new one."

Carmen shrugged one shoulder. "Then maybe people aren't paying attention."

"Maybe they're not all empaths." He seemed more amused than upset, and maybe a little resigned. "I do live with one under my nose most days. Never been able to scare her, either."

"Is that your goal? To scare me?"

"Not you in particular. The world in general? Maybe."

She watched him shuffle the tiles. "Your secret's safe with me."

"Is it?"

He was tense, nervous. Carmen frowned. "I don't spend a lot of time talking about other people's innermost feelings, if that's what you're worried about."

The nervousness tightened, then faded, and he shook his head. "It's not. It's not you. I'm just a crotchety old bastard."

Maybe he was less worried about gossip than he was about the possibility she'd report back to her uncle. "Just so you know, I don't talk to my family much, either. I'm not a spy."

"I don't think you are." His hands moved absently, flipping the tiles around and lining up all of the *one* ends in a row. "Not saying I never thought that. I considered it pretty hard, at first. But this would be one convoluted way to go about it."

She had to agree. "So what's the problem?"

His attention stayed fixed on the tiles. "Hard to remember I'm supposed to be a stone-cold psychotic bastard when you look at me like I'm a person."

She reached out to him before she remembered she wasn't supposed to, her fingers grazing the back of his hand. When she realized what she was doing, she pulled back and cleared her throat. "You're going to have to explain the rules to me."

She let the statement lie, hoping he'd take it at face value. It was just as well that he seemed to, since he sat back and began to outline the object of the game.

Chapter Seven

After two days of nothing but cooking and waiting, Carmen was jumping out of her skin. "I want to go for a run."

Alec didn't seem to find it an odd request. "There are a couple trails through the woods. The run to the lake's nice too."

She vaguely remembered it from the day she'd arrived. "Just let me change clothes."

Several minutes later, she stepped onto the porch and tried in vain to draw in a deep breath. The days were growing hotter quickly, with the sort of humidity she was more apt to associate with midsummer than early spring. "August is going to be miserable if this weather keeps up."

"This your first summer in New Orleans?" Alec was still wearing jeans, but had tugged on another tight black T-shirt.

"Except for visits," she confirmed. "But I've lived in Atlanta and Nashville for most of my life."

"Never spent that much time in either. They this muggy?"

"Just about. Georgia especially." Carmen tilted her head and sighed. "You don't have to go with me, you know. You must have things to do."

His sudden smile bordered on roguish. "Plenty. You going to make me do them instead of giving me an excuse to get outdoors?"

He'd told her to back off, and yet he kept flashing her those wicked looks, as if he couldn't help himself. "I'm not your mother," she told him. "I'm not going pace myself so you can keep up, either."

"That so? If you're going to invite a wolf to a chase, you'd better make sure you can outrun him. Unless getting caught is the point."

"I think you're forgetting something." She stepped off the porch and turned to face him. "I'm not entirely human."

Her vague memory supplied a general direction, and Carmen dug in her heels and ran.

At first she wasn't sure he'd followed. A quick glance over her shoulder proved he was following, all right, just keeping his distance. Not to mention checking out her ass.

She ran faster, something instinctive pushing her to push *him*. A gentle rush of empathy told her he was enjoying the chase and, surprisingly, so was she.

Because you know he'll catch you. He could deny it, fight it, and it didn't matter.

Carmen slowed and spun, walking backwards. "How long have you lived here?"

"This house?" He slowed too, to a casual amble. "Bought it...oh, nine or ten years back."

"And do you do this often?"

"Run? Or chase women through the woods?"

"That's chivalrous of you, to keep pretending you're the one doing the chasing here."

One eyebrow quirked up. "You're right. If I were really chasing you, you'd be under me already."

"Now there's a thought." She had to get used to the blatant, idle flirtation. She couldn't get aroused every time he said something like that, or she'd be perpetually horny—and frustrated. "I meant your obvious role as protector and mentor. Do you have a lot of new wolves beating down your door?"

"A few," he acknowledged with that infuriating little smile. "Someone has to take care of them, and I'm good at it."

And he needed it. She might never hear the admission from his lips, but she felt it plainly. "Thank you."

"You're welcome. You're going to trip and break your neck if you keep walking backwards on this path."

She stopped. "I was trying not to be rude."

He jerked his chin toward the path. "Quarter mile, maybe a little more. There's a nice clearing. I'll give you a ten-second head start."

The predatory glint in his eyes stole her breath and kicked her heart rate into high gear. "Head start for what?"

"Before I chase you. For real."

She had to be crazy to consider it, even if the thought made her body buzz. "And then what? More dirty talk because you can't sleep with me, but you can sure the hell torture me with your eyes and muscles and ridiculously hot voice?"

He actually laughed. "Can't do much to fix any of that. I could back off, I guess, but you're not going to like that much better."

"No, I suppose I wouldn't." She didn't feel like a crazed animal, but she'd never been quite so moved by feral instinct, either. "Go easy on me, would you?"

Pacing herself wasn't a problem, not if it was only a quarter of a mile, so Carmen ran hard, pushing herself almost at a sprint. Soon, the near-echo of trampled brush drifted from behind her, and she smiled through her panting.

He let her get three long strides into the clearing before he tackled her, somehow twisting their bodies as they fell so she sprawled across his chest. His low, delighted laughter curled around her, warm as the arms that circled her waist. "Easy as I get."

Too easy. Too intimate. She wiggled out of his arms and landed on the ground beside him. "You smile like you're not used to it, did you know that?"

Laughter died, and he twisted his head to stare at her. "It's been a while. Only other person willing to poke at me until I laugh is Kat. I always figured she did it because she knows I'm not going to kill her, even if I'm glaring like I want to. An empathy thing."

"Maybe." She wanted to reassure him with her touch, but she thrummed with a sexual awareness he could surely sense. "Is everyone else so careful with you because they're scared?"

"Some of them are." He slid his fingers over hers, his hand a heavy weight. "What do you feel? Beneath the sex, what does my power feel like?"

Dominant. Implacable. "You're strong, and you're intense." All things so wound up in her attraction to him that there could be no separation.

"And I'm a little crazy. Or I act that way enough that everyone thinks it's true. Better if most of the scary people in town are wary of pissing me off."

"Makes sense." His hand was huge, warm and a bit rough. She wanted to feel it on her body, sliding down her back and curling around her hip to hold her still for a hard, demanding thrust.

The mental image formed so quickly that all she could do was bite her lip as she blinked and willed it away.

His fingers tightened around hers. "I hate not knowing what to do. If I'll hurt you more leaving you alone, or by giving you what you crave. I don't want to hurt you at all. Do you have any fucking idea how long it's been since I didn't know what to do?"

"You're too hard on yourself," she admonished. "It isn't your job to keep me from hurting, and no one knows everything all the time."

"It's my job to keep from hurting you." He lifted his hand and hers with it, sliding it up until they pressed into the grass over her head. Then he released her and rolled to his side, propped up on his elbow so the bulk of his body loomed above her. "It's all a damn excuse. It's my job, and I'd be doing it anyway...but that's not why I'm doing it now."

It was the most nonsensical thing she'd heard in a while. "Are you saying you want to protect me?"

"I'm saying I *want* to protect you." His free hand landed on her stomach, skimming up to skip over her breasts and land on her collarbone. "You're not scared of me. Even when I'm acting crazy."

"Because you're not crazy." She caught his hand and held it still. "Don't do this just because you think I need it. It's not worth it."

His eyes looked so dark they might as well have been black. "Honey, I thought you were an empath."

"You know what I mean. If you still think I'm not in my right mind, the guilt would kill you, and I only want you to feel good about this."

He considered that for a moment, then guided her other hand up above her head. "I'm going to kiss you. Deep. Hard. You okay with that?"

He'd urged her into a position of submission—both hands over her head, her body stretched out beneath his—and it made her shake with anticipation. "More than okay."

"You want me to stop, you say stop." One hand curled around both of her wrists, gentle but unyielding. "You want more, ask for it. Okay?"

Carmen pulled against his grasp, not to free herself but to test his strength. He held tight, and her eyes fluttered shut under a wave of need. "Yes."

His free hand settled at her hip in a possessive grip. Power built in the space between them, a slow, steady rise that mirrored the dark heat in his eyes as he lowered his mouth, lips barely touching hers. "Let me in."

The command released something inside her, a tension she hadn't noticed before he eased it, and she closed her eyes again. Honesty was one thing, even a kiss...

Don't think, Carmen. Feel.

She obeyed, loosening her tight hold on control, gasping when the first waves of empathic feedback echoed off him to heat her own body.

His beard scraped her chin as he closed the distance between them with a shuddering groan. He kissed the way she'd seen him live, reckless arrogance and power and an intensity that bordered on intimidating. Lips and teeth and his tongue stroking her mouth until she parted her lips, then surging forward to taste and take, his hunger and satisfaction twisting between them on the threads of her empathy.

She wasn't prepared for the depth of her reaction to his satisfaction. Beyond the undeniable physical pleasure of the kiss was a whole world of intimacy, a power she'd flirted with but never really embraced.

She could give him everything.

More, he'd take it. There could be no doubt of that, not with his desires laid bare before her, the hot need for her pleasure dwarfed by the steely craving to be the only one who provided it. Nothing tentative there. Nothing tentative about the way he teased his tongue against hers, his pleasure spiking every time she moaned and arched closer.

It had to stop, even if depriving herself of his touch drove her mad. Carmen turned her head to break the kiss. "Oh God."

"Shh." He pressed a kiss to her temple. "How's the wolf instinct feeling now?"

Curiously silent, all things considered. She'd expected that part of her to be feral, riled up and ready for a ride, but everything in her that still strained toward Alec's touch was entirely human. "Quiet."

"She knows she's safe." The whispered words stirred her hair. "She ran. I caught. Claimed. Won't be the last time she pushes a challenge, but it might not be so bad next time."

She bit her lip to hide a smile. "You're still convinced that's all it is? That I wouldn't usually try to get a rise out of you?"

"Maybe not all of it." He nuzzled her cheek, working his way down until his teeth closed lightly on the line of her jaw. "In a week or two this magic should settle down, if we're lucky. Or Jackson will find a way to break it sooner."

"You make it sound so simple."

"It's not our first crisis. Don't think it'll be our last, either."

"It's mine." Her life hadn't been easy, but most of the pain she'd had to deal with had been emotional. "Nothing about my family has ever made me feel endangered before."

His body went tense beside hers, the fingers at her hip digging in for a heartbeat before his hand relaxed. "I'm sorry. I remember what it feels like the first time."

Pain accompanied the words, an agony that almost sickened her. Her first thought was to shut it out, but that would mean shutting Alec out, and she couldn't. So she took a deep, shaky breath and watched his face. "What did they do?"

He rolled away from her, landing on his back with his hand still above her head. His fingers curled around hers, an almost compulsive, instinctive movement, and that pain tightened, turned to a free fall of loss. "My cousin killed my wife. Because she was human."

There was nothing to say, no questions to ask. Prejudice had cost his wife her life, and Alec had been left to deal with an aftermath full of pain and emptiness. That wouldn't change now, no matter how hard anyone wished.

Nothing to say.

Carmen squeezed his hand. "Tell me about her."

"Her name was Heidi." The corner of his mouth quirked up. "Remember how I said my friend Karl fell in love with a cowgirl from South Dakota?"

"I do."

"Yeah, the cowgirl was on a date with me when that

happened. The worst first date in the history of men and women, and Karl stole her out from under my nose. Guess she felt guilty, because a few months later she introduced me to one of her friends from college. An art major who liked to make sculptures with a blowtorch."

He already looked lighter somehow, less bowed by guilt. "She sounds like a badass."

It made him laugh a little. "Only if you pissed her off while she was holding the blowtorch." His smile faded. "She made it easy to walk away from the supernatural world. To just forget it was there."

Except it always was for someone like him, no matter what, and his renewed guilt proved he knew that. "I'm learning now that you can't walk away from something that's part of you."

"No, you can't. You can hide from it for a while. You can tell it to fuck off..." His thumb stroked her wrist. "It's in my blood. It's in *your* blood. Maybe I just hate thinking that me and Heidi might not have lasted. Feels too much like saying I didn't love her enough."

"You tried," she said firmly, "and you were happy, right? Beyond that, who knows what would have happened?"

"No one, I guess. No one ever will." His arm looped around her, as if he needed the comfort of her touch. "My cousin never gave her the chance to walk away from me. He thought I should thank him for that."

It was barbaric. Unfathomable. She wanted to scream at the injustice of it, but all she could do was stroke her fingers over his skin. *I'm sorry.* It wasn't enough, but she murmured the words anyway.

Alec's voice dropped to a rough whisper. "It was a while ago. My cousin went to ground afterwards—even my family couldn't condone what he'd done. He was a member of a pretty radical group. They thought changed wolves were making us weak, that no shapeshifter should have the right to squander our precious blood on anyone who wasn't born to the gift. Humans were a thousand times worse."

"I understand." Hadn't Cesar demanded that Carmen's father abandon her mother for the crime of being a psychic, a human? And what might he have done if Diego had refused?

"The supernatural world is fucked up. All we can do down here is... I don't even know. Pick up the pieces?"

"I think so." She was living proof that avoidance only worked for so long, and it certainly never changed anything. "Did you find him? Your cousin?"

"Yeah. With Jackson's help." She felt his subtle withdrawal, though his fingers stayed on hers. "I found him, and all the people who'd encouraged him. Who'd been terrorizing other people. And when it was over, I was that crazy bastard no one wanted to piss off."

Carmen reluctantly slipped her shields back into place, sat up and leaned over him. "And that's why everyone but Kat tiptoes around you."

"That's why." The corner of his mouth kicked up in a tiny, morbid smile. "Plus all the crazy things I've done since."

"Crazy things?" The urge to kiss him again almost overwhelmed her, so she climbed to her feet and held out her hand. "Surely tackling women and kissing them stupid qualifies, so I won't argue."

He accepted her hand, but rocked to his feet with effortless grace without her help. "Nah, that's on the tame side. Last year I kidnapped a Conclave member's kid in someone else's truck."

Carmen laughed helplessly. "Somehow, the fact that it was someone else's vehicle makes it sound crazier."

"He wasn't thrilled at the time either, as I remember."

"The owner of said truck, or the person you kidnapped?"

"Neither, I guess."

"Uh-huh." She hadn't released his hand, and now she tugged him toward the path. "Let's go have a beer."

"In a second." He pulled her back and turned her, raising both hands to her shoulders. "You seem steadier today, so I want to try something tonight, after dinner. I want to try to guide you through the change."

"I told you—I don't feel that different."

"Then nothing will happen." A hint of sadness wreathed the words, perhaps explained by those that followed. "And then you can go home. Get back to your life."

She would never be the same, even if the magic he spoke of came to nothing. Not after the way he'd kissed her. "I don't live on another planet, Alec."

He shrugged and turned back to the path. "I do. A planet where angry shapeshifters kick my doors off their hinges and people need kidnapping and saving and killing. There's always something."

In other words, there was no room for her. Unsurprising—and understandable.

And it didn't matter anyway. It might have been one unforgettable kiss, but his busy, dangerous existence was far from the only reason getting involved with him would be a bad idea. He was inextricably tangled up in the fringes of a world she'd avoided her whole life.

Bad, bad idea.

Carmen caught up with him and slid her hand back into his. "There's always something—later. Right now, I want that beer."

She had a day, two at the most, and she wouldn't waste them.

Jackson had called him five times.

The text on his cell phone's screen indicated he had four new voicemails, and he'd bet all of them had come from his partner as well. With Carmen happily occupied putting away the groceries he'd had delivered, Alec felt safe enough stepping out on the back porch. Easier than staying in the kitchen with her smiles and her scent and her friendly chatter twisting him up into a confused wreck.

Fucking women was safe. Liking their company was asking for trouble.

He didn't bother to listen to any of the messages, opting instead to call Jackson back. There was no way the man didn't plan to yell at him, and he only had patience for one tedious lecture.

Jackson answered the phone with a short, particularly foul curse. "Okay, where the hell have you been?"

"Running." Mostly the truth, and Jackson wouldn't be able to tell either way. "She needed to burn off some energy."

"Her brother's been here, bitching because he showed up the other morning to quite the domestic-looking little scene."

The kid should be thanking any God he prayed to that it'd been domestic and not pornographic. "We're getting along decent enough. Nothing crazy's happened."

"Yeah, I told him you'd take care of her. No funny business."

"That a statement or a question?"

After a moment of uneasy silence, Jackson cleared his throat. "Is there something I need to know?"

Damn it. His own defensiveness had turned a statement into a question. "If she was stuck here for a few more days, maybe. But if I can't walk her through a change tonight, then I'm sending her back home. Franklin's practically shacking up with her roommate. He'll be on hand if anything happens, but I'm starting to think it won't."

"The longer it takes, the less likely it is to happen," his partner admitted. "Julio says there's no news on the whys-and-wherefores front. You gonna shuffle her off on Franklin and help him out? He tries, but come on. The kid's a firefighter. He doesn't think like a cop."

Long association with Jackson made it easy to follow the path of his thoughts. A cop might have found Alec's lack of subterfuge reassuring...but Julio Mendoza wasn't human. And Jackson didn't think like a shifter. "Wolves aren't so great at hiding that sort of thing. Especially if someone's charging into our territory and questioning our right to have someone. The only way I'm going to convince Mendoza that I'm not the latest big bad wolf come to gobble his sister up is to get her the hell out of my house."

"Then you're right, you need to do just that. We can't get down to real business with you stuck babysitting."

"Yeah." He was right. Getting Carmen away from him was the only thing that would give him the focus to find out what had happened to her.

Too bad it was the last thing he wanted to do.

"Still, couldn't hurt to stay in touch after she goes home. Make sure everything's all right. You can handle that, right?" Jackson's voice sounded studiously casual.

Meddling bastard. "Since when do you encourage me to stick my nose in other people's business?"

He could almost hear Jackson's shrug. "You've taken responsibility for her so far. May as well see it through."

"I take responsibility for everyone. And I always see it through. So butt the hell—"

Magic exploded.

The phone slipped from Alec's fingers as he staggered under the wave of sheer, undiluted power. It was so overwhelming that he couldn't even pinpoint a source, not until Carmen's voice rose in a scream of protest from the front yard.

He faintly heard Jackson's frantic voice spilling out of the speaker on his phone, but instinct moved his feet before he could stop to think. One hand landed on the railing of his porch and he vaulted it, four feet up and then ten down, enough that he gave into momentum and rolled before springing to his feet again.

Then he ran.

It was the witch. She stood in the yard, chanting, as one of the men from the house in Algiers lifted Carmen off her feet.

The rhythmic chanting paused as the witch turned her head. "Drop the girl. Deal with the shifter."

Carmen hit the driveway, and the burly man rushed him.

In the second before the huge body crashed into his, Alec caught the scent of blood in the air, distracting enough that he hit the ground, the muscle-bound shifter on top of him.

The man drew back a fist and drove it into Alec's jaw. Pain splintered the world into overlapping fragments, but at least it drew his attention back to the fight. Alec shook off the blow and used a move he'd seen Zola pull more than once to get a larger opponent off of her. A feint to the left, as if trying to throw the man off him, then a lightning-fast change in direction the second the bulky man started to pull right.

They rolled together and Alec got a knee in the shifter's gut and smashed his fist into his face. Bone shattered and a hoarse yelp of pain split the air, but it wasn't loud enough to cover Carmen's agonized moan as magic lashed through the still evening.

The man cursed over the sound of metal clearing a leather holster. Nickel plating glinted in the fading evening light as he lifted a pistol to Alec's head.

No time to be flashy. Alec swung a fist and knocked the hand and gun to the side, then smacked it again, sending the weapon flying.

A meaty hand slammed into his face, a strong thumb digging hard into one eye. Alec choked on a curse and reared back, barely keeping the man from gouging out his eye, but he couldn't escape the painful pressure. The shifter huffed out a short, triumphant laugh, only to draw up short as a gunshot rang out.

The man let go to press his hand to a rapidly welling spot of blood on his shoulder. Alec rolled him, taking advantage of his opponent's pain and distraction to wrench his head and snap his neck. The man went limp, and Alec came to his knees in time to see Carmen, the shifter's gun held easily in both hands.

In that moment, she was the hottest thing he'd ever seen.

"Alec." Carmen's hand shook, and her relieved expression turned to one of horror as her arm moved, jerkily at first and then more smoothly. Her fingers twitched as if she wanted to drop the gun but couldn't, and she raised her hand, lifting the barrel to her temple.

Alec froze, both hands held out at his side. He didn't dare move, not even to turn his head and face the witch head on. "What do you want?"

"To finish my job." The witch's voice held a gentle, almost cajoling edge. "Ten minutes, and everything will be done."

"Everything what? What are you trying to do?"

The woman snorted, and the beads in her hair clicked as she shook her head. "If you don't understand, you shouldn't interfere."

His wolf battered against his self-control, frantic to break free and eliminate the threat. Alec choked back hard. "No one's interfering."

"I am," Carmen said angrily. Her trembling ceased as she rose and took a step back. "I'm saying no. No more magic, no more spells. I'd rather pull the trigger."

His heart damn near stopped in his chest. "Carmen—"

The witch spoke over him, her dark eyes narrowing in her pale face. "You're bluffing."

"Am I?"

For an eternity, the two women stared at each other. Finally, the older woman whispered something and magic snapped through the air. The gun flew out of Carmen's hand, and the witch turned to Alec, one hand raised as she whispered an incantation.

An incantation she'd never finish. Adrenaline gave him

speed. The need to shake Carmen until she promised never to bluff again—and dear God, she had better have been bluffing—gave him a vicious edge.

Alec crossed the space between them before the woman got three words out. On the fourth he pounced, flying through the air separating them.

She never got out the fifth word. She threw up both hands and Alec knocked them aside and caught his fingers in her braids. His palm slammed into her chin. One twist, one snap, and she hit the ground in a lifeless heap.

Carmen sucked in a harsh breath and fell to her knees. For a moment, everything was silent. Still.

Then she screamed.

Alec's heart tried to climb into his throat. He scrambled to his knees and lurched to his feet, covering the space between them in a few ragged steps. He hit the grass and skidded toward her. "Carmen, Carmen, it's okay, sweetheart. You're okay—"

Her hands clenched, fingers digging into the grass. She growled and lifted her head, her entire body trembling and wary.

Wild. She was wild. His instincts said feral, and he kept his body rigid. Ready to stop her from hurting herself. "Take a breath," he coaxed. "You're okay."

She growled again, part question and part warning, and moved closer. One hand hovered near his chest, and she pressed her cheek close to his and inhaled sharply.

Carmen turned her head and bit his jaw.

Lust burned through him, wiping away everything human and leaving the wolf in its wake, hungry and curious. Alec's hands swept up her back before he could stop them, curling in her hair so he could guide her head back.

He was supposed to guide her head back. He just couldn't remember why.

She released him, only to brush her lips and tongue soothingly over his skin. Her hand flattened against his chest, slid down past his stomach.

Alec caught her wrist when her fingers reached his fly. "Oh, no you don't, lady. This is not you."

She didn't snap or snarl. Instead, she made a soft, coaxing

noise and nuzzled his ear.

Christ. If he let go of her hand she'd find his dick rock-hard and willing, but the rest of him couldn't be. Not with her clearly out of her mind and a body on the ground.

Two bodies. *Christ.* "*Carmen.*"

She went rigid and jerked her hand free of his. Her eyes narrowed in confusion, and she rocked back, moving away from him slowly.

If she bolted, he'd have to chase her down. He only had so much self-control. He held out a hand, stopping just short of touching her arm. "Honey, let's go inside—"

Carmen slapped at his hand and scrambled out of reach. She opened her mouth as if to speak—then turned and sprang into a dead run.

He chased her because he had to. Because she was beautiful and wild, because she was hurting and he had to make it stop.

Magic must have been at work, because she was damn fast. She nearly hit the tree line before Alec caught her around the waist, dragging her body back against his chest. "Be *still.*"

She fought, her nails digging painful furrows into his arm, and she kicked. One blow bounced her heel off his shin and his knee, and she threw back her head and howled with rage and pain.

It shredded his heart, but he couldn't let her go. So he kept his arm locked around her body and summoned all the power inside him, setting it loose in a soothing rush that should have dropped her to the ground in a submissive heap.

She whimpered and fell still. He could taste her fear and confusion, but she didn't struggle anymore.

"That's it." Keeping up the press of power would drain the hell out of him, but he had a sinking feeling she'd start struggling the second he stopped. "I'm gonna pick you up, sweetheart, and get you inside. Then we'll make you feel better."

Her arms slid around his neck, and her breath blew hot over his cheek and ear as she nuzzled him again, more hesitantly this time.

He was going to hell. He was going to the lowest fucking layer of the darkest fucking hell, and she'd send him there personally when she came back to herself and realized what he'd done.

What he was about to do.

"That's right..." Slow. Soothing. No lies, just nonsensical murmurs as he bit the edge of her jaw. "Let's go inside, honey."

Carmen's whimpers melted into a moan, and she curved one hand around his cheek, petting him.

Forget her. His own damn dick was going to want him to go to hell by the time this was over. He slid his arm under her knees and lifted her, holding her tight against his chest. "You're safe, Carmen. I've got you."

Her breathing roughened, and she whispered something unintelligible, her voice shot through with lust and longing.

Alec walked faster.

By the time he reached his front steps, she'd begun trailing kisses over his jaw. He staggered up the steps and barely got the door open. "Hold on a second, sweetheart. Just—slow down. A little."

The caresses subsided, and she lay still in his arms, eyes closed, as he opened the basement door and walked down the stairs.

Hell was too good for him.

He eased the door to the cage open with his foot and froze, hating the fact that the scent of Kat's attacker lingered, thick with the stench of fear. As wild as Carmen was, she'd be sensitive to it. *He* was sensitive to it, even with most of his energy devoted to keeping her calm.

Her eyes flew open and her hand shot out, curling tight around the bars on the door.

No betrayal in her eyes, not yet. She trusted him. He made a soothing sound and kissed her, parting her lips with his tongue and driving deep, kissing her like it was going to be the last time—because it might be.

She shuddered and let go of the door to hold him tight, her fingers clenching in his hair. A soft growl vibrated in the back of her throat, and she wiggled in his arms.

The scent of her arousal hit him, and his resolve wavered. She wanted him. She liked him. A good hard fucking would make them both feel better about life. He could imagine the way she'd look, bent over, fingers tearing up his sheets in her eagerness, legs spread wide, *begging* for him—

And if she'd been drunk on tequila instead of magic, he would have thrown her under a cold shower instead of sticking his dick somewhere it might not be welcome.

Carmen trusted him, and that made it so easy to betray her.

She was still panting for him when he dropped her onto the cot in the corner of the cage. The fact that it was a bed of sorts seemed to distract her long enough for him to get out of arm's reach. The metal doors clanged shut and Mari's spells activated, apparently no worse for the wear even with Andrew's earlier abuse.

It took her a moment to sit up, and another to realize they were on opposite sides of the bars. She shot off the cot and grabbed the door, rattling it loudly. It held, of course, and she turned a disbelieving stare on Alec.

Leaving her there was going to break his damn heart. "I can't let you run off into the woods, and I won't fuck you when you don't have the wits to say no."

She stumbled back, her hurt melting into obvious anger, and she turned away to stalk the cage.

"Carmen."

She ignored him, and it hurt. It hurt more than it should, more than he'd thought possible. The ache in his chest made it that much more important to get his ass upstairs and call in backup, because it meant his judgment was seriously fucking compromised.

Compromised judgment would get them all killed, sooner or later.

He made a list of the people he had to call as he climbed the stairs. Jackson first, then Carmen's brother. No need to worry about Julio getting the wrong idea now—the hurt in Carmen's eyes had killed his hard-on and the silent treatment wasn't liable to bring it back anytime soon.

He should have been a lot more grateful.

Chapter Eight

They were hovering around the cage, talking about her again.

The blue-eyed wizard hissed a curse and dragged his hands through his hair. "We're back to square one. If I don't know how she was weaving her spells, it's dangerous for me to fuck around with it."

"Damn it, this is going to drive her crazy."

Alec. She remembered his name, though the wizard hadn't said it. It was branded in her memory, along with his taste and scent. He'd rubbed his hard body against hers, given her his mouth—and then he'd locked her up.

There had been no mocking in his eyes as he'd done it, and his voice now was rife with worry. He was scared for *her*, and it made it impossible to bare her teeth and snarl. To warn him off.

Her mind began to clear quickly, the feral anger dissipating. He'd tricked her, but he'd done it because giving her what she wanted was unacceptable. She knew that.

Still, the sting of betrayal lingered.

"She hasn't changed yet." The wizard stood—Jackson, that was his name. "There's one thing I can try, but only if you're pretty sure she isn't going to."

Alec shoved both hands through his dark hair, leaving the short strands standing on end. "I can try changing. That's what I was going to do tonight. Shift and see if the magic sparks something in her."

"If it's ever going to happen, it's now."

"Fine." Alec backed up a step, shooting Carmen one furtive look before he dropped his hands to his belt.

He looked like he wanted her to turn away, so she knelt by the bars and watched him as he stripped off his shirt. It revealed the ink on his arm and shoulder, dark indecipherable lines, and she let her gaze trace them boldly as he reached for his pants.

A challenge. He could answer it, or he could turn away.

Of course he answered it. Dark, expressionless eyes held hers as he jerked open his jeans and let them slide to the floor. He stood in front of her in boxers and an unwavering frown, but he didn't look away.

One of them had to give, but it wouldn't be him. The realization both soothed and excited her, and Carmen turned her head. "Can he leave?" she rasped. "The wizard?"

Alec kicked his jeans out of the way. "I'm not coming in that cage, whether he's here or not."

That chilled her even as it sparked sharp, hot anger. "I didn't ask you to."

The sudden wariness in his eyes faded to confusion, but after a moment he nodded. "Jackson, go upstairs."

He shoved his hands in his pockets even as he backed away. "Yell if you need me, Alec."

Carmen waited until his footfalls faded up the stairs and a door slammed to rise and reach for her own shirt. "Tell me what to do. How to find her. The wolf."

"All right. Can you close your eyes and feel my power?"

She could feel everything, the power of the animal inside him as well as his almost crippling concern. "I can feel you. Stop worrying so hard."

His rough laughter filled the room. "Oh, honey, we're way past that. I worry. It's what I do."

The last thing she wanted was to be yet another responsibility, a burden no good alpha would set aside. She opened her eyes. "Don't. Don't worry about me."

His hands fisted. His voice dropped to a whisper. "I worry about you more than I should."

Because he cared. She'd known he wanted her, but this was different. Something closer to what she felt, and insufferably dangerous for someone in his position, who lived the way he lived.

It burned through her anger, and it didn't matter that he

was mostly naked, that she was half-dressed in her shorts and bra. Carmen dropped her shirt and closed her hands around the bars. "You talk a lot about what you do, what your job is. What do you *need*, Alec?" She'd give it to him, even if it meant walking out and never looking back.

After a tense, endless moment, he opened his eyes and met her gaze. "I need you to be all right. I need to keep you safe."

"The only way to do that is to find out what that woman did to me and why." The possibility of Carmen killing herself had spurred the witch into a mistake, one that had cost her her life. "She needed me to be two things—alive, and a wolf. That means my family has to be behind this. There's nothing else that makes sense."

He gave a short nod, then tilted his head. "You're feeling steadier?"

"I feel—" The vicious bite of magic had already faded. "How long has it been?"

"An hour. Maybe a little more."

Last time, it had been longer than that before she'd come back to herself enough to recognize her surroundings, much less carry on a conversation. "How bad was it?"

One dark eyebrow swept up. "You're in a cage, sweetheart."

Her cheeks heated. "That was a stupid question."

"A little bit." But he smiled and brushed his hand over hers. "You were pretty mad at me. I wasn't sure you were going to forgive me. I didn't put you in there willingly."

What he didn't say made her blush even harder. "I tried to jump you."

The first hint of true amusement made his eyes dance. "I'm used to it. Women can't resist a brooding loner."

"I'm sorry."

"Do it again some time when you're *not* high, and all will be forgiven."

Will it? Asking seemed like asking for trouble, so she stepped away from the bars. "Show me how it's done, and we'll see if you can let me out of here."

Alec stepped back and hooked a thumb under the edge of his boxers. "I'm about to be really naked. Watching with your eyes won't do you much good, but I don't care if you do."

Carmen tracked her gaze down his hard body to where he'd

dragged the fabric low. For a moment, temptation nearly got the better of her. "I shouldn't, since I have to keep my hands to myself." Reluctantly, she turned away and leaned back against the bars. "What about the rest of my clothes? Will I have time to get rid of them if I start to feel like something's happening?"

"Probably not. It'll be over before you can count to three. Doesn't hurt either, so you don't need to be scared."

"Right. Are you—?" She swallowed hard, her hands on the waistband of her shorts, and almost glanced over her shoulder. "Are you watching me?"

"Does that bother you?"

"No." It excited her, feeling the weight of his gaze on her, his interest and arousal spiking every time she moved.

Part of her wanted to put on a show, send that twisting desire of his through the roof, but it didn't seem fair to tease. Instead, she unhooked her bra and slid the cotton free of her arms. After tossing it across the cot, she pushed her shorts and panties down her legs in one quick, efficient movement.

"All right." His voice had definitely gotten lower. "Your empathy might help. Close your eyes and kneel, and try to feel what I'm doing."

She bit her lip and slid to the floor, wincing at the hard bite of concrete on her scraped knees. "I feel..." Worried. Determined. Turned on.

Then the lust bloomed into something primal, something she recognized on an instinctive level. It was the magic that had always lived in her, just cranked up to an overwhelming intensity.

It called to her, inviting and wild, and she clenched her hands into fists. She wanted to join him, release that sleeping part of her and *run*—

Nothing.

"Damn it." The magic that had flared up in reaction to his settled, and Carmen rubbed her hands over her face. "I don't know, Alec. I just don't *know*."

A quiet yip answered her.

He was right behind her, and she turned to look at him. Dark fur covered his large frame, muzzle to tail, and she smiled in spite of herself. "It's weird how it's impossible to predict what shifters will look like, but then they always look like themselves somehow. They look...right."

The wolf stretched slowly, then magic shimmered in the air again. It happened so fast it seemed like a blur, the wolf rising on his hind legs before the shimmer became too much. A heartbeat later Alec stood before her—

Aroused.

Her breath caught in a gasp as need washed over her. This time, she couldn't look away. "Alec."

"Shh." He wrapped his hands around the bars of her cage, fingers clenching so tight his knuckles looked white against his dusky skin. "Shifting is... There's no high like it."

She had to get off her knees, so she climbed to her feet. "So I've heard."

"I should leave."

"I should make you." The tables had been turned, and now he was the one crazy with magic. But she touched him anyway, sliding her hands over his. "You keep protecting my virtue. What about yours?"

"The only way I'm keeping my virtue is if you stay in that cage." A rumbling laugh escaped him. "Even that might not save us."

She felt no confusion, no doubt that this was what he wanted. That she was what he wanted. "You can stay or go. Either way, no regrets."

Something feral sparked in his eyes. "Turn around."

It was firm and forceful, and the command weakened her knees. She obeyed, standing so close to the bars that she could feel the heat of his body.

His breath skated across the back of her shoulder. "Lift your hands. Above your head."

She raised her arms and gripped the cold metal bars, feeling curiously exposed by the position. "It's as natural as breathing for you, isn't it?"

"What?" His fingers brushed hers, then started a slow, wicked glide down her arms. "This?" He curled his hands to cup her breasts, palms abrading her nipples. "Or this?"

Carmen whimpered at the sudden rush of pleasure. "Dominating your lover."

"Don't need a cage for that," he agreed as one hand swept lower, spreading wide over her abdomen. "The only reason you're still in there is to keep me from dominating you. Can't fuck you through the bars...probably."

"I think you're a liar." She pressed back, reaching through the bars to tangle her hands in his hair. "You could find a way."

"Maybe." His fingertips brushed her thighs. "There are people upstairs. You have to keep quiet. Believe me, honey, you wouldn't be quiet riding my cock."

He had a dirty mouth, and she had to check a moan. "I don't think I can be quiet with your hands on me, either."

"What if I give you something to bite?"

The sensual possibilities left her dizzy. She could sink her teeth into him. She'd have to, because he'd touch her and he'd make her come so hard she'd forget everything, including the people roaming around his house.

Including the dead bodies they'd left outside.

She let go of his hair and pulled away with a ground out curse. "You wouldn't be doing this if you were in your right mind."

Alec snarled, but he didn't disagree with her.

It strengthened her resolve. She bent to gather her clothes, still trembling from his caresses but determined. "Sometime when you're not high, Alec, and that's a promise."

"A promise." He turned and snatched up his jeans. "I need to go upstairs. I'm going to pop the lock on the cage. Come on up when you're ready."

The urge to call him back consumed her, but what would it accomplish? She had nothing to explain, no reason to justify being unwilling to take advantage of his magical arousal when he'd spent the last few days doing the same for her.

And she *had* done it for him. Because, sooner or later, he'd come back to his senses and find a way to blame himself for losing control.

Carmen dropped her clothes on the cot and pulled on her panties. "I'll only be a minute or two."

He didn't answer, just stopped at a number pad mounted on the wall and typed in a code that resulted in a soft *click* from the cage door. A moment later he was gone, his feet barely making a sound on the wooden stairs.

She finished dressing slowly, taking the extra time to steel herself. It was insane to feel as though she'd done something wrong, but that didn't change facts.

She felt like hell.

Shut up, Carmen. It was karmic payback for sniping at Alec every time he pulled away, unwilling to take advantage of her heightened instinctive drives. He'd only been trying to do what was right, what was best.

I need you to be all right. I need to keep you safe.

Best for her, not himself, and that was the key. She climbed the stairs, her mind racing. Alec would hurt himself before he hurt her, and it was more than a platitude or something he'd try to do, except when he fucked up.

It was who he was.

Alec wasn't upstairs, but the pretty brunette who'd picked Kat up from the clinic sat at the kitchen table, fidgeting. Carmen smiled and hoped she'd already stopped visibly shaking. "Hi, Mackenzie."

"Hey. Good to see you again."

"Want some coffee? I could make some." It probably wouldn't help Mackenzie's fidgeting, but it would keep them both from sitting at the table, twiddling their thumbs. "I get the feeling it might be a long night."

"Sure, coffee's great." Mackenzie rocked to her feet. "I would have already made some but I don't know where anything is in Alec's kitchen. Or if he has coffee."

"After the last few days, I've figured out the lay of the land." She rinsed and filled the carafe. "If I hadn't, by Alec's own admission, I would have starved by now."

"Yeah, I get the impression Alec eats a lot of takeout. God knows no one would deliver all the way out here. He's pretty well in the middle of nowhere."

Carmen paused in the act of settling a fresh filter into the pot. "I have no idea where we are. South of the city?"

"Southwest." Mackenzie hesitated. "You were pretty out of it, I guess. But you seem to be doing a lot better."

"I don't think it worked," she confessed. "Or maybe it did, it's just not finished. The witch said she needed more time."

Mackenzie hopped up onto the counter and crossed her legs, bouncing one foot so that her sandal dangled. "I'm not a magical expert or anything, but based on my experience, you'd know. I had some big badass spell cast on me to keep me from shifting, and when it started to fall apart... Well, there weren't exactly lucid periods. First I tried climbing the walls, then I tried climbing Jackson."

Suppressing the blush that rose was impossible, so Carmen kept her gaze riveted to the coffee maker. "The, uh, climbing. Yeah, I'm familiar with that part. What happened to you...afterward?"

"They had to reinforce the spell, but the second it was gone, I shifted. I couldn't have stopped it."

It sounded nothing like the way she'd had to strain and grasp for the slightest flicker of magic. "Definitely not, then."

"Well, congrats." Mackenzie hesitated, her foot frozen mid-bounce. "Right?"

"Right." Even as she spoke, Carmen shook away the tiny, inexplicable frisson of doubt that rose. "Right. I mean, this isn't something I would have chosen."

"Then it's good. And the rest will shake itself out."

"Of course it will." Carmen leaned one hip against the counter. "Are Jackson and Alec outside?"

"Yeah. Jackson's got Kat on the phone about something and Alec's dealing with..."

"Oh." She grasped the edge of the counter and tried not to babble. "Seems like I should help him, doesn't it? They came here because of me. Alec wouldn't have two dead people in his front yard if it wasn't for me."

"That's not—" Mackenzie leaned forward and dropped a hand to Carmen's shoulder. "I don't know if this is going to make you feel better or worse, but either way you deserve to hear it. This isn't anything new for him."

Another warning. "Don't worry, Alec's already taken pains to explain to me exactly what his life is like. I know."

"Then let him take care of it. Let him do what's going to put him on solid footing."

She'd spent years avoiding her father's family and all other lasting connections to wolf society. Yet here she was, with a man who knew nothing else, treading the line between casual involvement and something that could change her life.

Carmen didn't know whether to laugh or cry.

Mackenzie slid off the counter a second before the front door swung open. "I'm going to go check on Jackson."

Which meant it was Alec coming through the door. "Later, Mackenzie." Carmen ran her hands through her hair and reached into the cabinet for two mugs.

Footsteps sounded behind her, but Alec didn't touch her before he spoke. "You okay?"

She turned to face him, and her heart skipped at the implacable look on his face. "I think so. What about you?"

He shrugged one shoulder, then looked away. "Nothing kills a hard-on like burying bodies."

Harsh words that covered something, though Carmen couldn't tell what. She reached back and gripped the edge of the counter to steady herself. "I could have done it."

"It's not—" Alec sighed. "I'm sorry. That was a shitty thing to say."

The space between them was more than physical, a palpable emotional distance that left her feeling awkward. "Do you want me to go?"

"I don't want you to." That at least had the emotional punch of honesty, but it didn't erase the tension vibrating off him. "I think—I think maybe you need to, though. Franklin can keep an eye on you, and I'll be a lot more effective at finishing this shit with your family once I've got my head on straight."

"Once you—" Once she was gone, and he didn't have to think about her anymore. Carmen shivered and crossed her arms over her chest. "That's it, huh?"

"It has to be it." He took a step toward her, filling the small kitchen with the intensity of his power. "When you're in a room, seventy-five percent of me is focused on you. The rest of the world might as well not be there. I can't be effective like this. I can't protect you."

He'd already told her that was what he needed more than anything. More than being close to her. "I understand."

"It's not about you. You get that, don't you?"

"Yeah." If anything, it made it hurt worse. He wasn't pushing her away because she wasn't what he wanted, or because they didn't fit. She simply wasn't worth fighting for. "I'm not going to sit around, Alec, waiting to be convenient for you. If I leave, I'm moving on."

It hurt him, and he couldn't hide it. But he didn't admit it, either. "This isn't how I wanted it to go. I wanted—" A breath.

His shoulders slumped. "Doesn't really matter what. My life's never going to be safe. There's always another crisis."

Then you're always going to be hiding. She didn't want to torture either of them, so she took a step toward the door. "I hope you find—" The hard lump that formed in her throat choked off the words.

He stared at her in anguished silence until the front door crashed open. Mackenzie strode in, bright-eyed and smiling and riding a wave of sympathy. "Hey, Alec. Sorry, should have knocked, but Jackson's got some stuff for you in the car and it can't wait."

Alec pivoted and leveled a glare on her, one so sharp it should have flayed her skin. Mackenzie just stared back, completely unperturbed—and clearly unwilling to leave. After a tense few moments, Alec stalked past her, pausing at the door to look at Carmen. "I'll be right back."

It didn't matter, because she wouldn't be there, even if it meant she had to walk home. "Excuse me, Mackenzie. I have to pack my things."

Alec slammed the door behind him.

"Well." Mackenzie folded her arms over her chest and eyed Carmen. "I'll hit him, if it makes you feel better. Probably won't do much damage, but it pisses the hell out of him that I'm faster than he is."

Of course Mackenzie would have heard. Carmen flushed and shook her head. "I just need to go. Can you give me a ride?"

"Not a problem. I'll even help you pack."

The faster she could leave, the better. Maybe, if Carmen was lucky, the other woman wouldn't want to talk about it, and she could lock down until she got home.

She just had to make it home.

Alec talked to Jackson long enough to make sure he and Mackenzie would get Carmen home safely. Then he got in his truck and drove.

The coward's way out, but he was feeling cowardly. Way too weak to watch Carmen pack her things and walk out of his life, even if letting her was the right thing to do. It had been so clear outside, with the stench of death in the air and the proof of danger at his feet. Carmen needed to be safe, and she wouldn't be safe around him. No woman ever had been.

But when she looked at him...

He drove twenty miles before he was sure he could relax without turning the truck around and going back to stop her. His wolf clawed at him, furious that he'd let the female they both craved slip through his fingers. There'd been a hunt. A chase. So close to claiming her, and now she was gone, and they were alone.

Always alone.

At least someone else understood his pain. He called Andrew from fifteen minutes outside of town. A half an hour later they faced each other across the wooden floor of Zola's second-floor sparring area.

Words weren't important. They'd never needed them anyway, not when Andrew had been reborn with instincts as overpowering as Alec's own. Usually those instincts gave Alec the advantage, but today they felt fuzzy, compromised by his need for Carmen and the lack of her ripping its way into his soul, like she'd taken chunks of him with her when she'd gone.

It slowed him down. Not so much that a lesser fighter would have been able to take advantage of it, but Andrew wasn't just another wolf. He fought with a vicious edge and didn't hold back. Pain blurred the edges of Alec's misery. Frustration mounted every time Andrew spilled him to the floor, and that helped distract him too.

They fought for an hour before Andrew took him down with a right hook Alec should have seen coming long before it landed. The younger wolf stepped back, panting. "What the fuck is going on, Alec? I telegraphed the hell out of that move."

Alec lay on his back and stared up at the ceiling as his jaw throbbed. Andrew was younger than him. A protégé. A successor. But he was other things too. A dominant wolf. Pack.

With the world spinning out of control, Andrew was a steady presence—someone who didn't need his protection. It was safe to show weakness. "I lost her before I should have even wanted her."

"What?"

Shit. It had gone down so fast no one even *knew*. "The doctor. Carmen Mendoza. I went sideways stupid over her, and my instincts went with me."

"Oh." Andrew dropped to the mat beside him. "You like Carmen?"

Like was a stupid word, one that made him feel a thousand years old, and it highlighted an uncomfortable truth. "Sure, I like her. *Like* isn't what makes the world tilt ten degrees every time she walks into a room. She's only half wolf, but I guess that half packs a punch."

"Huh." Andrew flashed him a quizzical frown. "I'm trying to wrap my brain around it. She seems so...nice."

"She is nice. That's probably why she's already walked out on me. I'm too much of an asshole to make a nice woman happy."

"Well, what happened?"

Alec covered his eyes with his hand. "I damn near lost it. More than once. You think what you did to Kat was bad? You had a fucking excuse. I'm just out of control. Drunk on instinct and stupid."

Andrew snorted. "Speaking from experience, I don't think you'd be this fucked up about it if *she* walked out on *you*. If that happened, you'd be relieved, not beating yourself up."

He wanted to ask Andrew how relieved he'd be when Kat started going out on dates with smooth-talking Miguel Mendoza, but he didn't have the heart to rub salt in that wound.

At least there was one thing he could ask. One thing where Andrew was the expert, because Alec's instincts had never been this out of control before. "Is your head clear? When Kat's not around, when you're not having to deal with her... Does all the instinctive shit go away too?"

"Most of the time." He shrugged. "Never goes away, not completely. What you've got to do is make peace with it. The pain's yours. You hurt her, right? That means you deserve it."

A chillingly succinct summation that told Alec more about Andrew than himself—and held up an unpleasant mirror. This was where Alec was headed. Straight to Andrew's personal hell, where he sacrificed everything and gave up the woman he loved because it was the right thing to do. Whether anyone could see it or not, Andrew was still bleeding.

Bleeding, but clear-headed. Alec was anything but, which meant he was facing a different problem all together. Carmen had taken parts of him. His rationality, his higher-thinking processes. Some sort of magic had tied them together, and walking away might not be enough—assuming he could stay away.

Even lying on his back, bruised and aching, he craved her with an intensity that bordered on madness. Assuming he could walk away might be the dumbest thing he'd done all day—and that was saying something.

Chapter Nine

The next morning, Carmen woke to the scent of brewing gourmet coffee, and she knew she was in trouble when her first thought was disbelief that Alec was up before her.

She wandered into the kitchen and into the middle of a spirited conversation between Lily and Franklin, who sat with the morning paper spread across the table.

"Thank you, Jesus." Lily latched on to her presence. "Carmen, tell this man why I couldn't come get you by myself yesterday. I plugged the address into my GPS and—hand to God—the thing laughed at me."

Carmen forced a smile as she poured a cup of coffee. "It's not that far from town, Lil."

Franklin's eyes followed her, narrowed and slightly assessing, but his voice was light. "Lily's a city girl. Keep trying to get her to come camping with me, but so far no luck."

"We don't have to sleep in the woods. We can build houses now."

Carmen slid into the chair across from Franklin's and avoided her boss's curious gaze. "Lily's never going to be your queen of the wilderness. May as well start shopping for a replacement."

"Oh, ha ha." Lily slid a plate of pancakes in front of her and propped both hands on her hips. "Shit, Carmen, you got kidnapped. Are you sure you're all right?"

"I'm fine." Different, and not entirely because of the spell, but okay. "Barely a scratch on me."

"And that's the way we're going to keep you." Franklin took a sip of his coffee, and the mug looked tiny in his rough, callused hands. "I'm thinking about getting a part-time guard for the clinic."

Carmen choked on her own coffee. "Did something happen while I was out?"

"You got kidnapped. Things are unsettled, and I'd rather not take chances. Not with you, or anyone else working there."

Her kidnapping had had nothing to do with the clinic, but he was right about one thing—he couldn't afford to take chances. "If you can spare me, I think I need some time off." She could deal with her family, at least, and make sure no one else was put in danger because of her.

Franklin glanced at Lily, who raised both eyebrows and flashed him a pointed look.

Carmen set down her mug. "Okay, what's going on?"

It was Franklin who finally spoke. "I didn't want to put this on you, not on top of everything else, but your uncle's been throwing his weight around."

Rage rose at his words, sudden and breathtaking, like a punch to the gut. She closed her eyes and counted backwards, a trick she used to soothe herself. "Did he threaten you?"

"People threaten me all the damn time, Carmen. Keeping the clinic neutral is a full-time job. And sometimes I piss people off, like I'm going to hack your uncle off." His mug hit the table with a thump. "So guards, when I'm not there. Just until things settle down a little."

"Julio always says this is the kind of stunt Uncle Cesar pulls when he feels out of control. He shakes trees just to see what falls out." Carmen smiled, the feral edge of anger still sharp inside her. "He's shaking the wrong one this time."

Lily watched her with wide blue eyes. "I recognize that look, Franklin."

"Which is why I didn't want to tell her." Franklin braced his hand against the table and leaned forward. "I don't get to tell you how to deal with your family, but you need to leave the clinic out of it. I don't go a week without someone pissing in my Cheerios over something, and my place'd be shut down if I smacked everyone in the face simply because they have it coming."

"Oh, I have plenty of reasons to punch Uncle Cesar in the head." Carmen picked up her fork and stabbed at her pancakes. "We can start with the fact that he tried to sell me to your army buddy like a purebred poodle."

It was Franklin's turn to choke. "He tried to sell you to Jacobson?"

"Maybe sell isn't the right word, since I'm pretty sure there might have been cash incentives readily available if Alec had agreed."

Franklin shook his head. "Your uncle's an idiot, and lucky he didn't get his jaw broken. Alec's sisters got to pretty much choose their husbands because even his father doesn't dare cross him on the topic of unwilling arranged marriages. Granted, Alec's father is a boot-licking lackey and not hard to bully."

Even if his father had been strong, he might not have stood against Alec. "Cesar's not stupid. He's just utterly convinced that he's right, and that the world should fall in line."

"Then he'll be sorely disappointed. In Alec, in you and in me." Franklin pinned her in place with a stern look. "I'm fond of you, Mendoza, and not only because you work for me. You've got to promise me you'll be careful."

She could reassure him on that count, at least. "Trust me, Franklin. My family has a vested interest in keeping me safe and well enough to smile pretty for my engagement photo in the society papers."

He didn't smile. "That'd be a hell of a lot more reassuring if we were all human. A psychic could make you smile pretty for all the pictures they wanted to take."

A week earlier, she would have denied the possibility. She would have been sure there was nothing her family wanted from her badly enough to go to such extremes. Now, she knew better. "I won't let that happen."

"Lily?"

Lily bent and kissed his cheek. "She'll be careful. Carmen likes herself well enough to want to stay safe."

She dropped her gaze so she wouldn't have to look at them. "I'm planning on sticking close to home for the next few days anyway."

A hand fell on her shoulder. Franklin's, warm and comforting. "Alec's in a damn pissy mood. Does that mean he did something dumb?"

She took her time chewing. "If you're curious, you should talk to him about it."

"Not a chance, Mendoza. Throwing myself on a grenade sounds like a better time than asking Alec Jacobson about his feelings. If you don't want to share, I'll stay curious."

"Fine." She dropped her fork and reached for her orange juice, wishing the glass also contained its fair share of vodka. "He's an asshole who can't make up his mind what he wants."

Franklin's expression turned serious. "Of course he can't. That man hasn't spent more than twenty seconds thinking about what he wants in a long damn time. He's probably out of practice."

Out of practice and scared by what could happen to her. "I'm an asshole too. It's a bad situation, all the way around."

"Yeah. And shitty timing, with your family." He smiled, a little lopsided. "Sorry, Carmen. You've had a week from hell, haven't you?"

"Could always be worse." She just wasn't sure how.

Alec was running a red light when his cell phone rang.

At least it was at an intersection so deserted he didn't feel guilty about slamming down the gas when the light turned yellow. He fumbled for his phone as he zipped through the intersection, then swore when he read the display.

Nicole Peyton rarely called him by choice. Jackson was her best friend and she was married to Kat's cousin—if she had a message for him, it usually went through one of them. The only time she called him directly was when shit was going to hell fast—

—or the Alpha had a message he couldn't officially give to a rogue bastard.

Alec fumbled for the answer button. "Yeah?"

"You have a problem," Nick said without preamble. "The guy who attacked Kat disappeared from Conclave custody this afternoon."

His first thought was, *shit,* followed closely by the more puzzling question. "How?"

"Oh, I thought I covered that part. He *disappeared,* as in a teleporter popped into his cell and popped right back out, with him in tow."

"Jesus Christ, Nicole. Are you shitting me?"

She made a strangled noise that almost sounded like a laugh. "This isn't my idea of a rollicking good joke, Alec. A Conclave guard watched it all happen, so it was either teleportation or one badass glamour affecting about a hundred people, because no one else in the building saw or heard anything."

"Damn." Not good news, considering he'd never heard of a teleporter strong enough to move themselves more than a few hundred feet, much less take someone else along for the ride. Then again, psychics with strong gifts that could be put to sinister uses had good reason not to make their presence known. "I can't tell if that's related to my current shitstorm or a completely different shitstorm."

"The thing with the Mendoza kid?" Nick hesitated. "Look, Alec, I don't say this a lot—mostly because you can take care of yourself—but watch it. Cesar Mendoza isn't good people."

Life really was circling the drain when Nicole Peyton started worrying about him. At least she was too distracted to ask painful questions about Carmen—questions Alec wasn't in the mood to answer. "I know Cesar Mendoza's a jackass, which is most of the reason I think this mess with Kat has to be separate. Mendoza wouldn't send someone on a risky job if they needed rescuing. Maybe if they needed killing, but this... Shit. Does your husband know?"

"Not yet. I thought I'd give you the heads-up first."

"Don't suppose you'd consider holding off for a bit?"

"Nope. I like being married."

Married people were a pain in the ass. "Fine. At least tell him that his cousin's fine, she dropped a shifter with a stun gun all by herself, and we're taking good care of her."

"I will, but don't be surprised if he shows up anyway."

"If he does, I'll deal." Alec whipped his truck around a corner and swore. "I'm on my way back to meet Kat and Jackson at your bar. Maybe I can convince her to call and fess up."

"Works for me. In the meantime, I'll keep an ear open for news."

"Thanks, Nicole. Give me an hour to convince Kat she's

busted before you spill the beans to Derek, would you?"

"One hour. Talk fast." The phone clicked.

Shit. One hour to get to the bar and convince Kat that independence didn't need to mean cutting her cousin out of her life entirely.

Alec buried the needle.

Forty-seven minutes later, Kat capitulated and took her cell phone outside into the April sunshine to call her cousin.

Alec blew out a breath and wondered if it was too early to drink something stronger than beer. "She seems to have bounced back just fine. I think Zola's stubbornness is rubbing off on her."

Jackson finished his beer before answering. "Really? I think she's getting more and more like you."

"I hope not." It sure as hell wasn't a compliment, especially considering the mood he'd been in since Carmen had left his house—and left him regretting half the things he'd said.

"Oh, come on. Don't get all wounded. It's a good thing."

"Uh-huh." Alec tilted his beer bottle toward the leather satchel on the seat beside his partner. Carmen might not want to talk to him, but he'd still do what he could to keep her safe. "So what's the news? Kat finally figure out what Cesar's been doing with his money?"

"Yeah." Jackson's eyes shadowed. "You're not gonna like it."

"He buy a witch?"

"No. He didn't spend it at all." He reached into the satchel and drew out a sheaf of papers. "He's been transferring it— cash, money market, even real estate assets. All to his brother's kids."

"*What?*" It didn't make any sense, unless... "Oh, shit."

"Yeah, looks like he's sheltering his assets in anticipation of a challenge. Which, if I recall correctly, is a big cowardly no-no, right?"

"Christ, yeah. Assuming it even works." A few generations ago, it wouldn't have mattered. An underhanded attempt to escape the consequences of a lost challenge would have been brought before the Conclave, and retribution would have been swift and brutal. The Alpha would have taken his share of the wealth as penalty, and the wolf in question would have been lucky to escape with his life.

John Wesley Peyton might have the strength to be Alpha, but he abhorred unnecessary brutality. The man had been fighting a losing battle for years, trying to drag the wolves into the civilized twenty-first century. Cesar Mendoza might be crazy enough to think he'd get away with a stunt like this.

Jackson tapped his empty bottle on the table. "Kat tracked down the paper trail on the rental house in Algiers too."

The bottom of Alec's stomach damn near fell out. It had been the first thing they'd looked into, but the paper trail had gone in endless circles obviously meant to protect whoever had paid for the place. If Kat had been restricted to legal channels, that would have been the end of it.

Thank God it wasn't—though confirmation of Carmen's suspicions might make her feel worse, not better. "Was it her father?"

"Hate it like hell, but yeah. Diego Mendoza secured the rental six months ago."

"Jesus. Wasn't a spur-of-the-moment decision, was it?"

Jackson smiled mirthlessly. "I don't think you can hit up the phone directory and find the kind of caster he needed for this shit. I'd be surprised if it took him less than a year of planning."

That was going to break Carmen's heart. "Did Kat include that in the paperwork?"

"Nope. I figured you could decide which parts to tell her."

"She suspects already." Alec sat back and scrubbed a hand over his face. "Suspecting isn't the same as knowing, is it?"

"Not about something like this, it isn't."

He'd pushed her away because she wasn't safe in his world. It had seemed stupid enough during the lonely nights he'd spent wishing she was in his bed. It seemed even stupider now, with proof in front of him in black and white—Carmen wasn't safe in her own world, and it had nothing to do with him. She'd be in danger whether she was with him or not.

Hell, she'd be a whole lot safer *with* him. "I'm an idiot, aren't I?"

"Yes," Jackson replied instantly. "What are we talking

about, specifically?"

Alec made a particularly rude gesture and earned himself a glare from the woman polishing the bar. "Acting like Carmen getting tangled up with me is more dangerous than the shit her family's dragging her through. I blew her off like an asshole."

"Oh, that. Yeah, you did." The waitress delivered another round, and Jackson thanked her with a smile. "Good news is, there's probably still time to fix it."

"Yeah, these files will make a great peace offering. 'Hi, honey. Your dad tried to kill you and your uncle's a spineless coward. Wanna screw?'"

His partner spewed beer all over the table. "And here I thought you were smoother than that."

He was, usually, but Carmen scrambled his brain. She made the world blurry, like the mating urge was trying to take hold even though she wasn't a wolf. Maybe the urge had been driving him the whole time, tying him in knots that nothing would ever undo. Making him dumb.

Only one way to find out. "I'll polish my charm."

"Good. I'm still putting out feelers about the witch but, like as not, we won't hear a peep."

"Dead ends and stonewalling. Business as usual." Alec finished his beer and shoved the bottle away. "Anything else I need to know? Plagues? Rain of toads?"

"Nah, pestilence must have taken the week off."

"Smartass. Just for that, you get to deal with Kat and her cousin. Keep Derek from storming the town and stirring up shit, would you?"

Jackson grinned. "You underestimate me."

"Let's hope."

"Mm-hmm." His partner slid the papers back into the satchel and handed it over to him. "In case Dr. Mendoza wants to see it for herself. I'm going to give Kat a ride and head home."

"Sounds good." Now all he had to do was learn how to grovel.

Chapter Ten

Carmen had just finished showering and dressing and was considering the Chinese takeout menu in her hand when the doorbell rang.

She peered through the window by the door, and her heart jumped. Alec stood on the porch, a leather folder in one hand. He was simply but neatly dressed in jeans and a black button-down shirt, and she looked down at her own clothes. Cotton lounge pants and a tank top had seemed fine for an evening in, but not with company.

Especially company that had fucked up and should now eat its heart out.

She opened the door, but held the edge instead of inviting him in. "Alec."

He didn't even greet her. "I'm sorry. I'm a jackass, and I'm sorry."

Franklin must have put him up to apologizing. "I said I understood, and I do." She raised both eyebrows. "Is there something else?"

Alec closed his fingers around the edge of the door, as if he was afraid she might jerk it shut. "You can't possibly understand. I don't even understand."

Looking at him hurt, so much more when he looked at her that earnestly. "I don't know what you want me to say. I forgive you? Just...go away, all right?"

"I can't." Uncertainty crept over her—his emotions, tinged with something almost like fear. "It was supposed to be clearer without you, but it's not. Just hurts more."

Part of her wanted to slam the door and retreat to a place

where he couldn't wound her again. "I can't do this, Alec. What happens in another week or two when you decide that yes, you were right, your life is too dangerous for me?"

"You're not Heidi." His fingers tightened on the door until the wood creaked. "I could have walked away and kept her safe, but I'm so fucking self-involved I never realized that none of this shit came to your door because of me. I didn't put you in danger, but I can protect you. Let me protect you."

Had he really thought he was at fault? "My family's been interfering with my life and my happiness for years. It's not you."

"I know that now." He held up his other hand, revealing a portfolio. "Jackson rubbed the proof in my face. Sometimes I'm stuck in my ways. I need to have the truth smacked into me."

She swung the door open and let him in. "I don't understand."

Relief flooded the room. Flooded his face. He stepped past her, his shoulder brushing her arm. "Kat figured out who paid for the house where the witch brought you."

She opened her mouth to ask him to explain, but a flash of memory slammed into her, stealing her breath. She'd talked to her father the day of her kidnapping, had stood in the too-warm spring sunlight and argued with him.

We're not talking about political alliances, Dad. We're talking about the rest of my life, and I'm not for sale.

I'm sorry to hear you say that, honey.

The sadness in his voice had held a finality that made her hair stand on end. And something else he'd said had been enough to scare the hell out of her. Enough to make her call Julio.

I have to go now, but I'll see you soon.

"It wasn't Cesar," she whispered hoarsely. "He didn't know what Julio was talking about because he had no idea."

"Your father rented the house six months ago."

My father. Call—call my father. Please.

Where do you think we're taking you?

Her knees wobbled, and Alec caught her with one arm. He pushed the door shut and twisted the lock, then swung her up into his arms and carried her to the couch. "Carmen? Stay with me."

The exact words she'd wanted from him before, and the circumstances under which they came now made her laugh. It came out sounding hysterical, so she pressed the heels of her hands to her eyes. "Franklin said it. This has been the week from hell."

"Yeah, it has." He settled with her in his lap, one hand rubbing between her shoulder blades. "And I haven't made it any easier on you by being an asshole and a coward."

"Shut up." She'd had the week from hell, all right, and being in his arms had been one of the few bright spots in it. "I don't want to hear about how stupid you were. Just tell me you're not going to do it again."

"I'm not going to do it again." It held the ring of truth, but regret still lingered. His fingers spread wide on her back as he sighed. "I don't want to lay anything else on you...but there's something else you need to know. About your uncle, and what he's been up to."

"Uh-huh." It had to be more important than kissing the side of Alec's neck, but that was what she found herself doing.

"Christ, Carmen." His knuckles brushed her neck, and his fingers slid into her hair. "How are you feeling? Magical crap mostly gone?"

Her body responded too quickly to his touch, and she didn't care. She'd been hungry for him before; now, she was starving. "I feel better," she answered breathlessly. "Good."

His eyes sparked with an interest echoed in the subtle shift of his emotions. "Good's good."

There was nothing between them this time, no reason to turn and walk away. Carmen took his other hand, folding both of hers around it. "This is going to sound—" No, she wouldn't apologize, and it couldn't be ridiculous, not with him looking at her like that. "I missed you."

The corner of his mouth kicked up as he stroked his thumb up and down the side of her throat. "Don't hear that very much from women who've spent more than a couple hours with me."

"So you keep reminding me." She tilted her head, baring more of her neck. "I think they haven't figured you out yet."

"And you have?" The callused pad of his thumb swept down toward her collarbone, then up the front of her throat. His fingers were warm against her nape. "What have you figured?"

She swallowed hard. "That you're not crazy. You just hurt."

His smile faded, and his hand stilled. "I think I've hurt so long that I might be a little crazy."

Maybe they both were. It couldn't diminish the heat that blazed inside her at the thought of his mouth on hers. "I'm an empath, remember?" Even as she spoke, Carmen reached up to guide his head closer. "I'd be able to tell."

He froze with his lips almost touching hers, and no amount of urging could budge him. "What else can you tell?"

Dominance pulsed between them, and every beat of her heart answered it with growing arousal. "You want me to submit," she whispered. "To let go of everything that isn't you and feel."

"Mmm." His fingers tickled the back of her neck as he twisted his wrist, twining the damp strands of her hair around his hand. "Just enough wolf in you to bring it out. This isn't a human game. It's not about power. It just *is*."

"I know." He evoked it like no one else ever had, that quiet instinctive need to belong completely to someone. "It's not control. It's caring."

"Always." Hot breath spilled across her cheek as he shifted his lips to her ear. "It's always about caring, but it can be about dirty goddamn fucking too."

Blood roared in her ears, and her hands began to tremble. "You say that like they don't go together."

Laughter spilled out of him, low and dark. "Oh, sometimes they do. But not everything is about fucking."

No, not everything. "Alec?"

He tilted her head back with the fingers curled in her hair, and his short beard lightly chafed her jaw as he pressed a kiss beneath her ear. "Yeah?"

"Sometimes, you talk too much."

"That so?" His teeth scraped against her skin. "And here we are, doing the one damn thing I'm not half bad at talking about. But if you don't like it..."

Before she could respond, he bit the spot where her neck curved into her shoulder, a rumbling growl of pleasure washing over her along with his intense satisfaction.

The forceful caress stole her breath, and she whispered a curse. "Just to clarify, we're not starting something we're not going to finish, right?"

"Not unless you decide to stop it."

It was all she needed to know. She rose on shaky legs, his hand still clutched in hers, and tried to pull him up beside her. When he resisted, she growled and climbed onto his lap. "Maybe I'm going to bite you now."

Alec just smiled and slid one hand around to the small of her back, edging her shirt up. "Take this off."

Nothing less than a command. She watched him as she drew the thin cotton up, hesitating just before it bared her breasts. He narrowed his eyes, his gaze dark and hot, and she shivered and stripped off the shirt.

He leaned forward without a word and tugged his shirt up and over his head, baring tanned skin marked by one or two thin scars and the black ink that curled around his arm and the back of his shoulder.

She ached to taste him, so she traced the hard line of his shoulder with her fingertips, then followed the same path with her mouth.

An approving noise vibrated up from deep in his chest as he caught her hair in one hand and stroked the bare line of her spine with the other. "Gonna bite me or not?"

"Impatient." She breathed the word against his skin. As soon as it was out of her mouth, she bit him—hard. He sucked in a breath. His hands tightened, one pulling her hair and the other dragging her hips to his.

He was hard under her, aroused. Nearly giddy with her own arousal, Carmen licked his shoulder before lifting her mouth to his ear. "You make me hungry."

"Good." He tugged lightly at her hair. "Come here."

He kissed her, at once sating and inflaming that hunger. His tongue drove past her lips to slide against hers, his own ardor so deep and sharp that it shook her. She tilted her head, fusing her mouth to his, and battled the urge to lower her shields so she could feel every reaction that shuddered through him.

But she couldn't keep them up forever, not like this. She broke the kiss, her head spinning. "Have you done this before?"

That earned her a hoarse chuckle. "Am I that bad at it?"

It took her a moment to realize what she'd said, and her

cheeks heated even further. "Not sex. Sex with an empath."

"Once." His mouth found her jaw, and he left a trail of teasing nips down the line of her throat before dragging his tongue along her collarbone. "She wasn't very strong. Couldn't project at all."

With his tongue on her skin, she could barely manage a husky murmur. "Then this might be different."

"You holding back?"

"For now." She licked her lips. "Unless...you want me to let go."

He urged her head back again, and his mouth found the top of her breast. "Let go. Let me feel what you're feeling."

Her breathing hitched. If she did what he asked, it could be fast, maybe even rough, a blinding blur of carnal pleasure.

It might be like that anyway.

Carmen closed her eyes and released her tight hold on control. He'd leaned her back so far that the only thing keeping her from tumbling off his lap was the steely strength of his hand at the base of her spine.

He would hold her.

She arched farther, shuddering through her pleasure *and* his when her nipple brushed his mouth. Teeth scraped the tender bud, followed by the hot swipe of a tongue, so good it left them both groaning. "Christ, you like the teeth, don't you?"

It was her turn to laugh, and she scratched her nails over the spot on his shoulder where she'd bitten him. "So do you."

"Most places." He closed his teeth on her this time, increasing the pressure until just a tiny bit more would have made her squirm away. Then the biting edge of his teeth vanished, replaced once more by the soothing heat of his tongue.

Most attentive men could gauge a woman's reactions, figure out when to apply a softer touch here, a quicker stroke there. Alec was going beyond that, using empathic feedback to give her exactly what she wanted.

She could do that too.

He was new to the give and take of empathy, but she'd lived with it her whole life. She'd already felt his libido stir at the sight of her on her on her knees, submissive and eager, and she knew they wanted the same thing.

It was part of what made him perfect for her.

She moved slowly, climbing off his lap only to ease between his legs and slide to the floor. She knelt there, her hands resting lightly on his knees, and waited.

Something dark stirred in his gaze, feral and hot. "You're cheating."

"But you like it." She trailed one hand up his leg and closed it around his belt buckle.

Alec dropped his hand to cover hers. "You wrap your lips around my dick, and there's a good chance I'll be fucking you over this couch. You ready for that?"

The image made her body throb, and she let the slightest hint of challenge show as she held his gaze. "If I get you in my mouth, I'm not stopping until you come."

He smiled and released her hand. "We'll see."

"Yes." And then he would know how quickly a storm of ecstasy could gather, how fast and hard it could sweep them away.

Carmen tugged open his belt and unbuttoned his jeans. Desire had built to a roar by the time she closed her hand around his erection, and she moaned as she stroked the pad of her thumb along the underside of his shaft.

He liked it, and it showed. In the twitch of his hips, the way his eyelids drooped and his jaw tensed. Small signs, so small compared to the vastness of his desire simmering just beneath the surface.

She used her tongue first, soft strokes meant to tease more than satisfy, and she trembled when a little more of his calm demeanor cracked, his fingers finding her hair.

He'd wait as long as he could to unleash the full force of his passion on her, and that only made her want it more. To see on his face and hear in his voice what she could already feel burning inside him.

"Harder," she whispered, and rubbed her head against his fingers for a moment before sliding her lips around him.

His hand did tighten, enough to drag her head back up. Another crack in his control. His eyes blazed, and his breath came too fast. "Take off your pants."

Carmen rose, her knees weak with anticipation. Her fingers fumbled on the drawstring, but the loose cotton fell easily, leaving her clad only in plain white panties. She half-wished she'd known to don something more provocative, but the feeling vanished when she met his eyes again.

Desire. Hot, pure desire that would burn bright enough to claim them both. "Those too, unless you want me ripping them."

Yes. She gasped and clenched her hands into fists at her sides.

It happened fast. His hand curled in the fabric and yanked it away with one violent jerk. He pulled her down to his lap just as fast, her back against his chest and her bare legs spread wide over his jean-clad thighs.

His skin was hot against hers. She arched, need riding her with a grating, almost painful edge. "Bedroom?"

Instead of answering, he gathered her hair and tilted her head to the side so he could close his teeth on the curve of her throat.

Claiming. Marking her as his.

His.

Carmen cried his name, all thoughts of moving from that spot gone in an instant. "Please. Alec, please—"

He spilled her from his lap to the couch as he rose. "You've got until I get my boots off." The words bordered on a growl. "Then I'm taking you where I catch you."

One boot hit the floor, and she shoved her hair out of her face and stared at him. He was dead serious—and undressing fast.

She ran.

She made it to her bedroom, but not to the bed. He caught her around the waist and dragged her the last few feet, bending her upper body over the mattress. "I've only got one condom. I sure as hell hope you've got more around here."

"In the medicine cabinet." She laughed, giddy with anticipation and relief. "Lily just bought some. I'll steal the whole damn box."

His gruff laughter almost covered the sound of tearing foil. "I don't know if that's a warning about your stamina or confidence in mine, but it's fucking hot."

"I'll have to steal them. I don't have any that aren't dangerously close to expiration." She swallowed hard. "It's been a while since—since I did this."

Alec's hand smoothed along her spine, down to her hip and then farther, curling around her thigh as he guided her legs apart. His other hand hit the bed next to her head, and he leaned over her until his voice came from behind her left shoulder. "Want me to ease you back into it?" Wide fingers slipped against her, pushed inside. "Or do you want it fast?"

She couldn't answer at first, not with his fingers stretching her, intensifying the ache building inside her. "Don't make me wait."

His fingers vanished. His cock replaced them, hard and pressing into her, so slow, even though she could see the effort control cost him in the tense arm next to her, could feel it in his steely, unbelievable determination.

He needed to make her feel good, and the strength of that need sent her spinning. "This is what you do to me," she whispered hoarsely. Then she came, pleasure twisting tight inside before exploding, shaking through her in a rain of fire and satisfaction.

One hard, startled thrust pinned her hips to the bed, and he groaned and slapped his other hand down on the mattress. Both fisted, crushing the quilt as his chest slicked over her back with every panting breath. "Christ, woman. Do you have any idea what *that* does to *me*?"

"No. *Yes*." Carmen shuddered and bucked, desperate for more. "You're the one holding back now."

His hips rocked, a slow glide out and a faster, harder return. He nuzzled her hair from her ear and bit the lobe with a pleased noise. "No making me come before I get to enjoy being inside you."

"Sex with an empath." She reached up and clenched her hand in his hair. "It doesn't have to stop when you come."

His next thrust inched her along the bed. "Sex with a shifter means it just starts again."

"See?" She pushed back against him and bit her lip when white-hot ecstasy rebounded through her. "We *are* perfect."

He made a rumbling noise of agreement and straightened, dragging his fingertips over her shoulders and down her back until his hands found her hips. "Don't hold back. Let me feel it all."

It was a habit more than anything, rebuilding those walls. As soon as she dropped them again, she hissed a curse as the full force of his appetite swept over her. He yearned for her, hungered—

Craved.

Under it all, a fine blade of fear lurked, and Carmen made a soothing noise. "I can take you. You won't hurt me."

He began to move, and it wasn't gentle. His fingers tightened, lifting her hips until every thrust rubbed her G-spot. Her hand slipped and her elbows crashed to the bed, arching her back even more. The next time he drove into her, the hot ache inside her twisted tighter, almost to the breaking point.

Almost.

"God, Alec. *Please.*" She was begging, and she didn't care. It didn't matter. Only him, inside and around her, so much desire. "So much—"

Satisfaction trickled through the pleasure spun out between them, and he whispered one word. Just one, rough and needy and without doubt a command. "Now."

Ecstasy lashed through her, wrenching a scream from her throat. In that moment, she was completely, utterly open to him, and she relished it. He'd taken her, marked her skin and claimed her—and that made him hers.

Mine. More than a thought, and she felt it shudder through him a split second before he tightened his grip on her hips and dragged her back into a hard, unsteady thrust. Her orgasm had barely faded when his began, and with no barriers left she felt it too, every pulse, every spike, all of it in reaction to her.

If he hadn't been holding her, she would have slid to the floor. Carmen turned her cheek to the light quilt, cool under her flushed skin.

Alec slumped over her, his elbows digging into the bed as his forehead dropped to her shoulder. "Jesus."

Joy bubbled up in her chest and escaped as a laugh. "I think I figured out what our problem was."

"We had a problem?"

"Mmm. Talking, and fighting." Her brain whirled, and she laughed again. "Fighting this."

He eased away, only to lift her up and lay her on the bed. "Seemed like a good idea at the time. Now I'm kicking myself a little."

She rolled onto her back. "Don't. Plenty of time now."

"Mmm." He crashed next to her, stretched out and hooked one arm over her waist. "I turned off my phone. New Orleans will have to survive without me for the night."

It didn't seem like the sort of thing he did often. "I don't mind if there's an emergency, Alec. With my job, believe me, I'm used to it."

"Eh, if there's an emergency, they'll find me anyway. Can't hide from psychics and wizards. But if it can wait, I'm going to make it wait."

She traced one finger over one of the dark lines of ink that curled around his shoulder. "Thank you."

"For what, honey?"

The stern, serious set of his face had relaxed, and it made it easier to confess the truth. "I don't know yet, but I'll think of something."

A tiny smile curved his lips. "Down payment for what I'm going to do to you when I recover in fifteen minutes?"

"I think...for not fighting anymore."

"I was never fighting you. You know that, right?"

No, he'd been fighting himself, his own demons and the magic that had bound her. But the end result had been the same. "Doesn't matter."

He caught her hand against his chest. "Yeah it does. One's about not wanting to want you. The other's about not wanting to hurt you."

Carmen sat up and leaned over him. "I know who my family is. If you didn't have any reservations about getting involved with me, then you just weren't thinking."

Alec shrugged. "Sure. I had reservations while I was wondering if you were a femme fatale sent to mount my balls in your trophy case. As for the rest of it, hell. If anyone should have reservations, it's about my family. And yeah, I have my share of those."

Because of his wife. Even if she wanted to talk about it, that was definitely a conversation for another time. So Carmen propped her chin on his chest and affected a sigh. "Shows what you know. I don't even *have* a trophy case."

His smile widened as he lifted a hand to toy with a lock of

her hair. "So where do you keep them? Bookshelf? Bathroom cabinet?"

"Interestingly enough, I usually let men leave my acquaintance still in possession of all their most beloved parts."

"Makes sense. We're more useful that way."

"Exactly." He was a beautiful man anyway, but when he let his guard down and really smiled... "You're gorgeous."

He twisted his finger in her hair and tugged a little. "Not as gorgeous as you."

Warmth unfurled in her belly. "You want to argue about that now too?"

"Maybe only a little. Unless you've got something else in mind?"

She feathered kisses over his chest, from one shoulder to the other. "Maybe. Since you still have all your parts and all."

If he gave her the night, she'd take it. If he gave her more, she'd take that too, and worry about everything else—including both of their families—later.

After twenty-four straight hours of sex, sleep and a silent cell phone, Alec knew the blissful vacation had to end.

Still, he didn't expect it to end with eleven voicemails. "Jesus."

Carmen set an open beer on the table in front of him. "What's wrong?"

"This." He held up the phone with its damning message count. "Not sure if the shit hit the fan, or they really missed me."

She bit her lip. "Just Jackson, or others?"

"Guess we'll find out."

First was a message from Jackson, an update that he hadn't found anything. The next two were from Kat, both accusing him of having forgotten to charge his phone but not leaving any real information. He deleted the one from his father without listening.

The fifth message made him sit upright, apprehension unfurling in his gut. His cousin's voice—the only cousin he actually liked, and the one who lived on a ranch in Wyoming. The ranch where the Alpha's daughters lived.

"Hey, Alec. It's Gus. Michelle wanted me to call and ask if you can bring someone named Dr. Mendoza up here to the ranch as soon as possible. She didn't say much else, just that the magic stuff could be bad, and coming from Michelle..." He'd paused to clear his throat. "Well, it's the stuff she *doesn't* say that scares the hell out of me. So watch yourself, and be careful."

Alec hung up the phone without listening to the other messages.

Carmen stood, one hand clenched around the back of a kitchen chair, staring at him. "Alec, what is it? What happened?"

He needed to stay calm. Not panic, and not make her panic. "You know about Seers?"

She nodded jerkily. "Of course. Shapeshifters with magic. The Alpha's daughter is one."

"Michelle Peyton. She sent a message through one of my cousins. She knows a little about what's happened to you, and thinks it might be a good idea if you come up so she can take a look."

Carmen's chest rose and fell with rapid, shallow breaths, but she only said, "I'll pack a bag."

Damn it all. He could hide his alarm behind all the straight-faced stoicism he wanted, but Carmen would be able to feel it. "I overreact," he said quietly. "Worrying is what I do. Doesn't mean things are dire."

"I know." She smiled, a shaky expression that she didn't try to hold. "I should probably hit Google, see how cold it is in New York this time of year."

"Right idea, wrong place." Alec shoved his chair back and rose. "Wyoming. Michelle lives on a ranch there. It's a long story."

"It always seems to be." Carmen caught his hand and stared up at him. "I should have already thought of it. I, of all people, should know that feeling fine doesn't necessarily make you fine."

Alec leaned down and brushed his lips over her forehead. "No should-haves and could-haves now. I know someone who can fly us up to Wyoming tomorrow morning, first thing. If your stomach can handle tiny planes, that is."

"I don't get airsick."

"Or nervous?" He tried to find a smile. To pretend everything was going to be fine. "Ever had a wizard pilot?"

"If so, I didn't know." She released him and stepped back. "Do you need to go home and pick up some things too?"

It would be easier to make all the necessary arrangements, but the thought was surprisingly unappealing. He didn't like the idea of leaving her, especially if something might go wrong at any second.

And if it could go wrong at any second... Gus had said as soon as possible. "Maybe we could leave tonight. I'll call my pilot friend and we can swing by my house and pick up my stuff on the way."

The words startled her, but she covered well. "I'll get my bag now." She wrapped her arms around her body as she turned and walked out of the kitchen, leaving behind a faint echo of fear and guilt.

Alec wanted to follow her. Comfort her. Hold and soothe her, as if hugs and kisses could protect her from whatever magic might be curled inside her. Waiting.

A danger he couldn't fight, and it made his skin itch. If he made it to Wyoming without driving himself half-insane, it would be a goddamn miracle.

Chapter Eleven

The sun was still tucked behind the distant hills when Nelson set his tiny plane down on the landing strip Luciano Maglieri had built on the outskirts of his ranch. Marriage to the Alpha's daughter had brought Luciano a small fortune—and a father-in-law anxious to visit his first grandchild.

Carmen had fallen asleep somewhere over Oklahoma, driven by exhaustion and lulled by the warmth and silence provided by the Cessna's magical enhancements. Nelson made a tidy living as a supernatural taxi, and Alec couldn't blame the shifters who'd rather pay for a private flight than endure hours in a cramped space, surrounded by humans.

Of course, it meant Nelson didn't have time to stick around waiting for them. He pulled off his headset as soon as they were stopped and nodded toward the two trucks pulling toward them. "Looks like Maglieri's waiting for you. I've got to get out to California for a pickup, but y'all just give me a holler when you need a ride back home. I'll juggle things around. Make it work."

Alec nodded and twisted in his seat. "Carmen, honey? We're here."

"I'm up." She blinked and lifted her head, the red imprint of the seat standing out on her cheek. "Yeah, I'm up."

She was rumpled, red-eyed and entirely disheveled, and it was adorable. Endearing. Less endearing was the fact that he was a forty-four-year-old man thinking words like *adorable* in the middle of a damn crisis. *Get a grip, idiot.* "Don't have to stay up for long. It's not even five. I'm sure no one will mind if we sleep for a couple hours."

"I used to be able to do this," she said ruefully. "Now I have regular shifts with occasional call. Working for Franklin has spoiled me."

Nelson laughed. "Jake and Frank have gone soft. All this nice, cushy civilian living. I could tell you some stories from back in the day..."

God only knew what Franklin had already told her about their less-than-glorious days as supernaturals hiding in a very human army—or worse, their even less glorious days as guns for hire. "Thought you needed to get to California."

Carmen chuckled as she gathered her bag and rose. "Mr. Nelson, if you consider them soft, then you must be far scarier than you appear to be."

Nelson flashed her a flirtatious grin that had Alec's fingers curling toward his palm. The urge to hit him didn't diminish when he affected a southern drawl so "good ole boy" it even out-did Jackson. "Well, ma'am, that's 'cause all that growlin' just lets people know they're comin'."

Alec bit back a growl—barely. "We'll call you." Then he got the hell out of the plane before he punched his friend in the face.

Luciano climbed out of the first pickup, bleary-eyed and unshaven, and stopped short when he got a good look at Alec's face. "Welcome to Wyoming. Got the guesthouse all set up for you." He nodded to Carmen. "Ma'am."

"Carmen Mendoza." She held out a hand.

Luciano glanced at Alec again, a quick, almost furtive look, before shaking her hand quickly. "There's room for all of us in this truck, but Dr. Mendoza'll have to squeeze into the backseat."

Shoving her into the back wasn't the polite thing to do, but it would put her farther away from Luciano, and the boy wasn't a fool. After thirty-six hours together, Carmen had Alec's scent on her skin in a way a shower wouldn't erase, and his temper was legendary.

Plus, he *had* kidnapped the kid and locked him in a cage.

Everyone was watching him, waiting for a response. The wind held a bitter edge, a hint of snow even in mid-April. The most important thing was getting Carmen someplace warm. He took her bag and his own and dropped them into the bed of the truck. "I'll be fine in the back."

"Your legs are longer," she urged. "Sit in the front."

Luciano ignored them both in favor of climbing into the truck, and Carmen followed suit by opening the half-door that led to the tiny backseat. Once in the truck, Alec did his best to polish up his manners. "Thanks for letting us come up here with no notice."

Luciano laughed. "I thought Michelle as much as ordered you up here."

"She lit a fire under Gus's ass, but I wasn't sure if that was on purpose."

The other man's humor faded with a quick look at the rearview mirror. "I think it might have been, yeah."

So much for that hope. Alec forced a change of topic to keep his fear from growing strong enough for Carmen to sense. "I tried to call Nicole before we left, but it went straight to voicemail. I'm guessing Kat couldn't talk Nicole and Derek out of flying down there to check on her?"

"They left yesterday. Last night."

He wished Kat all the luck in the world talking her cousin down. At least it would keep her out of trouble...and he wouldn't have to deal with Nicole's smartass commentary on his too-obvious concern for Carmen. "What about the Alpha?"

"Someone escaped from Conclave custody, Jacobson. The Alpha flew back to New York to deal with the fallout."

So the disappearance of Kat's attacker was being taken seriously. One less thing he had to worry about. "Michelle didn't want to see us right off, did she? I could use a couple hours of shut-eye."

"She's asleep." This time, he looked away from the rough ranch road long enough to turn back and smile at Carmen. "Late breakfast around ten?"

"Thank you," she murmured.

Five hours to get some sleep. Alec could only hope that would be enough to deal with whatever came next.

Michelle Peyton Maglieri didn't look like she'd been up all night with a two-week-old baby.

Carmen never would have known, except that the proof of it lay beside Michelle in a white bassinet, drowsing as she sipped her herbal tea. He was small, maybe too small to have been delivered at term, but he looked healthy. Strong.

She forced her attention back to the Seer. "You didn't have to see me so early, but thank you."

Michelle smiled, warm but a little worn around the edges. "He'll be up in a while anyway, and you would have heard him from the guesthouse."

"He's beautiful."

"I think so." Michelle set down her cup and reached out to smooth the edge of the blanket before touching her son's cheek. "I admit to my share of maternal bias. But you didn't come all this way to see my son."

"No," she admitted. "I'm here because of magic I didn't ask for and know nothing about."

Michelle faced Carmen. A tiny crease appeared between her eyebrows as she narrowed her eyes. "Yes. It's still tangled around you. Powerful magic, and reckless. I was afraid of that."

How could she explain the lengths to which her father had gone, whatever his reasons? "Is it...dangerous?"

"Yes." Gentle, but uncompromising. "Trying to make a shapeshifter with magic is no safer than trying to turn a human through violence. It's a hundred times more dangerous when there's already magic involved. In your case, more than one kind of magic."

Carmen willed her hands to wait until she'd set her cup aside before they began trembling. "Dangerous to me or to others?"

"Potentially both." Michelle held out her hands. "If you let me, I can put shields in place. A temporary measure, but it will protect you and the people around you until I can figure out how to unweave the spell."

The Seer was a brand-new mother, and a closer look revealed the beginnings of dark circles of exhaustion under her eyes. "Will it wait?"

"For a day or two. Mahalia is still here, and she has experience and finesse that I lack."

The spell her father had paid for was fractured, broken. It would take a Seer and another witch, one Alec had talked about with deep respect, to dissolve the shards of magic that could still make her bleed.

Carmen knew she should be frightened—*needed* to be—but

all she felt was numb. "You and your husband are very kind for having me here."

Michelle's lips pressed together, and the first hint of emotion broke through her excellent shields—pain. "Our society seems to have no boundaries in how far it will go to protect status and prejudice. My child lost his father, Alec lost his wife...and you could have died. Anything I can do to stop them is more selfish than selfless, believe me."

"Whatever your reasons, I'm grateful."

"It's noth—"

A tiny cough drifted up from the bassinet and, in one heartbeat, the confident Seer melted away, replaced by a frantic new mother who lifted her son into her arms with an expression that bordered on panic.

The baby fussed at being woken so unceremoniously, and Carmen watched Michelle for a moment before rising from her chair. "May I look at him?"

"He's had a cough..." After a split-second hesitation, Michelle held him out. "I know you're not a pediatrician, but do you think I should call for the doctor? There's a witch my father has on retainer."

"Nah, let's see the little guy." Carmen nestled the baby in one arm and peeled back his blanket. His skin was a healthy pink, with none of the blue tinge that would accompany inadequate oxygenation. "Has he been wheezing with the cough?"

"No, no wheezing. It hasn't been too bad, but he was born early..."

The baby looked okay, but Carmen asked a few more questions, more to be thorough than anything. Michelle's answers confirmed her suspicions, and Carmen smiled as she tickled him on the cheek. "He's healthy. Yeah, you're doing just fine, aren't you?"

Michelle dropped back into her chair with a relieved sigh. "The witch has politely warned me against overreacting. Intellectually, I understand, but it doesn't make it easier."

"They're tiny and helpless, and that's scary all on its own." Carmen rocked the baby slowly and turned her attention to Michelle. "What about you? How are you doing?"

"Fine, aside from the lack of sleep. Shapeshifters can heal

from a lot, but not exhaustion." Her brown eyes drifted shut. "I'm told this is a natural state for a new mother."

"I was almost a teenager when my mother had her youngest. I remember."

Michelle rubbed at her face and smoothed her hair. "It's making me scattered. I can't remember if I've explained *why* the spell they've tried to use is so dangerous."

"Because I'm already part wolf?"

"Yes. And not just that—you're from a strong bloodline." Michelle opened her eyes and gave Carmen a look that seemed almost apologetic. "One of my jobs as the Conclave's Seer was knowing everything about the council members. Strengths that could be used and weaknesses that could be exploited."

It wasn't a secret. It couldn't be, not when her uncle made sure everyone knew about Julio, the wolf born to a fully human mother. "My family doesn't try to hide the strength of that blood. Quite the opposite."

"I know. Which is why this was incredibly reckless. There's a reason wolves don't have their human offspring changed. The power in the change is all consuming. Someone with only a bit of shapeshifter blood might come through all right, but the magic in the change is linked to the one who made you. If their magic has to fight the magic already inside you, there's no room for anything human."

It was the most authoritative discussion of the spell that she was bound to get now that the witch was dead, and some tiny flame of hope within Carmen died. It shouldn't still hurt, damn it, because she'd already told herself the hard truth about her family and her place in it, already forced herself to face it.

A gentle hand settled on her arm. "I'm sorry."

Carmen shook her head and shifted the child she held back into his mother's arms. "It's not news. It's—it's something I should have understood a long time ago."

"But not something easy to understand. Not something you should have to understand."

Definitely not, but it didn't change reality or the truth of her situation. "If this magic is going to be taxing for you, then you should wait as long as you can. I don't want to trespass on your hospitality too long, but if you might hurt yourself doing this—"

Michelle shook her head and cut her off. "No, not at all. I have the power to spare, even as tired as I am. But Mahalia... She's the magical equivalent of a scalpel. I'm more of a claymore. You need a little bit of both."

"Okay." Carmen took a deep breath. "When?"

"Tomorrow, I think." Michelle rose and tucked her son back into his bassinet. "A day to prepare, and a day afterwards to be sure there are no lasting effects. Can you spare three days?"

"If I won't be in the way."

"Only if you don't mind living at the whim of a two-week-old who can be heard halfway to Laramie."

Carmen's cheeks heated. "Your husband told me I could put my things out in the guesthouse, if that's all right."

Michelle pursed her lips, almost as if she was holding back a laugh. "Shapeshifter boys don't always play well together. Luciano and Alec have...a bit of a rocky history. Alec will probably be more comfortable in the guesthouse, and more comfortable with you there too."

Of course, the Seer would have figured out their situation just as quickly as anyone else. "It seemed to be a bit of a territorial issue."

"So much of our lives can be." She hesitated, then tilted her head. "May I ask a personal question?"

"Of course."

"Will you regret not becoming a wolf?"

It stopped Carmen cold, because she hadn't considered it. She'd thought about how she might handle it if it happened, of course, but only as how she would deal with the inevitable complications. Only how she'd survive with her sanity intact.

She'd never thought she might want to become a wolf, not once. She'd spent too much time avoiding what it meant that she carried wolf blood at all, and becoming part of that society...

Isn't that what you've done? Inviting Alec into her bed, her *life*, meant that she would never be able to truly separate herself from wolf society. He existed on the rebellious edge of that world...but he was still *in* it.

And he'd already told her it was a dangerous place. Maybe becoming a wolf would help her stay safe in the midst of that chaos.

Carmen found herself shaking her head. "No. No, I won't regret it. There's only one reason I'd even consider wanting to become a wolf and—and it's a bad reason. I can't change myself like that for someone else. I won't." And if Alec cared about her at all, he wouldn't want that either.

Michelle's smile held more than a little relief. "I'm glad. Because it could be that the only way we can fix this will be to twist the spell in on itself. Turn it from danger to protection. It would mean you could never be changed, not even if you chose to."

Even with her decision made, Carmen expected a measure of panic at the finality Michelle described, but it never came. "I'm okay with that."

A short nod. "Do you have any more questions?"

She probably wanted to rest while her baby did, so Carmen shook her head and rose. "Thank you, but no. I think I'll go lie down for a while."

"Make yourself at home. If you need anything at all, please let me know."

With Carmen safely ensconced in Michelle's sitting room and Luciano off dealing with some sort of ranch emergency, Alec sought out the one familiar face he hadn't seen in far too long.

He found his cousin in the kitchen, wrestling with a pan, packages of cream cheese piled high on the counter beside him. "Making cheesecake tonight."

Gus hadn't changed much. He was still large, blunt and about as pretentious as a stack of bricks. It made him a welcome relief from the rest of the Jacobson clan. "That's a lot of cream cheese."

Gus snorted. "I guess that means asking you for help with this damn springform thing is out of the question."

As if he knew what a springform thing *was*—presumably the round pan Gus was glaring at. "Depends on what you want to do with it. Carmen could probably set you on the right track, though."

"Yeah? She good in the kitchen?"

"Kept me from starving."

Gus dropped the round piece of metal on the counter and

eyed Alec. "Are you gonna let me meet her?"

It shouldn't have brought protective rage bubbling to the surface. Maybe the magic was affecting him too, triggering an instinctive reaction that went far beyond hot sex and enjoyment of her company. Hadn't he spent hours explaining the mating urge to Derek and Andrew, fighting to explain the inexplicable? Carmen might not be a wolf, but she felt like one.

A nice, easy explanation that would give him an excuse for running through half a box of condoms with her. It didn't explain the fact that his cousin—his friend—felt like a threat.

"Settle down, Alec. I didn't ask if I could see her naked."

Maybe he could break the pan over his cousin's head. "Back off. It's been a weird fucking week."

"Don't doubt it in the least." Gus smiled, a rare expression that made him look ten years younger. "It's good to see you."

Alec's aggression faded a little. "Good to see you too. When you're not jabbing at me just to see if I'll snap."

"Is that what you think that was?" He laughed. "Everyone down in Louisiana goes too easy on you."

"They probably do." Alec leaned against the counter and took in the industrial kitchen, with its large, heavy pots that would make it easy to cook for dozens. "I never realized just how serious Luciano took this ranching business. I always thought he was a city boy, playing at being a cowboy."

"Luke? Hell, no. It's a solid operation. He's got one Crabbet that's fetching a stud fee you wouldn't believe."

He'd long since written Luciano off as a spineless mama's boy, but the kid had showed some pluck in the last year. He'd stood up to his family and the whole damn Conclave by marrying Michelle and taking another man's child under his protection. That their marriage was one of convenience and polite distance was well known. That Luciano had feelings for the woman who had made it gently clear she could never return them was more of a secret.

And a tragedy. It was hard not to respect a man who'd stomp on his own heart to do the right thing. "Sometimes I almost miss ranch life. I haven't been back to Texas in...ten years, maybe."

"Me neither." Gus picked up the pan again. This time, he managed to fit a piece of glass in the bottom and lock a lever mechanism in place. "You'd think the damn state would be big enough for us to go and still avoid our family, wouldn't you?"

"My father's probably got spies posted on every road in, waiting for his chance to ambush me on his turf."

"Good reason to stay away, if you ask me."

"Agreed. You could come down and visit me, you know. New Orleans is..."

"Interesting?" Gus supplied with a raised eyebrow. "I've got some time off coming. Maybe I'll do that."

"And maybe I'll put you to work, helping me save the world." Alec glanced at his watch, then toward the door. "I suppose if I go and check on them, I'll get kicked back out."

"If you're lucky." A large bowl clattered on the countertop. "Your woman's safe. Michelle will help her."

"My woman." He said it without meaning to, and Christ, it felt too good. "Better not call her that where she can hear."

"Why not?" The question was more matter-of-fact than probing. "Hasn't she figured it out yet?"

A good fucking question, and one he wasn't feeling a pressing need to discuss with her. "She's not a wolf."

"Does she know wolves, though? And, more to the point, does she know *you*?"

"She's getting there." Alec crossed his arms over his chest and gave his cousin a look. "If no one scares her off."

Gus cracked an egg with a chuckle. "If you haven't terrified her with your scowling, she's not going anywhere. Trust me on that."

"You're awful amused. Truth be told, I thought you'd be a little more pissy about me taking up with a Mendoza."

The second egg disintegrated in Gus's hand, and he turned a shocked stare to Alec. "Tell me that's not Diego Mendoza's daughter."

Oh, shit. "You thought she was a random Mendoza tied up in a shapeshifter mess?"

"Hell, all Michelle mentioned was some sort of magic spell gone wrong. I didn't put two and two together." Gus rinsed his hand with a grimace. "You don't do things by half, do you?"

Alec watched his cousin pick eggshells out of the bowl. "Didn't plan to do it at all. It's complicated."

"Guess so." Gus dropped the shells in the sink and cursed

again. "Couldn't think of a more dangerous place to stick your dick? There's a garbage disposal right here. I'll give you two a minute alone."

Gus wasn't stupid, which meant he couldn't have been surprised when Alec drove a fist into his jaw.

Carmen waited for Alec in the front room of the guesthouse. When he returned, one eye was swollen and bruised. There were red blotches on his cheeks and jaw, and split skin on his knuckles that had barely healed over.

She took a deep breath and asked the last question she wanted to hear the answer to. "What happened?"

Alec frowned. "What happened when?"

"What happened to your *face*?"

"Oh." He poked at his bruised cheek and made a rude noise. "Gus is faster than he used to be—or I'm slowing down. I used to whup him nine times out of ten when we were kids."

Don't be paranoid, Carmen. "Do you two beat each other up a lot?"

Alec's amusement faded, and he reached out and looped an arm around her. "A fair bit. Sometimes the only way to deal is to blow off steam."

"Okay." The temptation to lean into his embrace was great. "Michelle thinks she's figured out a way to fix the spell."

"Yeah?" He gave her a little tug and guided her toward the cozy living room and its worn but comfortable furniture. "What'd she say?"

"That she has to do something to the magic. Turn it around on itself and make it into something else."

Alec dropped onto the couch and pulled her down, tucked close against his side. "You're nervous about something. You wanna talk or is it easier to just let it be?"

"I don't think I have that option." She had to stand, to get a little space so she could order her words. "When Michelle and Mahalia do whatever it is they're going to do, that's it. The end of the spell. No more potential for me to become a wolf. In fact, it can't happen. And I'm good with that...I think."

"You think?" His expression remained inscrutable. "Something's still holding you back?"

"I thought it was you." She'd make them both crazy if she tried to talk while she paced the floor, so she perched on the edge of the coffee table. "I mean, the first thing that occurred to me was that you might want it. But then I started wondering *why* I thought so."

He stayed very, very still. "I'm a controlling bastard to be sure, Carmen, but not that much of one."

Her heart skipped. She was fucking it up, making it sound like she was placing blame when she was only trying to explain. "The night my father left my mother, I heard them arguing. She told him there was no way he was going to take her kids, and he said he only wanted Julio, of course."

The line of his jaw tightened, and his fingers curled around the back of the couch, like it was the only thing keeping him from reaching for her. "No offense, sweetheart, but your father's kind of an ass."

So calm, but she could feel the rage brewing beneath that façade. "That's not the bad part, Alec." Her throat ached, and her eyes burned with tears. "I ignored the seriousness and danger of this spell because my father is responsible for it, and surely my own father wouldn't do something that could kill me, no matter how little he cared. And then I realized what it meant."

His eyes said he knew too, but he just nodded. "And?"

"It means I spent twenty years thinking I was nothing to him, but it's worse. I'm less than nothing." The tears spilled over, but she couldn't stop them. "My own *father* thinks I'm better off dead than the way I am."

"Oh, honey." Strong hands slipped around her. "C'mere."

She fell into his arms, into the way he held her and the comforting strength he represented. "I know you're not like that. Really, I do."

"You know it," he agreed. "But do you believe it?"

She wanted to, so badly. "I believe you're a better man than he could ever be."

"I'm a different man." His hand came up, fingers lifting her chin. "I'm not a good man, Carmen. But even so, I wouldn't change you."

She felt the undeniable truth of it, saw it in his eyes. "I know."

"Good." A smile finally curved his lips. "I'm out of practice at dating, but I'm pretty sure we're going about it a little backwards."

"I think we're doing all right. Well, except that I just cried on you. Then there's the ton of childhood trauma I unloaded."

Alec shook his head. "And I gotta say, I don't usually lock a woman in a cage until the third date."

He was nervous, odd when she was the one burning with embarrassment. "What's wrong?"

For a long time he didn't speak. His hand fell to her hip, a strong grip that kept her body tight against his. "I follow my instincts. A lot of times, I get accused of doing it without thinking, and some of those times it's true. Now, it's true."

"You mean me," she said slowly. His admission didn't scare her, but the bewilderment and fear lurking behind the words did.

"Not just you. Everything. I've charged into your life and I've dragged you halfway across the country and this isn't a fucking date and we both know it."

"I wanted you in my life, and you haven't dragged me anywhere. But you're right." Her rational mind clamored for control, but it couldn't overcome her heart. "It's not just a date. I'm falling in love with you."

His fingers tightened and purely masculine satisfaction swelled through him. Then came a slash of fear, and he shook his head. "Not now, not yet. Part of what's got me turned around is knowing the only time you've ever seen me without magic clouding things up is the first day we met."

She couldn't fault him for doubting, not under the circumstances, but his words provided an uncomfortable reminder. "The converse is also true, isn't it? Your instincts might tell you something entirely different about me once the magic is gone."

"Maybe." He touched her cheek. "A couple of rational people might think that was a good reason to slow the fuck down."

The words made sense, but every last bit of his body language defied them. "But this isn't a fucking date."

"Because you're already mine."

Carmen laughed even as a shiver of satisfaction ran

through her. "Now *I'm* all turned around."

"Welcome to my world, honey." His fingers crept under the hem of her shirt, warm and rough against her skin. "There's no up or down, but clothing's optional."

No sense in fighting it, not when the slightest touch flooded her with heat. "Take me to bed."

Alec rose and lifted her with him, hoisting her up until she wrapped her legs around his hips. "I can do that."

In a more familiar place, she would have kissed him, trusting him to find his way blindly. Instead, she bit the side of his neck, a little harder with every step until they reached the bed.

He growled and dropped her to the mattress. "Making sure everyone knows I'm taken, are you?"

"It'll heal." The reality was blunt, simple. "I want you to know."

If anything, his eyes darkened. He pulled open his belt, dragging the smooth brown leather free of his belt loops before dropping it to the floor. "Might have to do it again, just to drive the message home."

"Whatever you need." She whispered the promise as she unbuttoned her shirt. Alec watched her movements, and he didn't hold himself back. She felt the spike in desire when her shirt gaped open, and the twist of hunger as his gaze traced the satin and lace of her bra.

He needed *her*.

All their talk had been just that—talk. Desperate words detailing what they should have been doing instead of what they wanted more than breath. Rational people would slow down, Alec had said, and it was true.

But they weren't rational people, not about this.

She held out her arms, and he came to her.

Chapter Twelve

Alec was on his third cup of coffee by the time Mahalia made her appearance.

She looked good. Her smooth dark skin bore a few more wrinkles, and her dark eyes held hints of worry, but some of those wrinkles were smile lines and there was peace in her gaze along with the sorrow.

Alec lifted his mug in greeting, then nodded to the window. "Just admiring the view."

"You should see those mountains in the wintertime, after a heavy snow." She sat in another of the rocking chairs with her own steaming cup, but the scent that wafted out of it was herbal tea. "No coffee for Michelle," she explained. "I've switched out of sympathy."

There was something comforting about her presence. Mahalia had been there for him during the rockiest time of his life, and the soothing timbre of her voice still gave him the hint of peace his own mother's had never managed to. "Next you're going to tell me you stopped smoking. For real."

"It's not good for babies, especially premature ones, even if they are shapeshifters."

It looked like Mahalia finally had someone to play doting grandma to. Alec hid another smile beneath a sip of his coffee. "Not good for grown-ups, either. How many times did I tell you to quit?"

She flashed him a look and arched one dark eyebrow. "Do we want to talk about all your bad habits now?"

Bluster wouldn't fool him, but it made him feel better. "Sure. Haven't heard the list in a week or two."

"And here I was, trusting Jack to take care of that in my absence."

"Jackson's busy making big eyes at the kitty-cat who's got him wrapped around her dainty pinky finger." Alec grinned at her. "Your little apprentice is all grown up and thinking about engagement rings and picket fences. Poor guy."

"Uh-huh." She rocked her chair gently and smiled. "You know I see through you, right? Poor guy, indeed."

He wasn't going to say it. He wasn't going to give her an opening.

He *wasn't*.

Damn it. "And what do you see, Mahalia?"

Her smile faded. "If you don't poke a little fun, people might figure out how bad you want something like that again."

The words brought the expected pain, but tempered with something he'd never felt before—guilt. "I'm not supposed to want it again."

Mahalia's brows drew together, an expression of confusion that quickly turned to sympathy. "Oh, Alec. You really think your wife would have wanted you to stay locked up and alone for the rest of your life?"

No one ever said her name. Sometimes it grated on his nerves. "No, Heidi would rise from the dead and dent my head with a frying pan for even thinking it."

"But you think it anyway."

He didn't. Heidi had barely believed in marriage, but she'd adored love. She'd be the first to tell him to grab at any chance of it with both hands.

No, it wasn't about Heidi anymore. Maybe it hadn't been in a long time. Alec set his coffee cup on the wicker table. "You know what my mother told me when Heidi died?"

"I shudder to think, honey, I honestly do."

She didn't want to hear it, but Alec told her anyway, because he needed to say it. "She said she was so very sorry, and it was a terrible loss, but I should try to remember that someday I'd meet a nice shapeshifter girl and realize that what I had with Heidi wasn't real."

Mahalia cursed softly, then leaned over and grasped his hand. "I'm sorry. That is some ridiculous bullshit right there."

"Ain't it just?" Alec closed his eyes and squeezed her hand.

"Hard to think rationally about everything going on when Carmen's high on shapeshifter magic. Get it the fuck out of her, would you?"

"That's the plan, as soon as we can." Her chair creaked as she rocked. "I like Carmen. She's tough."

"You'd know." He opened her eyes and cast her a sidelong look. "Your poor house down in Boca Raton must be getting awful lonely. You've pretty much been in New York or Wyoming for the last year, haven't you?"

"Mostly," she admitted. "Retirement isn't all it's cracked up to be."

The temptation to tease was too much to resist. "The Alpha's been in New York and Wyoming for most of the last year too."

She blushed and swatted his arm. "Smartass. We could talk about Carmen some more."

Mahalia, blushing. Half of the supernaturals in New Orleans would have gaped. Most of the supernatural world would do more than gape if they suspected the leader of the wolves might have tender feelings for a spell caster. "You would pick the one man I can't intimidate with an angry glare."

"Hush. There's nothing like that going on."

Yet. "Of course not." He used his best bland I-believe-you voice. "How long does Michelle need to prepare Carmen for this damn thing anyway?"

Mahalia hesitated. "We didn't want to scare her, not if it has to be done anyway, but I think you should know. It's not going to be an easy process. That spell is a mess."

Fear clenched so tight, so fast, he thought he might puke on her shoes. "What in hell did they do to her?"

"It's not the spell, it's the loose ends," she said cryptically. "It wasn't finished, settled. So there's been all this—this extra magic, lashing around inside her. Latching on to whatever it can."

It sounded more like a disease than a spell. "Can you get rid of it? I thought Michelle said she was sure."

"She's sure we can change its focus, turn it into something else. A protection."

Which sounded like a nice, pretty way of glossing over whatever had Mahalia nervous. "Tell me about the loose ends."

"You already know. You've felt them, haven't you?" Her eyes darkened with sympathy again. "Magic seeks magic, even if it's in someone else."

So some of that desperate confusion twisting him up and dragging him back to Carmen *was* coming from the outside. It was relieving and horrifying, all at once. "So I'm a loose end."

"You're a complication, but one we can turn to our advantage. You care about her, and we're going to need that to help her."

"Whatever you need, Mahalia. Whatever the fuck you need. Just...make her okay."

She smiled then and patted his leg. "We will."

The worst, most damning part of all was wondering if he'd miss that magical pull. His life had been spiraling out of control since he'd found Carmen in that house, but the fear of stumbling from one day to the next had been blunted by the pleasure of falling into her.

Mahalia hummed softly. "Have a little faith, Alec. Don't give it more power than it really has."

Easy enough to say if you weren't a shapeshifter, and he would have told her as much if Michelle hadn't appeared in the doorway. It was the first time he'd seen her without her baby clutched protectively in her arms, but that wasn't what raised the hair on the back of his neck. Power pulsed around her, the kind he'd almost forgotten dwelled in her slight body.

Michelle Peyton was a dangerous woman. A determined one. Having that power on his side eased some tension inside him. "Ready?"

She nodded, then looked to Mahalia. "Does he know?"

"Enough to start," she answered. "He can do it."

Alec tensed. "Do what?"

"The loose ends," Mahalia whispered. "The ones tied up in you. You have to let them go."

Let go. Great. Something he was fucking fantastic at. "What happens if I can't?"

Her stare was steady. Implacable. "You have to."

"Because it will hurt her if I don't?"

"Because this won't work if you don't."

Well, at least he had motivation. He nodded and rose, offering Mahalia his hand. "Let's do this."

Every single step down the dark hallway seemed to take an eternity. Carmen waited in the middle of the floor in the den, her knees drawn up to her chest, though she scrambled to her feet when they walked in. "Hi."

Alec crossed the floor and ignored everyone else as he pulled Carmen into his arms. "Hey, sweetheart. How you doing?"

"All right." She clutched his shirt. "Michelle's very soothing."

Not something Michelle heard often, he'd bet. He smoothed Carmen's hair down and held her close, and now that he knew what he was looking for it was easy to feel the wild little curl of magic between them. Not so much, just enough to make the world a little fuzzier, to make everything that wasn't her seem distant. Less important.

Michelle stepped up beside them. "It's time."

Carmen pulled back, and the look in her eyes told him that she'd already heard the hard truth Mahalia had laid out. "I guess we'll know soon," she murmured. "What's real, and what's..." She trailed off and looked away.

"Hey." He turned her face back to his. "I like you, Carmen Mendoza. Mating instinct doesn't cause that. Keep that in mind, huh?"

"I know." She smiled, almost hesitantly. "Mahalia explained domino strategy to me, so I want a rematch."

It made him laugh. "Did Mahalia tell you I always win? Maybe you should get Kat to explain it to you instead."

"I'll figure it out." Her hand closed around his. "I'm smart."

"Yeah, you are." Alec looked to Mahalia. "So what do we do?"

"Don't move." She laid one hand on the back of his neck and the other on Carmen's, her eyes closed and her brow furrowed in concentration. "Relax."

Easier said than done. Magic brushed over him, an oddly insistent tugging, like someone plucking at the power just beneath his skin. Try as he might, he couldn't keep from tensing. "Mahalia, explanations make me relax."

"Right now, I'm trying to separate the two of you. Unweave where this magic inside her has latched on to you. That has to come first."

His hands tightened on Carmen, and he forced himself to relax. To hold her gently. "Sorry."

"Don't apologize," Mahalia said. "Concentrate on letting go."

The plucking grew worse, until he felt like a pair of boots with someone jerking at the laces. When he glanced at Michelle she had her eyes closed, her face serene as she held out both hands, palms toward them. A moment later, she frowned. "Alec?"

He fought the urge to snarl at her. He lost. "What?"

"Focus on the way you feel before a change. The way you make everything quiet, just before you reach for the magic."

Alec closed his eyes and tried. He concentrated on the wildness inside, the wolf who paced like an angry animal at the zoo, biding its time. The wolf didn't want to relax, didn't want to lose the wild, near-feral she-wolf it had marked.

Carmen whispered his name, her fingers squeezing his.

He had to let go, or he'd lose her in a far more devastating fashion. He smoothed his thumbs over her knuckles, using the soft, gentle touch as an anchor as the first knot of magic binding them together unraveled.

She made a soft noise of pain, almost a whimper, followed by a shaky sigh. Her hands turned, urged his to do the same, until they stood there, palm to palm, with the bonds between them quickly fading.

And then...nothing.

Quiet.

For the first time in nine days, his head cleared. The world snapped into focus, though he hadn't realized how blurry it had gotten. With instinct settled he could think again, and the wolf echoed his sharp relief. Control had never been a human ideal he imposed on his baser half—he *was* control.

Usually.

Now he had control. He dragged in a deep breath, filled himself with Carmen's scent—and found it no less arousing. Attraction was still there, even sharper now that he could find the boundaries of it. It was real. It was his.

She would be his too. *Soon.*

Mahalia dropped her hand from Alec's neck and stepped closer to Carmen. "I wish I could say that was the worst of it, honey, but that was only the beginning."

"I know." She stared up at him, the vicious bite of loss darkening her eyes. "But I'll be fine."

"You'll be fine," he repeated, making the words firm. "I'll be right here, Carmen. Through all of it."

"Sure you will," Mahalia cut in, "but later. You have to go now, Alec."

Everything in him, wolf and man alike, rebelled. "Like hell."

"It's too risky for you to stay. Right now, the only thing keeping her magic from latching on to you again is that Michelle and I are holding it at bay. We can't afford to expend that energy, not if we're going to help Carmen."

The woman knew how to cut his legs out from under him. Alec reached up to touch Carmen's cheek. "You gonna be okay?"

"Don't worry too much about me," she whispered. "I'll see you in a little while."

"Yeah, you will," he promised. He dropped his hand from her cheek. Stepped back.

Turning and walking out of the room was the hardest thing he'd done in years.

Nothing had prepared Carmen for how much it would hurt.

Another burst of pain splintered through her, and she bit her lip until she tasted blood. *Hurt* didn't describe the tearing that grew worse as each second ticked by. It didn't belong inside her, this magic, but it had rooted itself in her anyway, and every rhythmic word that fell from Mahalia's lips ripped away another layer.

The soft chanting faltered, and the witch blew out a shaky breath. "I think...we might need to stop for a minute."

Carmen opened her eyes, and marveled with slight detachment at the way her vision swam, with lights and colors playing at the periphery of the room. Then she realized it wasn't her eyes at all, but actual magic swirling around them. She wasn't used to such displays, and it made her shudder.

"Nothing to worry about." Even as Mahalia spoke, the sparkles died away, fading into nothingness. "Just a little flashy magic."

The woman's dark skin was ashen, and Carmen wondered what the hell *she* looked like. "Want to tell me why you really made Alec leave the room?"

Mahalia answered with a rusty chuckle. "Never can put anything over on the empaths. Y'all feel too much."

"Maybe." She'd seen her share of loved ones freak out at the sight of someone in pain, and sometimes ignorance was bliss. For a man like Alec, though, waiting would be torture. "How much longer?"

"Depends." She cast a look at Michelle. "What do you think?"

Michelle, at least, looked composed—if you ignored the tension around her eyes and the thin sheen of sweat on her forehead. "We're getting toward the end of the most painful parts, but there's a long way yet to go."

Carmen gripped Mahalia's hand. "She said this wouldn't harm the two of you. Was she lying to make me feel better?"

"Michelle doesn't lie, honey. It's not in her nature."

Michelle smiled. "I wouldn't say that's entirely true, but in this case...no, Carmen. It's not dangerous for us. It does take a lot of concentration, though, which is why a few minutes of rest won't hurt."

"Okay." The truth of the Seer's words was clear, and it allowed Carmen to relax. The echoes of pain had already begun to drift away. Her body expected more agony, some sort of lingering wound to show for it, but she felt fine, and the end result was disorienting. "It's strange, almost..."

"Easily forgotten. Not anything like physical pain," Mahalia agreed.

"It's all in your mind." Michelle smoothed a few stray hairs back into her otherwise immaculate bun. "The easiest pain to recover from."

In every way but one. Alec had left, and the ache of separation was fresh and sharp. It was useless to worry about it, to wonder what would happen between them with the magic gone. He would feel the same or he wouldn't, and foreknowledge of neither outcome would change the decision she'd made.

She had to be herself.

"You think too much," Mahalia observed.

"So I've been told."

Michelle tilted her head and studied Carmen, an odd curiosity in her eyes. "It's not a common tendency in the empaths I've known."

Something Carmen had heard time and again. "I was like this before I even remember being psychic. My mother used to tell me it was a good combination."

"Heart and mind. It is a good combination. A powerful one."

"Sometimes it gets me in trouble." Like when there were no rational answers to be had, only trust and faith. "Like when I can't shut my brain off."

"Ohhh." Mahalia lowered herself to a leather chair and shook her head. "At least you and Alec won't have the same problem in that respect."

"Be nice, Mahalia," Michelle murmured.

"I'm not being ugly, and Alec would be the first to tell you it's true. He's all about—"

"Instinct," Carmen finished for her.

"That's right, instinct." Mahalia leaned forward in the chair, bracing her hands on her knees. "Gut."

Michelle didn't relent. "Instinct's just another way of thinking. A faster way. Some of it we're born with, and some of it we learn. Instinct is experience reminding us of the things we've already thought about."

"You're right, of course."

"Alec thinks," Carmen told them. "All the time, about everything. Every single possibility in every single circumstance."

Mahalia smiled. "Michelle's definition of instinct."

"And while we're on the topic..." Michelle's smile faded. "My instinct tells me that the sooner we get this done, the better."

From the way Mahalia's expression sobered, as well, it wouldn't be pleasant. "I'm ready."

"Carmen?"

It won't last long. Get it over with. "Like you said, the sooner, the better."

Michelle stepped forward and held out both her hands. "This next bit will be the worst. Mahalia's laid the groundwork. She's separated enough of the magic to protect you for this. But now I have to tear it out."

A terrifying thought, because surely this had to be the dangerous part. "It's only in my mind, right? The pain?"

"It's only in your mind," Michelle confirmed. Then she

hesitated. "Are you a strong projective empath?"

"No, not usually. I have to try—" She broke off and bit her lip. "Should I take a few minutes, make sure my shields hold?"

"No. If you're not very strong, I can contain it. But if you'd been like Kat... Well, it would have been different."

"No." She'd felt the sheer amount of power that emanated from Kat. Even with shields and iron will, it spilled over. "Nothing like that."

"Good. In that case..." Michelle's fingers tightened. "Just hold on."

Oh dear God.

Everything before was nothing compared to the thick blaze of anguish that rocked Carmen. Her head pounded, and she wanted to scream but no sound would come. She felt as though she was teetering on the edge of a void, a deep, dark vortex, and with one more tiny push, she'd disappear into it.

It's in your mind. The voice, her own and not, echoed through her. *Meditate. Build your walls.* If it kept her in and the world out, surely it could protect her from this torment.

In her mind, Carmen made herself as small as possible, bent low against the screaming pain, and began to build.

When twenty-nine minutes of tense prowling ticked over into a half hour, Alec gave up pacing the hallways and went in search of Luciano.

The ranch was a sprawling building, a mix of older construction and new additions. It was easy to spot the money in the quiet decorations, understated in a way that usually meant someone had taste—and social status. Old money, like his mother, who had turned her husband's Texas ranch into the sort of place magazines fought to photograph.

Luciano's home was different. Tasteful, sure, but lived in. Photographs of horses lined one of the hallways, some artistic black and white, some more casual. Following Luciano's scent led him down another hallway, this one lined with more recent photos.

Kat grinned at him from one picture, an arm looped around her cousin's neck and a Santa hat perched crookedly on her head. Derek's smile was wide enough to split his face in two, and the next photo showed him and his wife, Nicole wrapped half around him, her brown eyes alive with joy. A third had Michelle and Nicole together in front of a Christmas tree, and even Michelle's usual sadness seemed less piercing.

Family pictures. Little Nicole Peyton had made a family here in spite of all of the odds. She'd told the supernatural world and its endless rules about who she could and couldn't marry to go fuck itself, and had picked the man she loved. Then she'd left.

For all his protestations, for all of his damn rationalizations, it was the one thing Alec had never done. He'd never just...walked away, not even when he'd married Heidi. He'd still played the political games. Tweaked the Conclave's tail sometimes just because he could. Because someone had to.

Maybe it was time that someone wasn't him.

The pictures ended at an open doorway, and through it he found Luciano sitting in a wide rocking chair beside a crackling fire, Michelle's baby cradled in one arm.

A touching domestic scene, if you didn't think too closely about the fact that the baby's father had died, a senseless sacrifice to the Conclave's rabid fear of Michelle.

Alec knocked on the doorframe. "Mind some company?"

"Nah, come in." Luciano looked up, a measure of quiet sympathy on his face. "I got tired of pacing."

In this case, solidarity didn't make Alec feel much better. He dropped into an armchair and leaned forward, resting his elbows on his knees. "Worried about Michelle?"

"Unavoidable, I think, but she knows how far she can push herself."

Michelle was young, but John Peyton would have secured his daughter the best tutors money could buy. Alec forced his thoughts away from all the things that could go wrong and focused on the baby. "How is he? No problems from him showing up early?"

Unmistakable pride and affection lit Luciano's face. "He's good. Better than we'd hoped, for being so early. AJ's strong."

The phone call when he'd heard about the birth came back to him. AJ. Aaron Junior. Alec didn't know enough about babies to know if the infant took after his tiny mother or his hulking father. AJ looked small, but not fragile.

Strong, just like Luciano said. Just like both of the kid's

parents. "I'm glad. I heard him yelling this morning, all the way from the guesthouse. Demanding little fellow."

"I've been trying to run interference. Let Michelle get a bit more rest." The baby yawned, and Luciano stroked his cheek. "It's hard for her to let someone else take care of him."

"All things considered, not surprising. But she trusts you."

"Yes." After a moment, he looked up, contemplative. "Mahalia said Carmen's family was responsible for the spell. Her uncle?"

"Her father, more likely." Alec's fingers curled toward his palm before he could stop them. "Her uncle's playing a different game. Ready to make a move on that open Conclave seat."

"Sometimes I think Derek should have taken it. He's a good person, and he could have done good things." He smiled ruefully. "Then I remind myself that he would have been miserable, him and Nick both."

Derek had challenged a Conclave member for love and vengeance, not out of any desire for power. "He couldn't have changed the world on his own. Rock the boat too bad, and you'll get challenged out of your place eventually. Whole damn system's built to keep the power where it is."

"I used to believe that. Now I wonder if it's only what we tell ourselves so we can sleep at night."

Alec lifted one eyebrow. "You took yourself out of the running pretty spectacularly."

"Yes, I did." His eyes were shadowed in the firelight. "I married the Seer. Even if that ends, they'll never trust me with any power now. And as much as I'd like to say I did it all for Michelle and AJ, I was selfish too. I knew exactly what I was doing."

For the first time, Alec looked at Luciano—really *looked* at him—and didn't see a kid. A man stared back at him, one who'd struck out on his own. Set his own path.

Of course, it made him feel old. He smiled anyway. "Honestly? I feel better knowing you've got a little selfish in you. Can't really trust selfless people."

"I'll keep that in mind." The baby fussed, and Luciano unwrapped the blanket around his upper body. "Cesar Mendoza will never land that seat on the Conclave, not unless he plays dirty. The bad part is that's about as likely as the sun rising and setting."

"All I care about is keeping Carmen safe from it. I can deal with the rest of it when the Southeast council gets done picking over each other's bones."

"The most they could hope for is to marry her off to someone, make an alliance. That's not likely."

He'd thought the same thing before he'd realized how far her father would go. "Let's hope."

Luciano tilted his head. "You think the spell was a bid for power?"

"I think I can't think like someone who'd sacrifice everything and anything for power, so I can't discount any possibility."

He nodded slowly. "Makes sense. Either way, it's a mess."

"That it is." Alec fell silent, watching as Luciano soothed the fussy baby. Soon enough, AJ's protests quieted, and Alec leaned back in his chair. "You're good with him."

"He's my son," the other man said simply. "Maybe I'm not supposed to think of him that way, but I do."

For once, Alec chose his words carefully. "I'd say the only one who should have any say in how you think of him is his mother. Screw the rest of the world."

"Michelle says that a shapeshifter son needs a shapeshifter father."

Because some things were instinct, but some had to be taught. Even to those who came into being shapeshifters as adults, like Derek. Like Andrew. "I think Michelle's right. AJ'll be better off than I ever was. Or you, for that matter."

"I don't think we have to be exactly like our kids," Luciano argued. "Any more than we have to be exactly like our parents."

Not a curse he'd wish on either of them. "Michelle's no less that kid's mother because she's different from him. That doesn't mean it won't be easier on both of them to have someone around who knows what a shapeshifter boy goes through growing up."

"I'll be here." A statement of fact more than anything else. Of intent.

Yep, Luciano was a man now. A man with a son, even if he wasn't one he'd fathered. "Good for you. I mean it."

A rustling from the hall drew their attention, and Mahalia

walked in, moving slowly, and sank heavily into the rocking chair beside Luciano. "I'm getting too old for this." She peered over at Alec. "Everything's done. It worked."

Alec was on his feet and halfway to the door before he realized his presence might not be welcome yet. "Can I see her?"

She waved him away. "Go. She'll be glad to have you nearby."

He found Carmen in the room where they'd cast the spell, conversing quietly with Michelle. The Seer rose as soon as he came in, a tired but pleased smile curling her lips. "She'll be just fine."

Carmen looked pale and exhausted, with dark shadows under her eyes. "Alec."

Michelle moved toward the door. "I'm going to check on AJ. Call me if you need anything."

"Thanks." When she'd gone, Carmen patted the sofa. "Michelle and Mahalia said everything went well."

He sat and lifted both hands to her cheeks, cradling her face. "You look beat, sweetheart. You okay?"

"Yeah." She leaned into his touch and closed her eyes. "It wasn't so bad."

A lie, and it hurt him. "But it's over now, right?"

She stroked his hands, almost as if in apology, as she nodded. "Done. The magic's protecting me now. Even if I'm bitten, nothing will take."

He'd dreaded the possibility of disappointment, but none came, only relief that she was safe. He smoothed his thumb over the soft skin of her cheek and smiled. "Good. That's good."

After a moment, she exhaled a single short breath. "It is, isn't it?"

"If that's what you want."

"It is." She dropped her head to his shoulder with a weak laugh. "That, and maybe a nap."

This time, the tenderness the words evoked wasn't instinct. Just her, and the growing awareness that he couldn't blame magic for the quiet tug of affection.

Later, he could be scared. Now, he needed to take care of her. So he gathered her against his chest and rocked to his feet. "A nap it is. We've got time before dinner."

Her arms slid around his neck, and she brushed her lips over his jaw. "Thank you."

"You're welcome, honey."

Chapter Thirteen

Dinner was a boisterous affair, redolent with relief and celebration. Luciano had helped Gus cook, and every bit of available space on the table was laden with food and wine.

Carmen barely tasted any of it with the distraction of Alec's leg pressing against hers and the hot weight of his stares. The way his hand brushed hers, gentle but firm enough for her to know it was no accident.

"Okay, that's it." Mahalia wagged her finger at Carmen and Alec as she reached for a nearly empty wine bottle. "You two, go."

Alec's sharp spike of satisfaction gave lie to the casual drawl of his words. "You kickin' us out, Mahalia?"

She snorted. "Luke's too polite to do it."

Luciano began to clear plates from the table. "Leave me out of it, May."

"We're going," Carmen cut in, unable to stifle her laugh. "Going right now, and we'll see all of you in the morning. Alec?"

Alec turned his attention to Michelle, who presided over the far end of the table with AJ in her arms and a sleepy but satisfied smile on her face. Under the table, his fingers found Carmen's as he smiled. "Thanks, Michelle. I mean it."

The Seer's perfect, serene expression didn't falter, not even when Carmen felt the stinging bite of her pain. "Take care of her," was all Michelle said. "We'll see you tomorrow."

The quickest path to the guesthouse was through the back door, and Carmen wrapped her sweater more tightly around her as they walked out under the stars. The night was crisp, clear.

Beautiful.

Alec didn't speak, and neither did she. There was a silence inside her, a peace that she hadn't realized had been disrupted until that afternoon. Now, freed from the low, constant buzz of magic, she could think again.

The house was dark, but the moonlight through the curtains showed her the way. She led Alec into the bedroom and gasped when he slammed the door behind them and spun her to face it. "Carmen."

No fear, even when he startled her, because he would never, ever hurt her. "Alec."

"Nothing in there but you." His hands landed on her shoulders and skated down, stripping away her sweater. When his fingers returned, they curled around her wrists and guided her arms up until her palms pressed flat against the door. "No magic. No instincts but what you've always had."

"Just me," she agreed, turning her head. "This is what you get."

"I'm not muddled anymore. Not fighting through the damn mating urge." He rocked forward, until she could feel the length of his erection even through their clothing. "I'm this hard for you."

Whatever else the spell might have done, it hadn't been the only thing drawing them together, and she shuddered at the reassurance. "Lift up my skirt and touch me, and you'll know how much I want you."

He chuckled, a low, dark sound that raised goose bumps on her skin and sent a tingle of arousal racing through her. "No. No orders from you, not tonight. None of that half-assed, out-of-control mating bullshit." One hand slid up her arm and then twisted in her hair, urging her head to the side. "Give yourself to me."

Her heart began to pound, and the mere thought of it weakened her knees. If he hadn't placed her hands so deliberately on the door, she would have sank back against him. "Completely?"

"Everything." A tickle of his breath was the only warning before he closed his teeth on the side of her neck with a low growl.

She almost fell anyway. "Everything." *Tonight. Forever.*

His tongue stroked over the place where he'd bit her, hot

and soothing. "No shields."

Nothing between them. "All right." Carmen closed her eyes and bit her lip. The habit of rebuilding them took effort to ignore, effort that would divert her attention away from him.

But she could let him in.

Slowly, she pulled down one wall, brick by brick, and built it back up around Alec. "They're not down," she whispered, "but you're inside."

Satisfaction swelled through him and curled around her as he released her hair and stroked his hand down her back, her dress barely protecting her from the heat of his touch. "I like being inside."

"In more ways than just this?" she teased.

His hand splayed wide across her ass. "In more ways than you've seen."

The implication made her catch her breath, and she wondered—for one tiny sliver of a second—if she was ready to belong to him, body and soul. Then the doubt fled, replaced in a heartbeat with the knowledge that she already did.

She rubbed the back of her head against his shoulder. "Show me now. No shields, mine *or* yours."

Leather whispered across metal. "Go lay on the bed. On your back. Leave the pretty little sundress on."

When she turned, he was pulling his belt from its loops. An image rocked her—of being bound to the bed, at his mercy, while he pleasured her.

Bed. She was shaking as she crossed the room and slid onto the mattress, but she hesitated on her knees. "My shoes?"

"Off."

She kicked them to the floor and stretched out like he'd instructed, her arms at her sides. "Like this?"

The corner of his mouth kicked up as he finally slid his belt free. "You know better."

How would she survive? Arousal already throbbed, heavy and low, in her belly, and it intensified when she raised her arms and crossed them at the wrists.

A moment later he was there, twisting the leather around and around as he leaned down to brush her lips in a teasing kiss. "You really *do* know better. Nothing new here, is there?"

She strained toward him because she couldn't help it.

"Some wolves like it more than others. The dominance, and the submission. So do some humans."

"Mine's not a human thing." He buckled the belt around her wrists and traced one finger down her arm. "I'm all wolf, honey. One-hundred-percent alpha bastard."

"And mine's not entirely a wolf thing," she warned. "I don't need it all the time...but sometimes I just want to let go."

He curled his finger under the strap on her sundress. "Whenever you want."

He meant it. Carmen rubbed her cheek against the inside of his wrist and hummed with pleasure at the warmth and protectiveness that surrounded her.

"That's right." The strap fell back against her shoulder, and the touches that followed were slow. Deliberate. He stroked her through the bodice of her dress, never giving her skin-on-skin contact and never lingering in one place for too long.

Her breasts tightened under his fingers, her nipples hard against the cotton of her dress. She tried to hold still but squirmed anyway, desperate to relieve the gathering ache. "Alec."

"Carmen?" His touch vanished, and he gathered his shirt in his hands and stripped it over his head.

He knew exactly what it did to her to look at the hard lines of his body, so she didn't bother to hide her admiring gaze. "You're a show-off."

"Only because you look at me like that." The mattress dipped as he knelt at the foot of the bed, both hands falling to her ankles. "Roll over. Onto your stomach."

He'd bound her hands together, but not to the bed. She rolled, the scent of warm leather filling her nose as she drew her arms closer to her body so she could rest on her elbows.

He started at the backs of her calves, smoothing his hands up her legs with long, languid strokes. He toyed with the edge of her dress where it fell across her thighs, then pushed it up. "I like the dress, but this has to go."

"What has—?" The sound of ripping fabric drowned out the words as he tore off her panties. "*Oh.*"

"Bad habit I have." Strong hands urged her to her knees, legs wide, with her dress pooled across her lower back. "Good thing I can afford to replace them."

Moira Rogers

It took her two tries to speak. "I shop at this place on Magazine. They might start to wonder what the hell's happening to my underwear."

He slipped his hands under the sundress and around her body, up to cup her breasts. The rough fabric of his jeans ground against naked flesh as he rocked against her. "Let 'em wonder."

The urge to tease, to return a little of the torment he was visiting on her, made her head swim. So she arched her back, insanely grateful that one movement could thrust her breasts more fully into his hands *and* rub her ass against his erection.

He groaned, a low, desperate noise that turned into a challenging growl as his fingers closed tight on her nipples.

"Fuck." The curse escaped before she could stop it, and she bit her lower lip hard to hold back her pleas. His grip tightened, pushed her just to the edge of pain, and eased off as he rocked against her.

Her nipples tingled, and she panted for breath. Every sensation was intensified because she couldn't move, couldn't reach for him, scratch him or pull his hair.

Instead, she squirmed while he dragged his nails along her skin, down her stomach and over her hips. Both hands followed the curve of her ass, and she felt his breath a moment before he bit her.

Heat streaked through her, a fire he had to feel as acutely as she did. "You're trying to kill me," she whispered.

"You know better." He soothed the bite with his tongue only to bite her once more. Lower.

He'd drive her mad, leave her dazed and trembling—and then do it all over again. With a jolt, she realized that such pleasure wasn't destined for a distant future, but now. "Is this what belonging to you means?"

"When it's what you need." He licked the inside of her thigh, his beard rubbing over her skin. "Belonging to me means you get what you need, whenever I can give it. Tonight it means me proving that you set off every dominant, animal urge I've got, whether you're stoned on magic or not."

"Don't need proof." She had it already, with each look and breath, and it meant so much more to her because they weren't bound together by an uncontrollable physical instinct.

170

They'd chosen one another.

"That's right," he whispered, a quiet answer to the feelings she hadn't spoken. He stroked her with his tongue, soft at first and then firmer, circling closer and closer to her clit without touching.

She dropped her head and breathed through the teasing pleasure. Keeping still was impossible, and her hips rocked, just a little, seeking a deeper caress. A sharper sensation.

Finally, he gave it to her, a hot, rough flick of his tongue, and she moaned and shook. He pulled back, smoothed a hand over her hip and brought his palm down in a sharp slap.

The juxtaposition between pain and pleasure drove her closer to the edge, and she threw back her head, gasping his name.

His groan rumbled through the room. "Fuck, woman, you have no idea how hot it is that I can *feel* how much you liked that."

"Yes, I do." Every one of his reactions seared through her, a fire burning them both.

"We're going to have a lot of fun learning what else you like, aren't we?" She heard the quick snap of a zipper jerked down too fast, and two fingers slid deep inside her.

This time, she almost screamed as she clenched tight around his fingers. Together, bound by her empathy, they could push boundaries to the limit, dance the edge between just enough and too much with dizzying precision. "I like *you*. Want you."

A soft groan. The tear of a condom wrapper. His fingers curled, stroking inside her until a maddening pressure built, one only he could relieve.

He pulled his fingers away and entered her with a single slow thrust that would have driven her to her knees if she hadn't already been on them. She whimpered and tried to stay still, but she couldn't stop the way her body arched toward his, yearning and hungry.

Instead of another thrust, she got a soft growl and the sharp slap of his broad hand across her ass.

She froze, though the sensation made her want to buck even harder, and when she spoke she barely recognized her own voice. "Tell me what you want."

His fingers dipped between her legs again. Rubbed. His other hand fell to her hip, holding her still as he brought those slick fingers up to tease her ass. "Don't hold back. If I don't want you to come, I won't let you. If I don't want you to move, I'll stop you."

It was control in its purest form, and she wanted to give it to him. She needed to.

Don't hold back. Carmen moved suddenly, grinding against him with a low cry. She made it only a few inches before his fingers tightened on her hip, keeping her in place with effortless deliberation.

Yes. "I take it you don't want me to move, then?"

Dark laughter rolled over her. "Didn't say I didn't want you to keep trying." His fingertip pressed against her. Testing. "I love to watch you writhe."

Just like she loved to hear him groan when she did something shocking. Instead of shying away from him touching her ass, Carmen eased closer. His finger probed deeper, arousing delicate nerve endings with an electric shock of sensation, and she shuddered through a moan.

His pleasure spiked along with hers, and he *did* groan, low and hoarse. Then he moved, rocking his hips back and driving forward.

"Alec!" Breathless, and still she had to speak. To tell him. "I need you."

"I know." Another thrust. Faster. Harder. His hand shifted until he was gripping both of her hips, holding her. Suddenly, he stopped, buried deep inside her.

Long seconds ticked by. Carmen whimpered as she tried to move, but he kept her still. She'd beg, plead, if only he would give her more, and she almost gave in.

Not yet. Instead, she closed her eyes and squeezed her inner muscles tight around his cock.

Icy deliberation shattered. Not for long, just a second, enough for a single, wild surge forward. His hands hit the bed on either side of her arms, and he pressed his forehead to her shoulder with a groan. "You're hell on my self-control," he whispered, voice trembling with need and affection and something deeper that eclipsed both.

Then he fisted his hands in the covers and began to fuck

her.

Rational thought vanished, not only unimportant but impossible in the face of such possession. Every stroke, every breath, was a new claim, one that drove her closer to the edge. Everything in her was his, and not because a hint of animal instinct hungered for him. Because he could give her what she needed.

And she could do the same for him.

The leather around her wrists creaked as she rocked with him. "Yours."

"I know." He kissed the back of her neck. Licked it. Bit it. "All mine."

Words, because they were habit, though they only echoed what she could already feel through the empathy that bound them. A connection, both primal and immediate, that plucked at something deep inside her and rendered things like language obsolete.

It was that connection that swept her away, up into a dizzying spiral of pleasure that shook her, body and mind. "Come with me. Come—"

He shook above her, the last fine threads of control unraveling as they fell into flames together. His hips moved erratically, every thrust urging her on until nothing remained but the way he made her feel and the words he rasped against her cheek. "That's it. You feel so good around my cock when you come. So goddamn hot when I'm fucking you."

"Fuck, Alec." Another orgasm swelled through her, and she slammed her head back against his shoulder. "*Fuck.*"

He came with her, roaring his pleasure as he drove into her one last time, hard enough to push her hips against the bed.

There was no beginning and no end to the sensations cascading through her, through them *both*, a chain reaction fed by pleasure and desire and even more pleasure. Carmen tried to slow it down, to separate what was hers from what was his, but it was useless. Everything was shared and doubled because of it.

"Shh." Alec was stroking her, his hand smoothing from her shoulder to her hip in slow, gentle movements. Her wrists were free, though she couldn't remember how they'd gotten that way, or when he'd shifted them so she was curled against his chest, her cheek pillowed on his arm.

She pressed an open-mouthed kiss to his skin and nestled into his embrace. "I love being in your arms."

"I love having you here." His hand followed her arm on the next stroke, fingers rubbing at her wrists. "Wasn't too rough, was it?"

"Mmm, no." She caught his hand. "I won't break."

A quiet, relieved sigh stirred the hair at the back of her neck. "Good."

"You were worried."

"Not really." He yawned and tugged her closer. "Don't have to worry so much with you. If I hurt you, I'll know. I'll feel it."

She'd known men who enjoyed the sexual feedback associated with her psychic ability, but never one who valued it as a way to ensure her well-being, and never one who understood her other needs so completely.

But did he, really? The doubt rose, unbidden, but instead of pushing it away, she took a deep breath. "Can I ask you something?"

"Of course, honey."

It was hard to find the words, but she tried. The last thing she wanted was to have her relationship with Alec fall apart because they couldn't talk to each other. "The dominance. You said it's not something you need in bed all the time, but what about out of it? Everyday stuff?"

"I'm a bossy fucker. That's never going to change." His hand settled on her hip. "But the nice thing about all those wolfy instincts going away? I don't need you to obey me. Don't even want it, unless we're in a dangerous situation where I need to keep us safe."

The fact that she wasn't a wolf hadn't mattered in the past, not to the other lovers she'd had to walk away from when their controlling behavior spilled over outside the bedroom. "Is that a typical alpha attitude, or are you unusual in that respect?"

"I'm more alpha than most, but that just means I don't have much to prove. It's the ones who aren't secure—they're the ones who have to throw their power around all the damn time."

Maybe that had been the constant conflict. Insecurity could drive people to make all sorts of demands, and obedience was one she'd never been okay with. "I don't need someone to control my life for me. It's not that I think you would, but it's caused problems in the past, so I wanted to get it out there."

His hand tightened on her hip, and he eased her over onto her back before propping his head up on one hand. "Dated a few controlling assholes, huh?"

"To put it mildly." Even her family didn't know the extent of it, how close some of her lovers had come to crossing the line.

The sudden feral gleam in Alec's eyes said she couldn't hide as easily from him. "Don't suppose you want to let me hunt them down and kick respect into them after the fact?"

"No, I do not." She wiggled closer. "I'd rather move forward, if you don't mind."

"Spoilsport." But he smiled as he leaned down and kissed her forehead. "Fine, I'll behave."

"Thank you." The line of his throat beckoned, and Carmen followed it with her lips. "You're an unusual sort of man, Alec Jacobson."

"It's okay. You can call me odd."

"Your word, not mine." She bit his chin. "I wouldn't say odd. I'd say...fascinating."

That earned her a smile. "I like that word. 'Specially when you're saying it."

She could have said so much more, and would have, except that his cell phone began to ring.

Alec heaved a sigh and rolled away. His phone sat on the night table, but when he picked it up, he frowned. "It's your brother. Julio."

"Want me to answer it?"

He passed her the phone in silence, and Carmen thumbed it open. "Hello?"

"Carmen." Julio sounded rough, almost hoarse. "Are you finished with your thing in Wyoming?"

"Yeah." She instantly regretted not telling him *why* she'd flown up on the spur of the moment, but she hadn't wanted to worry him. "What's wrong?"

"It's Miguel. This thing, this spell—they did it to him too."

A cold shiver took her, a curiously hot numbness on its heels. "They did what?"

"They turned him." His voice grew even scratchier, as if he could barely speak. "Miguel's a wolf."

Chapter Fourteen

Another night of travel, another pot of coffee.

Alec was on his third cup of the morning, and glad he was used to going without sleep. "So they did the spell the night before they tried it on Carmen?"

"Apparently." Julio prodded at one of the stale donuts he'd brought. "I tried to reach Miguel for days, but my father gave me the runaround. I guess to give him time to recover and adjust."

What a fucking mess. "And has he? Adjusted, I mean."

"As well as can be expected." His mouth firmed into a tense line. "Not like I've had a lot of access to him, though. Carmen? She'll be lucky if she gets to see him at all. Miguel inherited our father's love of avoidance when it comes to tough situations."

Alec had known Carmen long enough to know one thing. "She's not gonna like that much."

"She shouldn't." Julio glowered. "It's low and cowardly, and I hate that Miguel still looks up to the bastard. But he wasn't even born yet when Dad left. He won't ever really understand."

Maybe Alec had more in common with Julio than he'd thought. "Not too flattering, being the favored son because they want you to grow up into a bigoted asshole, just like them."

"No, it pretty much sucks ass."

Carmen stepped into the doorway, still clutching the cordless phone in her hand. "Miguel won't see me."

She looked so upset that Alec didn't care about dancing around Julio's likely disapproval. He held out an arm to her, and she slid onto his lap and buried her face against his shoulder.

Julio didn't look happy, but he appeared to be more focused on Carmen than anything. "I'm sorry, Car. If it's worth anything, he seemed fine when I saw him. Physically, anyway."

She lifted her head. "Even so, from what Mahalia and Michelle told us, that could change. Any minute, he could have an adverse reaction to the spell."

"The only thing we can do is get someone to look at him," Alec said. "Mahalia might be willing to come down. Maybe she knows a way to minimize the risk." Or maybe the kid would always be a ticking bomb, waiting to explode.

Julio gathered his keys and his cell phone. "I have to head over to your office," he told Alec. "Jackson's been helping me out with something. Are you—?" He broke off, then cursed. "Fuck it, Carmen can be mad at me if she wants. Are you going to stay here with her?"

It wasn't about brothers and sisters, or acknowledging that Carmen was older than Julio and fully capable of taking care of herself. It was a question from one shapeshifter to another, a tacit understanding that humans and psychics needed protection.

Not just protection. They needed a protector. Julio would have been that protector, whether he knew it on a conscious level or not. It had nothing to do with human chauvinism or gender. Jackson belonged to Mackenzie as sure as Derek and Nicole belonged to each other.

As sure as Carmen belonged to him.

Alec curled his hand around her hip and nodded once, the gesture for Julio even though his words were for Carmen. "Wherever she needs to go, I'll take her."

"Okay." Some of the tightness around his eyes relaxed.

"Go, Julio," Carmen said softly. "Alec is here."

"Yeah, Alec is here." Her brother said it with finality, and he smiled as he tucked his phone in his pocket. "Don't worry about Miguel. He'll figure out soon enough how Dad and Uncle Cesar operate, and then he'll come around."

Carmen returned his smile, though Alec could feel her sadness. "Shouldn't take long."

Julio left, and Alec turned Carmen until he could meet her eyes. "We'll take care of your brother. I promise."

"If he lets us," she corrected.

"Mmm." A nice, noncommittal response, because Carmen didn't need to know the truth. Not yet.

Miguel, though... Well, if the kid wanted to be a shapeshifter, he could learn the first rule of being a shifter in New Orleans.

No one got to refuse to see Alec Jacobson.

Alec finally tracked Miguel back to his apartment, where he knocked hard enough to rattle the door. "You've got five minutes to let me in, kid, before I kick in the lock."

After nearly a minute, the door opened a crack, with the security chain still engaged. "What do you want?"

Miguel's power vibrated in the air. Steady and strong, but not dominant. Not like his brother. Not like Alec himself. "You're a new wolf in my town, Mendoza. So open the damn door."

It shut, and the chain clinked. When the door reopened, Miguel backed away, his gaze lowered. "Come in, I guess."

Alec stepped inside, breathing a silent sigh of relief that he wouldn't have to kick Carmen's brother around the apartment to clarify their respective places in shapeshifter hierarchy.

Once the door was closed behind him, Alec crossed his arms over his chest and studied the boy. He looked tense, a little twitchy.

He snorted as he reached for an open bottle of beer on the coffee table. "Carmen didn't come with you?"

"No, because you—" Alec froze. Inhaled. Miguel's scent permeated the apartment, but it wasn't the only one. Hazelnut, vanilla and cinnamon, mixed with the distinct something that screamed—

"Kat." The name came out as a growl. "Why the hell has Kat been here enough for this place to smell like her?"

Miguel shrugged. "Why do *you* smell like my sister's been riding you like a pony?"

Blind rage made the room swim. Alec uncurled his fists, just to have something to do other than knock Miguel's teeth down his throat. "If you want to stay in this town, you will damn well show your sister more respect than that. And if you want to lay a hand on Kat and not lose it, you'll show her more respect too."

"So the truth is disrespectful?"

"You're not an idiot. Don't act like one."

"Neither are you, so don't ask me why Kat's been here so much the place smells like her. She's been here because she wanted to be."

Alec closed his eyes and counted. To five, because he was Carmen's brother, and a new wolf who'd probably been through hell. "Fine. Kat's not my business. Your sister is, though, and if I hear you talking about her like that again, I will beat some manners into you."

Oddly, the kid smiled. "Yeah, okay. I apologize."

"Good." Slightly mollified, Alec leaned against the kitchen table. "Just so you know, the reason I'm worried about Kat is because new wolves can have trouble adjusting. Instincts, unpredictable strength... You can hurt someone without meaning to. Especially if they're human."

"I appreciate the concern, but I'm not going to hurt anyone." His smile turned rueful. "I'm not new, not completely. I've always been half wolf, right?"

Which was part of the problem. "Did your father tell you how much more dangerous that makes it?"

"He didn't have to, Alec." He tapped his temple. "I'm psychic, remember? He told me what he wanted me to hear, but he couldn't hide what he didn't, and neither could the witch. Not from me."

Julio and Carmen hadn't mentioned the possibility, but maybe they hadn't considered it. "So you know this spell could take a nasty turn now or in five years?"

"I was willing to risk it." He sobered, his expression turning stormy. "I didn't know they were going after Carmen, with or without her permission. I would have stopped them."

He would have tried and possibly ended up in worse shape than his sister. "I took care of her. And as long as you're in New Orleans, I'll take care of you too. That's how this works. But it comes with a price. I'm the law in this town, and you don't get to flout that."

Miguel finished his beer. "You're not the law in New Orleans. Trust me, I've heard that from my Uncle Cesar enough times over the last week to have it drilled into my head. After he got tired of yelling at my dad for pulling this stunt with the witch, he was happy to expound. At length."

Tension made it hard to sound casual. "Oh, he was, was he? And what did he have to say?"

"The gist if it? That one day you were going to overstep your bounds just enough for him to nail your ass to the wall."

It sounded about right, like the blustering bravado of a man who was sure Alec would never force that confrontation. "I've crossed that line a dozen times this month, kid. Your uncle hasn't shown up with the hammer yet."

"He's glad you don't want what he has," Miguel said matter-of-factly.

Maybe having a psychic shapeshifter around could be useful. "I don't want what he has. But if he brings trouble to this town, I'm going to be the one who ends it."

"Only one way to do that. You're sure he never wants you to challenge him? Well, he's sure you don't want to." Miguel fixed a pointed look on Alec. "And you already *have* one psychic shapeshifter. Go talk to Julio and leave me out of your shit."

Shit. "It's rude to snoop."

"Yeah, about that. Number one, this is my apartment. Number two, you think pretty damn loud. It's hard to ignore."

"You are going to be a pain in my ass, kid." Alec straightened and let his power off the leash. Barely, enough to give the boy a taste of real magic. "And that's fine. But I'm not going to let you break your sister's heart. She's been through hell. Your father and uncle damn near got her killed. What is she going to do that's so bad you won't even see her?"

Remorse darkened Miguel's eyes, though determination steeled them. "I could tell her I'm okay, and that I knew, one hundred percent, what I was getting myself into. But telling her that is only going to remind her that she can't protect me, not the way she's always wanted to. Things like that hurt her, worse than thinking I'm being an immature jackass who doesn't want a lecture."

They were both caught in a trap with no good way out. Nothing new, except for the pathological need growing inside him. The need to protect Carmen from the world, from pain, from everything. Even her own family.

It was a need he'd have to get a chokehold on—fast. "You can't avoid her forever."

"I'm not planning on it. Just...a little more time."

"Fine. But I want you to do something for me."

"What's that?"

"See a spell caster I know. Couple times a month, make sure nothing unusual's going on. For your sake *and* your sister's."

He wanted to say no, that much was clear. But when he finally answered, he said, "Sure. I could use a new poker buddy."

Alec released the breath he'd been holding. "Thanks."

"You're welcome." He set his empty bottle on the coffee table. "Julio said Carmen's fine. Is she?"

"Yeah. She's fine, and she's going to stay fine." Might as well get one thing out there. "No matter what your father and uncle try next. I'm not in the habit of asking people to pick sides against their own family, but you're in a hell of a spot right now. If things get worse..."

"I'm with Carmen," Miguel said, not a shade of doubt coloring his voice. "Julio and I both, we're with her."

"Good." Alec straightened, then hesitated. "If you've got questions or problems with the wolf shit—and you don't feel like asking your brother—Kat has my number."

"Thanks, but I'll make it."

Maybe. There was one more thing the kid deserved to know. "Watch your step with Kat. I'm the least of your worries if you hurt her."

"Andrew Callaghan. She told me."

Kat had her own skewed perspective of Andrew's supposed indifference to her, one she seemed stubbornly unwilling to relinquish. "Kat's smart and empathic, but she doesn't get instinct, not really. Try to remember that."

Miguel nodded. "I'm keeping it in mind."

"All I can ask." Of Miguel, anyway. Alec made it out the door and into the parking lot before he allowed himself a frustrated growl. Kat had a lot of talking to do.

Carmen faced Franklin across a cup of coffee and the mounds of paperwork on his desk. "I'll even do administrative tasks if you let me come back. I'm going to go nuts at home."

"You want to do paperwork?" Franklin smiled at her, though the tension in the room didn't dissipate. "Did Mahalia hex you?"

She had to tread carefully. "Is there a reason I shouldn't be here right now? More trouble with my uncle?"

Franklin's shallow smile vanished. "He took advantage of Alec's absence to make his presence felt. He's not happy that I won't tell him who pays the bills, and we've escalated from threats to legal attacks."

"Damn it. What the hell is he trying to accomplish?"

"Beats me. Maybe it's about the money, or maybe it's about putting me in my place. Wolves don't tend to think much of the rest of us shifters."

"Will John Peyton intercede if he knows Cesar is harassing you for no reason?"

"John Peyton doesn't have that luxury. He's taken all the chances he can afford, right now. Going against one of the old wolf families on behalf of a coyote? He can't do a damn thing unless Cesar crosses a line that puts the rest of the wolves in danger."

Carmen hated the feeling of helplessness that assailed her. Franklin—and by extension the clinic—had no ready recourse. "I'll fix it."

Franklin shook his head. "It's bigger than you. And it's not the first time something like this has happened. The old leader of the Southeast council used to mouth half-hearted threats once a month or so. They can smell the money." He sat back and tilted his head, regarding Carmen thoughtfully. "You've seen the equipment we have. Haven't you ever wondered?"

"Of course I have. But I figured you're a stand-up guy with decent funding and a good head for money management."

"Not quite." He checked his watch. "Do you want to know?"

As far as she knew, no one at the clinic but Franklin himself was privy to that information. "Only if you want to tell me."

"You're the closest thing I have to a second-in-command, Mendoza. I've been thinking about making it official for a while. Your relatives aren't going to change that."

"Even if they're causing serious problems for the clinic?"

"Rule number one of the supernatural community in this

town? We don't hold each other's families against one another."

"That seems fair." Carmen held out both hands. "Lay it on me. What is it, the Conclave making secret donations? A cabal of wizards?"

Franklin shook his head. "Sit here another five minutes and you'll get to meet our benefactor."

Surely he didn't mean that the way it sounded. "You say that as if there's only one."

"Mysterious, isn't it?"

He was enjoying himself. "Franklin..."

But Franklin didn't budge, instead engaging her with small talk about what had gone on in her absence, until a rattling knock set his door dancing on its hinges.

He raised his voice. "Come on in, Wesley."

The man who walked in had been in a recent altercation. Contusions and scratches marred his face, along with a nice-sized laceration over his right eyebrow. His leather jacket was worn and had a very distinct grass stain on the shoulder.

Carmen forgot about Franklin's words as she rose and stepped away from her chair. "Jesus, are you all right?"

"I'm fine, I'm fine." The newcomer waved her off and peered at Franklin. "Finally, I get to meet her."

"And you're making a great first impression." Franklin sighed heavily and leaned forward. "Who was it this time? You weren't in the casino again, were you?"

Wesley snorted, then winced and prodded at his swollen lip. "Casinos won't let me back in. Could head up to Biloxi or something, but I don't like to drive."

"Might as well sit back down, Carmen." Franklin waved a hand. "Meet Wesley Dade. Our illustrious benefactor, and a degenerate gambler."

"Not really gambling if you know what's coming," Wesley said, his voice light and careless. He managed a half-smile for Carmen, even with his growing bruises, and sank into the chair beside her. "Nice to meet you. Officially, I mean."

"You too." She tried to make sense of his words, and the situation. "You're a precognitive psychic?"

Wesley tapped his temple. "I knew you'd be a smartie. Too bad you're not going to have time to help Franklin run this place."

The words would have frightened her, except that he didn't seem to deliver them with any sense of foreboding. "I just got the job, and you're telling me I can't do it?"

Wesley hummed cryptically.

"Ignore him," Franklin advised. "Sometimes I think he says that shit to stir us all up. If Wesley *does* know something, he's not going to spill unless it looks like the apocalypse is nigh."

The psychic's smile grew. "Happens more than you'd think around here."

She believed it. "You fund the clinic? By gambling and subsequently getting the crap beaten out of you?"

He touched his bruised cheek. "People don't like it when you win all the time. But no, back-alley poker games don't pay the bills. The stock market does."

"Wesley's a little superstitious," Franklin said, dry amusement lacing every word. "He can't seem to stop testing his luck, but he's convinced God will strike him down if he uses the money on himself."

As a basic personal philosophy went, it was similar to what Carmen's mother had raised them to believe. "My mom used to tell us the same thing about our abilities. That we'd be punished if we abused them."

"Fire and brimstone and a big angry devil tormenting you all day long." Wesley shrugged and gestured to his face. "Or a beat down because you tempted fate. Wherever our powers come from, someone doesn't want us using them to get rich quick. Unfortunately, I have a compulsive personality."

"So you make this place possible, and warn everyone when an apocalypse is on the way. That seems like a pretty big chunk of good karma."

"It would have to be. I really like gambling." Wesley slanted a look at Franklin. "I know when to hold 'em. *And* when to fold 'em. Even when to walk away."

It sounded like a long-standing joke. Franklin certainly groaned like it was and rubbed at the side of his face. "And someday we're going to teach you when to run. Carmen, take him to one of the exam rooms and fix his face up, would you?"

He'd need stitches, at the very least. "Beats paperwork. Follow me, Mr. Dade." She led him down the hall, but hesitated at the exam room door. "Does Franklin give you a chart, or does he keep this stuff off the books?"

"There's probably one floating around somewhere." He gave her a half-grin that utterly failed to be rakish. "You sure you want to find out how many times I've been punched in the face this month?"

"Pretty sure I don't, actually." She ushered him in and gestured toward the exam table. "I think you know the drill."

Wesley stripped off his jacket and settled in like an old pro. "This is nothing, really. You should see what happens to card counters if you cross the line in the wrong casino."

"Broken fingers?"

"And then some. Too bad, because it's an art. Not much skill in knowing the future, but card counters can guess it."

"Isn't it more about memory?" Carmen grabbed some gloves and gauze. "Remembering what's been played and extrapolating the rest?"

"Remembering what's been played, keeping the count, knowing the odds..." He raised one eyebrow at her. "If you stitch me up so pretty I don't have a scar, that's an art too. Not less of one just because you learned it like any other skill."

It sounded like Wesley Dade was trying to impart a life lesson, not talk about repairing facial lacs. "I'm a big fan of knowledge earned and hard work."

"Of course you are. Franklin respects that, and he respects you."

Honesty, Carmen. "I'm also a big fan of directness. I'm even okay with people being on the blunt side."

Wesley smiled and held out both hands. "Just talking about counting cards. I like to talk to distract myself when needles are about to become intimate with my face."

Whatever he was trying to say, he wanted—no, he needed her to listen. So Carmen dabbed at his eyebrow and smiled. "All right. Not everyone can do it, right? Count? Calculate the odds on the fly?"

"No, they can't. But even the best... If you do it by yourself, it's easier to get caught. You have to play the table, you know, and for that you need partners. If they're good, they can watch how you change your betting strategy and figure it out."

"There's another option, you know—don't do it. Find another hobby. Take up watercolors or knitting. Parasailing."

"Lady luck's a fickle lover," Wesley admitted, "but some of us can't keep from crawling back to her time and again. Funny thing about this instance, though, is that lady luck favors you if you bring a friend. Or two. Spotters keep count, and the big player drops in to strike while the iron's hot." He sighed. "Too bad none of my friends are good at counting. Alec Jacobson offered to make buttons out of my teeth if I tried to lure his mathematically gifted secretary off to a life of adventure and mystery."

Carmen bit her lip to hold back a laugh. "Except for that part about Kat, I have to say, Mr. Dade...I have no idea what you're talking about."

"That's the point, Dr. Mendoza." He smiled, just a little. "God's busy. He can't smite us for bending the rules. Someday, it'll make sense."

"Like when the iron's hot."

"Smart girl."

She hummed as she opened a suture kit. If she were a little smarter, maybe she could figure out the gambling precog's cryptic words, and whether they were a promise...or a warning.

Chapter Fifteen

There were definite advantages to having a girlfriend.

Carmen's skin was smooth and warm under his fingers, and he'd discovered he liked the feel of it. Tracing idle patterns on her back was better than any ritual when it came to quieting his mind. Granted, the soft sheen of sweat and the way her heart still beat too fast didn't hurt. Alec was honest enough to admit that regular, enthusiastic sex with a woman who always knew exactly what he needed was enough to make a man drunk.

It seemed to have done wonders for Carmen's mood too. She hadn't unraveled whatever psychic trick it was that brought him inside her shields, and her emotions tickled over his skin, a gentle pressure he was slowly becoming used to. Understanding those emotions had been tricky at first, but now he was learning to separate frustration from anger, and desire from happiness.

All of them were present now. Anger struggling to reassert itself, though happiness seemed to have taken over. Alec let his fingers drift in another lazy circle before speaking. "I like this thing you did. Letting me feel what you're feeling. Different way of seeing the world, huh?"

"Mmm, I thought about rebuilding everything, but I was dragging my feet." She propped her head up and smiled at him, her expression one of satisfied, sleepy pleasure. "I like it too."

Tenderness stirred inside him. He liked her. Not just the hot sex, or the admittedly unusual pleasure of being fed home-cooked meals on a regular basis. He liked *her*, especially when she had that lazy smile that was nothing but naked, open trust. "You look happy, but you still feel a little pissed off."

She groaned. "My uncle's a jackass. While we were gone, he mounted a legal attack on the clinic, all because Franklin threatens his manhood, or maybe his authority. Or both."

"Or because Franklin's been my friend for years, and I support the neutrality of his clinic." Not a pleasant thought, but he'd had it before.

"Whatever the reason, I'm starting to wonder if anyone is ever going to make him stop."

It wasn't where he'd expected the conversation to lead, and some of the warm, pleasant afterglow faded. "It's not that easy."

"Right. Because everyone else on the Southeast council is busy trying to figure out how they can snatch power for themselves."

"Not that. If you stop Mendoza today, then tomorrow you've got to stop Reed. And the next week, Hopkins will be banging down your door. It never *ends*, Carmen, and the person who tried to stop it would get himself killed, eventually."

She sat up and ran her hands through her hair. "I don't believe they're *all* as corrupt as my uncle. Maybe they're as corrupt as they're allowed to be. Maybe all it would take to stop them is one strong person standing up to them."

It was naive. Sweet. It would get her heart broken. "Maybe they're not all that corrupt. But enough of them are. The majority."

Her eyes shadowed. "I may not understand being alpha, but I understand taking care of people. Responsibility. Some of the council members have to remember that's why they're there."

He'd spent more than his fair share of time thinking about the Southeast council and the men who ran it, their strengths and weaknesses. "Alan Reed's not terrible, though he'd like to kick your brother's ass more than a little. William Levesque is a decent guy. But Hopkins and Hughes... They make your uncle look reasonable."

"Reed and Levesque, that's two. And it's something."

She didn't get it. "They're decent, but they won't stop Hopkins and Hughes from tearing apart anyone who manages to take on your uncle. Or stop your uncle from doing the same to someone who took out one of the other two."

"Then I guess you're right." He felt the sting of dejection

before he heard it in her voice. "The system's change-proof, and it's too late to fix it."

They could have been his words from her lips—and he wanted to disagree. He wanted to change it, for her.

Stupid. The system *was* change-proof. The people in power had designed it that way. Still, he couldn't stop himself from holding out a hand to her. "I'm sorry, baby."

Her hand trembled in his. "It's not your fault, and it's silly of me to get upset about it. I just don't understand how they can not *care*."

"A little bit at a time." He tugged at her hand, urging her to curl up beside him again. "Maybe they're born into it, raised with it. Maybe they start out thinking they can change it and realize how much there is to lose. Once you're on the council, losing a challenge can wipe out your whole life."

"Too much to lose, and not enough to gain." Her breath feathered over his shoulder as she spoke. "That's when it happens, isn't it? When otherwise good people start to do nothing."

That stung a little. "I'm not doing nothing. I picked my battle. New Orleans is one I can win."

She tensed and lifted her head to look at him. "That wasn't a dig, Alec, and I wasn't talking about you."

He tried to laugh it off. "Guess I'm feeling defensive."

For a moment, he thought she might not speak. Then she said, "Maybe you think you should be doing something more."

"Yeah, well, no one ever said I was bright."

"I say you are," she corrected, lifting a hand to his cheek. "I also don't think you should feel guilty about this. You're doing what you can."

It should have been enough. Reassurance. Instead it felt hollow. "So what lets me off the hook when all the other bastards are guilty for letting the world go to hell?"

"Because you're not letting things stay the way they are because it benefits you. You mean well, and you're *trying*." Her hand traced down until her palm rested over his heart. "I can feel how hard you're trying."

Alec slid his hand over hers and closed his eyes. "I try. And sometimes it's enough."

Carmen kissed his shoulder. "No, I shouldn't judge. All I've ever seen is the worst part of any of it, so I don't really understand. I can't. But you live it, every day."

The words struck at the heart of the anxiety that had been building in him for months. "Seems like all we've got are worst parts, these days. I don't think it was always like this. Or maybe I'm just tired."

"Both?" she whispered, pressing her forehead to his. "Shh. I want to show you something."

Pressure gathered, a low buzz he could feel in his bones. The brush of her power, curling around him. It rose in a gently cresting wave, passion twisted with infatuation, sparkling trust and a sweet kiss of longing. Her feelings, the way he made her feel, bathing the darkest, most jagged corners of him with something wholesome and beautiful.

Alec closed his eyes and dragged in a shaky breath that smelled of sex and skin and Carmen. "Thank you."

"Don't thank me." She stroked his arms, a tender, soothing touch. "Just see yourself the way I see you."

"Don't know if I can, honey." He lifted a hand and touched her cheek. "But at least you let me feel it, for a little while."

"Whatever you need." His own words, delivered as a promise instead of an echo.

Alec tugged her down into his arms and rolled them both, until she was on her side and tucked back against his chest. "I'm just afraid it might come down to a showdown with your uncle," he admitted. "That can't be easy for you to think about."

"No," she admitted. "But I know you'll only do what you have to do. Maybe...I could talk to him."

His wolf snarled. *He* snarled. "If he hurts you, I'll kill him."

"I wouldn't put myself, or you, in that position."

Easy enough to say, but Carmen had a streak of glorious optimism. "I don't care if this makes me an overbearing, irrational ass. Don't go see him by yourself. Please, Carmen."

"I wouldn't, Alec, I swear. Not without you or Julio."

Julio was an acceptable alternative. A strong enough wolf to face down his uncle, if he had to, and determined to keep his sister safe. "Good. Speaking of your brothers, I went to see Miguel."

"I know." She turned her face to his. "He left a message while I was at the clinic. He said he'd talked to you."

Uh-oh. "Yeah? What else did he say?"

"That you're a hardass and an impossible bastard." Carmen laughed. "He likes you."

The kid's world was likely tilted sideways. Even if he didn't know or understand it, the steadying presence of an alpha would settle anxieties he'd never had before. "Did he also tell you that he's been getting cozy with Kat?"

"He did. Does it bother you?"

Alec sighed and closed his eyes. "It's a messy situation. Your brother's a new wolf, going through a lot of shit, and Kat's... Well, she's pretty determined to take care of him. But I'm worried maybe it's not for the right reasons."

Carmen kissed the corner of his mouth. "No getting involved in other people's relationships. It'll just make them mad and you crazy."

Alec curled his fingers around the back of her neck, holding her steady so he could meet her gaze. "He's one of mine now, Carmen. It's not because I want to be involved, or I like being involved. New wolves and relationships can be trouble. Knowing that, worrying about that—it's always going to be who I am."

That gave her pause. "Are you worried about his safety? Hers?"

"I'm worried..." He struggled to put the indefinable into words. "Shapeshifter mating is about bodies, and bodies are the least important thing to us. They heal. Maybe that makes broken hearts hurt that much more. We forget we're not indestructible." With the fragile curve of her neck under his hand, his chest ached. "We forget that a human woman can still destroy us."

Her sympathy flowed over him. "Because we're not indestructible either?"

"That's part of it," he acknowledged, but for once he hadn't been thinking of his wife. He was thinking about Miguel, awash in the well-meaning concern that Kat had never been allowed to heap on Andrew. Then again, maybe a telepath wasn't in danger of misunderstanding. Maybe the swelling anxiety had more to do with the woman he held in his arms.

Losing Carmen would hurt. She didn't need to die to break something inside him. All she had to do was walk away.

"Alec." She mirrored his gesture, sliding her hand under

the back of his neck. "Trusting someone, sharing yourself... It's a risk, not one anyone has to take, but the alternative is a terribly lonely one."

"I know." With her lips so close to his, it was easy to kiss her. Slow, deep. He stopped fighting for words that would never come out right, that would never be articulate enough to give voice to things that weren't very human. Instead he felt it all, and knew she'd understand.

Carmen made a soft noise and smiled against his lips. "Me too."

There was a crazy sort of peace in a woman who knew his heart, even the dark places, and still wanted to kiss him.

Chapter Sixteen

Julio protested as he coasted to a stop in an empty parking spot along the curb. "We're already late, Car."

"This'll just take a second," she promised, already unbuckling her seat belt. "I promised Franklin I'd drop these papers off yesterday, but I didn't get a chance." She'd been too busy trying to figure out how to approach the situation when she confronted her father and her uncle.

"You know Cesar. Any excuse to say you're disrespecting him."

Carmen wished she could deny it outright, but part of her relished the opportunity to make him wait, wanted to seize it. "He deserves a little inconvenience, especially on the clinic's behalf."

Julio drummed his fingers on the steering wheel. "You want me to come in with you?" She flashed him a forbidding look, and he laughed. "Fine, I'll stay here."

"Thank you. I don't need someone holding my hand every second of every day."

"Is Franklin even still here?"

"His office light's on." It glowed through the frosted window at the back of the building. "His car's still here too."

"Lily must have stopped by after work to keep him company." He nodded through the windshield to the dark-gray BMW parked around the corner.

"Don't worry, I won't get stuck talking." Though it wouldn't hurt to let Lily know that Alec had invited her over, so she didn't plan on being home for the weekend.

"You're blushing." Her brother's eyes narrowed. "Why are

you—? Oh God, I don't want to know, do I?"

"Shut up." She climbed out of the car and bent inside for her bag. "I'll be right back."

The street was quiet even for the late hour, but there never was much traffic on the nights when the clinic closed early. Even Franklin should have been home already, but Cesar's complaints and harassment had lengthened his already considerable workdays.

Carmen's heels clicked on the sidewalk, and she smoothed her palm over the lightweight fabric of her pantsuit. She'd wanted to attend the meeting in her grungiest jeans, but she had to be reasonable. More than reasonable, because she and Julio had to pick up the slack left over from their uncle's irrational behavior. It left no room for pettiness, justified or no.

She stumbled and barely caught her balance. At first, she thought she must have tripped over jagged concrete or broken a heel, but a wave of emotion crashed over her a second later, nothing short of mind-numbing, inescapable terror.

She stood there under the streetlight, trying to make sense of the fear holding her riveted to the spot, knees shaking. The metallic taste of blood filled her mouth, though she couldn't tell if she'd bitten her tongue or if something more sinister was happening, if her body was ripping apart from the inside.

A car horn blared, familiar. Her own. Then Julio's voice, barely cutting through her petrified haze. "Carmen! Carmen, get dow—"

The glass doors of the clinic exploded with a roar that drowned out her own heartbeat. Time stopped, seconds stretching into a strangely frozen moment where everything was silence, the concussed hush of eardrums under so much pressure they can't even conduct noise. Her mind catalogued it and marveled even as broken shards rained down, cutting through the stillness.

A weight jerked her to the ground. *Julio.* He grabbed at her, and she realized she was flailing, trying to crawl across the glass-strewn walk.

"You can't go in," he yelled. "There could be structural damage. We have to wait for the fire department—"

If he'd survived the explosion without life-threatening injury, Franklin might be fine. But Lily... "She won't make it. I have to, Julio."

"*No.*" He dug his phone out of his pocket and put it in her hand, folding her numb fingers around it. "Call 911. I'll find them."

"Julio—"

"I'm trained, Carmen." His voice was steady, even. "I'll find them, and I'll come get you."

She swallowed her protest and nodded. "Be careful."

It took her two tries to dial the numbers, and she answered the dispatcher's questions in a fog, her gaze fixed on the dark hole that used to be the clinic's entrance.

An eternity passed before Julio reappeared, dusty and coughing. "I found Franklin."

She was on her feet already, the phone forgotten in the grass. "Is he—?"

"He's hurt, bad. Come on." He led her through the clinic, a path already picked out among the glass and debris. "There's no fire, but I'm not sure how stable the building is. I'd have brought him out, but shit."

Franklin was on his back, eyes open and feverishly clear in spite of the bloody mess of his body. "Lily. Where is she?"

"I'm going to find her," Julio promised, already moving down the hallway. "If you need me, yell."

Carmen ripped at Franklin's shirt. "What hurts? Your legs?"

"Eight-seven-zero—" He coughed, air rattling in his chest. "Write this...Sera's number. No one else knows."

You call her. The words wouldn't come. There wasn't always a chance, and insisting there was didn't help. "I'll remember it. Eight-seven-zero," she prompted.

He delivered the rest of the phone number in a relieved whisper. "I've never called her. I was afraid—afraid he'd move them if he knew I'd found her."

Franklin lay in a rapidly spreading pool of blood. His best chance—his only chance—was for her to stop it. Carmen repeated Sera's phone number like a mantra as she shoved a filing cabinet out of the way and dragged open the supply closet. Pressure bandages and an IV, and the rest—

The rest would have to wait.

She dropped the supplies beside Franklin and began to cut open the legs of his jeans. "Tell me about Sera."

"Her mother left when she five." One of Franklin's hands curled into a fist. "I was no good at raising a little girl."

"You were *there*." The superficial wounds on his legs had already begun to heal, but the bones beneath them were misshapen. They'd heal badly and have to be broken again, reset, but she couldn't help that. "Where does Sera live?"

"Arkansas." He hissed in a pained breath and started to lift his shoulders. "Lily—I need to find her."

Altered mental status. Carmen pushed him back down, firm but easy. "My brother's looking for her, remember? Julio. Did I tell you he's a firefighter?"

Franklin's brow furrowed, but he relented. "Sera's in Arkansas," he whispered. "The bastard she married took her there when she was seventeen. Getting the law involved was too dangerous."

Too dangerous because they asked too many questions— and she'd just called 911. "Shit." She hadn't dealt with an emergency in New Orleans that hadn't been funneled through Franklin first. As far as she knew, he was the one everyone called when they needed a doctor.

So what happens when the EMTs show up and load him up? What happens when they watch him heal under their hands like he is yours?

She fumbled in Franklin's pocket for his phone. The screen was cracked, with inky black blobs stretching across it, but the keypad worked.

She dialed and, halfway through the first ring, Alec's voice filtered through the crackly speaker. "Franklin? What the fuck is going on? McNeely just called."

At least someone had alerted him. "It's Carmen. I'm here at the clinic. Franklin's injured, and we're still looking for Lily."

"Carmen? Christ, you're breaking up. Where are you?"

"At the clinic," she repeated. "I'm with Franklin, and Julio's searching for Lily."

"Already on my way. There's..." The speaker crackled, distorting his voice. "...going to take Franklin somewhere safe."

Relief steadied her hands as she tucked the phone against her shoulder and began to dress the still-bleeding wound on Franklin's side. "I called 911."

A horn blared on the other end. Alec swore. "I'm five

minutes away. Madden might get there first. You can—"
Another crackle, longer this time, and when Alec's voice came
back it was fuzzier. "Carmen?"

"I'm here. We're—" A crash from the back of the building
cut off her words, and fear flared anew. "We have to get out of
here."

"You're *in the clinic?* Get the fuck out, Carmen, right now—"

The phone beeped as it dropped the call, but another crash
drew her attention. There was no way Franklin could walk, even
if he could stand, and a wheelchair would never make it
through the busted block, fallen light fixtures and sheetrock
that littered the hall.

A clatter and a shout echoed around the corner, and Julio
came into view, Lily cradled in his arms. "She's unconscious.
Go outside with me and check on her, and I'll come back in for
Franklin."

"I can't leave him."

Franklin's hand shot out and curled around Carmen's
wrist, hard enough to bruise. "Go. Call Sera," he rasped, a
command in no way tempered by the weakness of his voice.
"Tell her I need her. *Go.*"

Not a command at all. A plea. "Okay."

Carmen followed close behind Julio, moving as quickly as
she could. The sooner they got out, the sooner he could bring
Franklin, and then they'd be safe, and nothing else would
matter.

Sirens wailed in the distance, and Julio hurried across the
street with Lily. "Stay over here," he instructed. "No matter what
happens, don't come any closer."

Carmen dropped and reached to help him lay Lily out on
the sidewalk. "I'll stay put." Help was coming and, even if
something went wrong, going back inside would do no good.

He nodded and took off again, running across the street
with more speed than he should have possessed.

Lily stirred, her eyes fluttering open only to close again,
and a quick check revealed a nasty bump on her head and a
gash on her cheek.

An ambulance arrived first, a tall, bulky man hopping out
of the back as it coasted to a stop. His gaze fell on her, then
dropped to Lily. "You Mendoza? Alec Jacobson said you were

here."

Alec had said something— "Madden?"

A short nod. "One of the dispatchers recognized the address and pulled some strings, but we don't have a lot of time. Need to get anyone who's supernatural and injured out of here. The first cops on the scene will probably be ours, but we can't control something this big."

She looked down at Lily. "She's human, but Franklin Sinclaire is inside. My brother went back in to get him."

Madden crouched next to Lily. "If she's his girlfriend, we need to bring her with us. Won't be able to settle him if we don't."

Carmen squeezed her eyes shut. "Of course. I don't know what I was thinking." Except that she *wasn't* thinking, not with her brain pulling her in three different directions. "I'll help you."

The driver's door of the ambulance clicked open, and boots hit the ground lightly before a vaguely familiar feminine voice cut through the night. "I got this, Madden. Go get Franklin."

A strong hand landed on Carmen's shoulder for just a moment. "There's a secondary location waiting. Franklin had it set up a few weeks ago. Maybe he's got a little precog in him, huh?"

Or Wesley Dade had instructed him to do so. "Someone does."

Madden squeezed her shoulder, then rose and bolted across the street, moving so fast his form was a blur. The woman who'd spoken before appeared at Lily's side, a sturdy blonde Carmen had seen at the clinic from time to time. "Hey, Doc. Help me get her loaded up, would ya? Madden'll get the others out."

Together, they eased Lily onto the backboard, and Carmen stabilized her neck while the blonde—Diane, maybe—made room in the back of the ambulance. They lifted her into the vehicle, and Diane climbed in after her.

Tires screeched behind them. Brakes squealed. The stench of burning rubber preceded a slamming door, then Alec appeared at the back of the ambulance, eyes as wild as the dizzying press of his emotions.

Relief sent Carmen tumbling into his arms, relief and a need she hadn't known existed until just then. "They're still inside. Julio and Franklin and—"

"Shh, it's okay." Warm hands smoothed over her hair. "What happened? Tell me what happened."

"I don't know. An explosion. Julio told me to get down, and it just—it blew up."

"Franklin?"

"He's hurt. They're going to take him to another clinic."

Alec frowned and glanced at Diane, who shrugged one shoulder without looking up. "Don't ask me. I didn't know Franklin had a backup facility until Madden told me."

"Madden's inside?"

Tension and fear spiked inside Diane, strong emotions that went wild at the mention of her partner's name. "It's only been a few minutes. Maybe—"

A loud noise that sounded like a pop shot through the night, and the building groaned as part of it folded, collapsing in on itself with a shudder. Carmen lunged, a scream caught in her throat, and Alec's arms locked around her body, unyielding as steel. "Carmen, *no*."

Either Julio had lied about the threat of fire or something else had happened, because orange fingers of flame began to lick out of the clinic's ruined facade. "*Alec*."

"Stay here." He released her, only to strip off his jacket and shove his keys and phone into her hands. "I can try to find a way in."

Fear melted into terror, but she didn't have time to voice her protest before Diane stepped in front of them both. "There they are."

The EMT led the way out of the smoke with Julio just behind him, Franklin balanced on his shoulder. Madden carried an IV bag, and Diane rushed to meet them with a collapsible gurney as more sirens pierced the night.

Julio's shirt was ripped, and the blood soaking the fabric didn't all belong to Franklin. "What happened?" Carmen asked.

"The ceiling fell." He winced as she pulled his shirt away to reveal a gash across his back. "A beam almost caught us."

Alec eyed the ambulance, then his truck. "We need to get the fuck out of here. Where's this second clinic?"

"Outskirts of town, near the airport." Madden spoke from where he sat, hunched over Franklin. "You three follow behind us."

Alec was already urging Carmen toward his truck. Normally, she would have fought to ride along—she was board-certified in emergency medicine, for Christ's sake—but this wasn't a normal situation. Her boss and her best friend lay in the back of the ambulance, and she couldn't treat them with the same necessary detachment as the EMTs. "Okay, we'll follow."

She ended up in the front of the truck, wedged between Alec and Julio. Pain, fear and tension made the front of the cab nearly unlivable as he gunned the engine and followed Diane. One cop car careened around the corner toward them, but Alec's stream of curses cut off abruptly when a dark arm thrust out of the window and waved them on. "McNeely. He'll cover as long as he can."

Julio peeled off his shirt, and Carmen helped him tie it into a makeshift bandage around his wound. "What will he tell the others?" she asked.

"He'll figure something out. McNeely's quick on his feet." The truck swerved as Alec took a corner too fast. "There are a few like him scattered across the city. Your brother probably knows."

"Like hell," Julio said. "If there was some sort of underground supernatural cover-up system in Charleston, no one ever clued me in."

Ahead of them, Diane flipped on the ambulance's siren, clearing a path. Alec frowned as he took the next corner. "Maybe Reed takes care of it."

"No idea."

It could be a measure of how far out of the supernatural loop Julio stayed—or an example of just how much Alec did in New Orleans in the absence of any official leadership. "I can't even worry about any investigation right now," Carmen whispered. "I only need them both to be okay."

"I know, honey. I didn't get a look at Franklin." Tension threaded Alec's voice, and true concern. "How bad is it?"

"His legs were broken. He'll need surgery."

Another soft curse. "I stay out of the clinic as much as I can. I don't know who to call. Who we need."

Neither would Wesley Dade, who had no doubt funded this

other clinic, as well. "I know an orthopedic surgeon we can call. If it's for Franklin, she'll drop everything. There should be space where we can set up an OR, but I'll have to make some calls, see if we can find a spell caster who can negate his healing while we work on him."

"My phone's in my pocket. Jackson's on speed dial—number three. He's got magical contacts. And he can round up Kat. Someone needs to track down Franklin's kid, and Kat's the one she's most likely to listen to long enough to realize she needs to get her defiant little ass back to New Orleans."

"Franklin gave me her number." She reached into his pocket and retrieved his phone. "I can handle the call."

Alec's voice turned rough, tension bleeding through. "Don't call Sera from my phone. Her prick of a husband will make them both disappear if he thinks anyone knows where they are."

Her hand found his knee, seeking to soothe more than anything else. "I'll do it in a little while, when I know what to tell her."

"All right." He glanced past her, at Julio. "You holding together?"

"It's a scratch," he answered simply. "I think it's already knitting up."

A quick check under the bandage revealed as much to Carmen. "I'll still have to check it out."

"Yeah, I know." He went back to staring out the window.

Cold certainty settled over Carmen. "You knew, didn't you?"

Julio grimaced. "Knew what?"

"What was going to happen." More than anything, she remembered the fear that had paralyzed her. "When you got out of the car, it was because you knew."

His skin had gone ashen. "Not soon enough," he whispered, a small sound full of self-recrimination.

He'd seen it in time to stop her from walking up to the clinic doors. In her mind, she traced her steps, tried to judge how close she would have been to all that jagged, flying glass if Julio's terror hadn't frozen her in place. "I could have been killed."

Alec's low, furious growl rumbled through the cab as the truck lurched. He bit off an angry noise and steadied the vehicle. "Precognition?"

Her brother snorted. "You have no idea what I'd give to be rid of it sometimes."

A familiar lamentation, one Carmen had heard from their mother dozens of times over the years. Even when her visions encompassed something she could change, a course she could alter, the lingering images had given her nightmares, sometimes for months.

Alec's fingers tightened on the wheel. "I don't want to ask this. I really don't."

Julio turned his head suddenly, his expression set, his gaze angry. "We were supposed to be at Cesar's hotel. A meeting, me and Carmen, at eight sharp, not a second later. He said that— not a second later."

A sob rose before Carmen fully processed his words. "*What?*"

Alec's quiet, vicious curse cut through the cab. More alarming was the way his anger and worry circled inward, vanishing like water from a tub after someone pulled the drain. In moments, he was shut off from her. Quiet.

His voice was quiet too. "That's it, then."

"No." Carmen repeated the denial, shaking her head. "Cesar wouldn't have gone that far. Peyton could strip him of his council seat for something this careless, and you said it yourself, Alec. They won't jeopardize their positions because they have too much to lose."

"There's one fatal flaw you're missing in that equation. The one that got Noah Coleman killed and opened up this damn Conclave seat to begin with."

"He's not human, Car. None of us are." Julio sounded as bleak as he was pissed off. "You can't say Uncle Cesar wouldn't have done it because he might have. If your boss challenged him enough, he could have completely lost it."

Worse, Alec didn't disagree. "We can plan. We can plot. We can have all the best fucking intentions in the world. If someone pushes the wrong button, none of it matters. We're monsters when it counts."

Any other time, Carmen would have tried to deny it. Now, she closed her eyes. "If Cesar did this, he's going to pay."

Alec's steely façade cracked—just for a moment—and she

felt the vastness of the rage gathering inside him. "I'll add it to his bill."

She wished she could feel more from Alec than blankness with the occasional flash of anger and pain. More than that, she didn't want to face the fact that he'd pulled away from her again, or the possibility that this time he might have done so for good.

Chapter Seventeen

Nicole Peyton was five feet of snarly alpha wolf who looked nothing like her identical twin. Oh, on the surface Michelle and Nick shared similar features—big dark eyes, long brown hair and their mother's slight stature—but Alec had never seen anyone mistake one for the other.

Maybe it was the clothes. Nick arrived at the block of mostly vacant warehouses in jeans and tiny little tank top that wouldn't have looked out of place on a hip college kid. Or maybe it was just attitude. The Seer had spent years trying to fade into any background she could, but when Nick entered a room, you knew it.

Her husband herded Kat and Miguel toward the other end of the warehouse, to the bare-bones clinic where Carmen had begun organizing chaos through steely willpower alone. Alec gestured Nick over to the folding table where he'd spread out every cell phone he could get his hands on, along with his list of contacts.

Her frown deepened. "You look like hell, Alec."

"You're a ray of sunshine as always, Peyton."

"I'm not here to blow smoke up your ass. I'm here to help, and I'm starting off by saying you look like you're barely hanging in there."

At least one thing in his life hadn't changed—she was still an obnoxious alpha bitch. The constancy was almost soothing. "I'm trying to figure out how to challenge Cesar Mendoza without ending up with a council seat I don't want."

To her credit, she didn't look surprised. "It'd be tough to pull off, especially if you expected the council to leave you any autonomy in New Orleans. They'd see denying the seat as weakness, for sure."

"And if I leave another hole in the Southeast council, God knows who'll fill it, or which one of those bastards will use the advantage to climb over the rest and onto the Conclave."

"An unenviable position." She sat on the edge of the table and nodded toward the other side of the cavernous warehouse. "Is that her? Carmen?"

Alec tensed, unsure if the emotion pounding through him was protectiveness or defensiveness. "Yes. That's Carmen."

"Damn." Nick blew out a breath and flashed him a sympathetic look. "Puts you in an even tougher spot."

Stress made him pissy. "You mean the part where I'm probably going to have to kill my new girlfriend's uncle?"

It didn't intimidate her. "Yeah, that part. It'd be hell on a relationship that *wasn't* new, but this... This really sucks."

His life in a nutshell. "Even worse, it's tomorrow's problem. Tonight's problem is that the only safe place for supernaturals to get medical treatment just blew up, and I have no idea if we've got enough people to bury the weird details. Like the pool of Franklin's blood we left behind, or who might have witnessed people dragging him out of the collapsed building."

"Jackson and I are already on it. You're not the only one who's been a busy boy tonight."

"Two-thirds of the shifters and spell casters in this town make their way through that bar of yours on any given weekend. You spreading the word?"

"In a manner of speaking."

"As long as it gets done." One more thing to cross off his mental list. "Does your father know about this yet?"

She bared her teeth in a fierce grin. "Cesar Mendoza can sidestep you all he wants because you're not the boss of him. Incidentally, my father *is*."

John Peyton would come down on Mendoza like a brick wall. Censure would be swift, and punishment would follow. Its severity would depend on how outraged the rest of the Conclave was, and it would be a slow process. It would take time, because if the Conclave loved one thing, it was listening to themselves talk.

Alec didn't have to wonder where it would end. They'd bicker. They'd fight. John would push for civilization. Some would side with him for favor. Some would oppose him out of pique. The Conclave would fail to find a consensus or present a united front, and whatever sentence they handed down wouldn't be enough.

The Conclave wouldn't solve the problem. But they'd keep Cesar busy. They'd keep themselves busy.

He'd use every god damn minute of that time to come up with a way to end this bullshit once and for all.

Nick watched him, her eyes wide and nervous. "You look scary." Instead of turning it into a joke, she made the observation solemnly. "Alec, don't do anything stupid, okay?"

For all her dominant tendencies, Nick wouldn't understand. Her battle had been for a quiet life, the right to live outside her father's legacy and her society's rules. She had her people—her tiny little pack—all those faces in the cheerful family photos that lined the walls of Luciano's ranch. Keeping them safe was her job, and she'd fight for it. She'd kill for it, if she had to.

Alec envied her that clarity. Not even thirty and she'd found her life's purpose. He was on the wrong side of forty and only starting to realize he'd been hiding from his.

He looked away from Nick, toward the opposite end of the warehouse. The jumble of two-dozen voices made it impossible to sort out one from another, but his gaze found Carmen like she was magnetic north.

The helpless terror he'd felt in her earlier was gone—or so well hidden no one would believe it was there. She'd taken control of the makeshift clinic with the unwavering steel of any good drill sergeant, and people went running in whatever direction she pointed them. Life could knock the woman down as many times as it wanted, and she'd still get up and save the world.

God help him, he wanted to save it with her. *For* her.

"*Alec.*" Nick sighed. "Jesus, I hope Cesar Mendoza knows what he's opened up."

"Don't think he could, Peyton." Alec glanced back at her and smiled. "Because I'm going to do the stupidest thing there is. I'm going to fix our world."

Carmen dragged her hair back into a sloppy ponytail. "Okay, Miguel. Clark needs help moving equipment out of the storage area and into the finished rooms on this end of the warehouse."

He hopped off the desk immediately, moving with a grace he hadn't always possessed. "Got it."

She turned to Kat, who'd already pulled a sleek silver laptop out of her bag. "I hope you brought your own Wi-Fi, because there are a few things we need to find, and quick. They're not in the inventory Franklin already stocked, but we need them in the next day or so."

"I brought everything." A boxy white MacBook and two tiny netbooks joined the first laptop on the table. "I figured you might need more than one computer online for the next few days, until I can set up something a little more permanent. I've got a mobile hotspot. The range isn't great, but I might be able to boost it enough so that you can get a signal from anywhere in the building."

"Thanks, Kat."

Tara waved her cell phone at Carmen. "You said you called Sokolov up in Shreveport, right?"

"That's right. She'll be down first thing in the morning."

"I know a guy who works in anesthesia at Our Lady of the Lake."

"In Baton Rouge?"

"Yeah. He knows plenty of spells that could come in handy, including one that can slow Franklin's shifter healing long enough for Dr. Sokolov to operate."

The only member missing from their specialized OR team. Alec's partner Jackson had offered to try if they couldn't find anyone else, but the last thing any of them wanted to do was take chances with Franklin's well-being. "Offer him whatever he wants if he can be here tomorrow."

Tara grinned, already dialing. "I'll talk him into it."

Carmen slid her hand into her pocket, closing her fingers around the borrowed cell phone there. Kat had handed it over readily, without question, and it was time for Carmen to use it.

The offices that occupied one end of the warehouse had been modified and outfitted as exam rooms or meeting spaces. When she found one with a large desk and a single folding chair, she sat down to dial the number Franklin had given her.

It rang five times before the call connected. Carmen heard

rustling, then the sound of a door clicking shut before a quiet, tense voice answered. "Hello?"

"Is this Sera Sinclaire?"

The sound of water filled the background. A shower, maybe, or a sink running. "Kat? Is that you?"

"Kat lent me her phone. My name is Carmen Mendoza. I'm calling because your father's been hurt."

Sera's breath caught. Hard on the heels of the gasp came a protest. "He's not—if you know Kat, you know...what he is?"

"I know." Carmen swallowed hard. "I work with Franklin at his clinic."

"Oh." Her voice sounded young and afraid. "Is it—how bad is it? Is he going to be okay?"

"He's all right. Stable. He needs surgery, probably tomorrow." She hesitated. "Your father told me you live in Arkansas. Can we send someone to pick you up, or—?"

"No!" Something clattered in the background, then paper crinkled. "I've got a pen. Give me the address, and I'll come."

Carmen rattled off the address she'd already memorized. "If you need help finding it, just call Kat's phone and someone will answer. I think most of us are going to be here all night."

"Okay. How did—was it Kat? Did she track me down?"

Lying might have been easier, but Carmen refused to do it. "Your father gave me your number and asked me to call."

Sera let out a soft breath. "Are you sure he wants to see me?"

A heartbreaking question, and so simple to answer. "I don't think there's anything he wants more."

"Okay." Relief, for a moment, but tension wreathed the words that followed. "I just need to talk to my husband. I'll be there by tomorrow morning."

"Sera." Instinct—and Alec's words—prompted Carmen to speak. "If you need help, if you need anything, call us. Please."

"I will." A muffled male voice called out in the background, and Sera swore. "I need to go. Tell him I'm on my way, okay?"

"Be safe." Carmen disconnected the call and rubbed her hands over her face. So much left to do, and all she really wanted to do was hide.

Her uncle, her *family*. All this pain and destruction, just because Franklin had flouted an authority that wasn't supposed to extend to him in the first place. And now Alec—

She stomped on the thought, pushing it down with absolute determination as she rose and made her way back down the half-lit hallway. There was no mistaking Alec's intention; he planned to make sure that nothing like this ever happened in his town again.

His town.

She pushed through the exit and into the controlled chaos of the main warehouse. Alec still sat at a table near the entrance, talking to Nicole Peyton. Though his glowering had subsided into a sort of quiet thoughtfulness, she didn't doubt that rage still boiled inside him, high and hot.

He would challenge Cesar and end up with his council seat. He would do it because he had no other recourse, even though he'd lain in her bed only days before and told her that anyone who went up against the Southeast council would die trying to change it.

His town.

He'd survive the first round of challenges, maybe even the first few. But no one could stand alone against an establishment, against so many who wanted to keep things exactly the way they were.

Lady luck favors you if you bring a friend. Or two.

Wesley Dade's words. Days old, but they echoed in her ear as if he stood beside her now, bringing painful clarity to the core issue at hand—Alec couldn't change the council, the Conclave, by himself.

Spotters keep count, and the big player drops in to strike while the iron's hot.

He couldn't do it alone, but he didn't have to.

"Carmen?" Alec's fingers brushed her shoulder, bringing the warmth of worry and protection. "You all right?"

She must have been staring, so lost in thought that she hadn't even noticed him crossing the warehouse. "I'm fine. I was...I was just thinking about something someone said to me the other day."

Worry intensified. "What'd they say?"

"That counting cards is a group activity," she answered absently. "What if you didn't take on the council alone?"

Alec's fingers closed on her chin and tilted her head back.

"Honey, you're scaring me more than a little. Do you need to sit down?"

"No, listen." She grasped his upper arms and looked up at him. "One person they don't want on the Southeast council? That person's a target. I'm talking about bringing backup. Majority rule."

Alec blinked. Frowned. "I'm trying to think of a reason why that wouldn't work. It *feels* like it wouldn't work. It feels..."

"It would take special people, ones you trusted. Ones who wanted to help, not take what you had."

"And here I was about to say it seems too easy." Alec's gaze unfocused. "Strong enough to get on the council. Strong enough to hold against challenges. Willing to lead, but capable of following too."

"My brother." He'd kill her for even thinking it, much less mentioning it to Alec, but it was true. "You need Julio."

He laughed suddenly. "Hell, if we're going to break all the rules, why go small? Andrew. Andrew can damn near take me out. He can win a challenge."

Carmen's heart began to pound. "It isn't breaking the rules because the rules are already broken."

"Oh, it's breaking all of the rules," he whispered. "All the ones no one ever wrote down because they just *are*. The rules that need to be smashed into pieces."

Exactly what she'd meant, but it didn't matter. She moved without thinking, sliding her hands up to his face. "Could you do it? If you weren't alone?"

"Depends." He gripped her hips and pulled her close, seemingly unconcerned with the attention they were attracting. "Will I have you?"

It was so much more than anything they'd discussed before, and it took her the span of a breath to know the answer. "You'll have me, no matter what you do."

He smiled, a smile full of warmth and excitement and *hope*, and then, in front of half the people they knew and a dozen they didn't, he dragged her to him and kissed her.

He kissed her as if nothing had ever been more vital, as if he would never stop, and nothing penetrated the haze of pleasure and possession until she heard both of her brothers calling her name in unison.

She broke away and turned to Miguel, who held the neatly lettered list she'd made for Kat. "Hate to break it up," he murmured, his cheeks red, "but you told us you'd put this in order so we knew what to track down first."

"Right." They had twelve hours to find most of the equipment, eighteen at the outside. "I have to do this, Alec. Can you go see if Franklin is awake? Even if he's not...tell him Sera's on her way, would you?"

"Will do." Alec smoothed back her hair and smiled. "We can do this."

"Yes." The council, the makeshift clinic, all of it. "We can."

Chapter Eighteen

Someone had brought a banged-up old card table upstairs. Someone else had provided flimsy folding chairs. Kat had given him one of her stupidly small computers, one with a keyboard so tiny he could barely type on it. A handful of cell phones lay scattered across his makeshift desk, tangled with phone lists and the files he'd had Jackson retrieve from the office.

A humble beginning for a revolution, but Alec supposed people had started with less.

They'd certainly started with less manpower. The room he'd claimed was a good twenty feet long and half that across, but with Julio, Andrew and Derek standing around the table, the place bristled with tense, uneasy power. It was almost a relief that Nick and Mackenzie had gone to raid Nick's bar for food and supplies—six dominant shifters in so small a space would have been damn near unlivable.

Not that it was comfortable now. Only Derek seemed at ease as he sprawled in one of the chairs. "So. This is how coups start?"

Julio snorted. "I'm sure the new, civilized Conclave would call it a hostile takeover."

After the last couple years, Alec suspected John Peyton might call it cleaning house, if he were allowed to express such sentiments out loud. "I put out a few calls. Tried to see if anyone could remember anything like this happening in the past."

Andrew leaned one shoulder against the wall. "And?"

"Not at the council level. And not by people with good intentions." Gangs, mostly, taking over local cities by challenging their way through the power structure and eliminating resistance in their path. Petty criminals who used the force of numbers because they didn't have the power to stand against the council wolves, and whose own unsuitability worked against them. The one united front the councils and Conclave could muster was their response to criminals working their way up the food chain.

Maybe they don't like the competition.

Derek crossed his arms over his chest. "So when I beat Coleman and refused to take his Conclave seat, I pretty much fucked up the whole system, didn't I?"

"They wouldn't have let you have it," Julio told him. "You won his *council* seat. Leadership on the Conclave isn't transferable, not like that. You would have still had to win out over the other members of the Southeast council."

Alec nodded his agreement. "The hole on the council didn't help matters, though. None of 'em dared jump until they knew who'd be at their backs. There's no system set up for something like that—Coleman's challenger should have taken his seat. If he'd died in an accident, his son might take his spot, but they're weren't going to let his daughter have that seat, even if she wanted it."

"My cousin, Veronica." Julio shook his head. "It's the last thing she ever planned for. Don't think Uncle Cesar never considered the Maglieri precedent, though."

Andrew's brows drew together. "What does that mean?"

"When her husband died, Enrica Maglieri took over his council seat—and then his spot on the Conclave. Cesar would like to do the same thing with Coleman's wife—my Aunt Teresa. The Mendozas would have two council members."

Understanding dawned in Andrew's eyes. "And she could back all of his plays."

"Yeah," Alec said. "Except Enrica Maglieri is a stone-cold alpha bitch who had the strength to trample over all the men in her council." Teresa Coleman—Teresa Mendoza, again, he supposed, with Noah finally gone—was a woman beaten down by time and her own brutal husband. She'd never have the strength to take a council seat, or the ruthlessness needed to keep one.

Derek seemed to make the same connection and took it to the next logical step—the same one Carmen had seen so clearly from her vantage point outside of the system. "So you need someone to back your plays." His gaze found Julio, then Andrew. "Two someones."

Julio groaned and covered his face. Andrew, on the other hand, seemed oblivious as he nodded. "Derek's a logical choice. That empty seat is already his by tradition."

Any hint of easygoing relaxation vanished from Derek's face. "I'm married. And my wife's sister is the one person these wolves pretty much universally fear and loathe. I'll be damned before I do *anything* that'll draw that much attention to Michelle and her kid."

"Then I don't understand."

"You, Andrew." Derek leaned forward, his gaze intense. "Alec wants you to take over the world with him."

He must have understood after all, at least on some level, because his answer was immediate—and absolute. "Like hell."

Alec choked back a sigh. "Julio, Derek? Would you two give us a minute?"

Julio held Alec's gaze as he backed toward the door. "I'll stand and I'll fight, Jacobson, but I hope you know what you're doing."

The first test of leadership—and one he was long accustomed to. He knew how to be confident for the people counting on him. "Wouldn't start a fight I couldn't end. Count on that."

Derek was slower to leave. He met Andrew's gaze, ignoring Alec completely. "Say the word and I'll stay."

But the blond man shook his head. "I'm good. Go."

The door clicked shut behind Derek, and Alec turned to face Andrew squarely. "This isn't some tiny thing I'm asking of you. Julio's got legacy. I've got legacy. You'd be rocking their pretty little world to its core."

"Yeah, no kidding." Andrew dropped to a chair with a snort. "Will it help? Is this stunt something that could put you—all of us—in place to really *change* some shit?"

That was the question. "I could hold my own against the Conclave, if I needed to. Give the Alpha someone at his back who wants the same changes he does. He's been fighting on his own for a long damn time. But I can't focus on that if I've got to worry about the Southeast council sticking a knife in my back."

"And that's where Julio and I come in, right? Make sure the

rest of them aren't planning to dogpile you."

"That, and keep this region running." Alec turned to the desk and dug through the stack of files until he found the one pertaining to the various councils. He'd kept up with the information because knowing was important if you wanted to stay safe outside the system, and now he could use it to get in.

A worn and creased map was tucked between two lists of council members, and Alec pulled it out and unfolded it on the table. "Southeast region," he said, jabbing his finger at Louisiana. "Us. Arkansas. Tennessee, Mississippi, Alabama, Georgia, Florida, both of the Carolinas, both of the Virginias, and Kentucky. Right now there are council members in DC, Memphis, Miami, Charleston and Atlanta."

"Jesus." Andrew studied the map, his jaw set in a tense line. "What does a council member do?"

"When they're doing their job? Mediate disputes between cities, sometimes within cities. Use tithes collected from the packs under their protection to provide resources. Fund clinics, like Franklin's. Deal with problems that might expose us, pass judgment on minor infractions. Just...keep people safer."

He sat back and flashed Alec a disbelieving look. "You already do half that stuff here."

"Yeah. I do." He gave Andrew the truth. "And I was thinking you'd step up to help me, sooner rather than later. Julio would be a lot of help, but you're the one I need at my back. You're the one I trust with my city."

Andrew made the logical leap easily. "If you take the Conclave seat, you'll be spending most of your time in New York. Like Nick's dad."

Something else Alec could only hope Carmen had realized. Uneasiness stirred, and he fought it back. "I'd have to be there a lot. But that doesn't mean we can't run things differently. Hell, if I give Kat enough money, she'll build some magical computer shit that'll make it seem like I'm on hand 24/7."

"It doesn't matter anyway, does it?" Andrew rose and paced across the room. "I'll do it. We'll all do it, because there isn't anything else to do. We have to take care of things."

"It's who you are now. Who you'll always be."

He turned his gaze on Alec. "No time like the present, I guess. I'm in."

Alec should have left it there. He should have counted his victory. But Andrew was more than just a mentee. More than a trusted lieutenant. Andrew was a friend, and he hurt, whether he could admit or not. "Is it going to be too much? Having to work with Julio when his little brother's..." *Climbing all over Kat.*

"He's not responsible for what his brother does."

Andrew's voice held an implacable edge that made it clear the topic of Kat was off-limits. "Fine. Stick your head out the door and drag those other two back in here, would you?"

Only Julio came back in. "Derek had to go find Nick. I think it's just us, anyway."

Better to keep Derek out of it. Alec shuffled through the files again, remembering what he'd said to Carmen the other day. "Drummond Hughes is the worst of the lot. He's the one who claimed Coleman's empty seat. He did it by killing every challenger who came against him, even though challenges at the council level are almost never to the death."

"He's a vicious bastard," Julio agreed.

"Then he's mine." Andrew growled the words.

No more protecting him. Alec nodded and handed over the file. "You should go to Zola and Walker. Walker's got experience in fights to the death. I'm sure he knows things neither of us would consider." And if they were about to bring down the wrath of the wolves, it was only fair to warn the only lion pride in the United States. Zola might even be an ally—*if* she thought the risk was worth it.

Two more files lay on his desk. Alec glanced up at Julio. "I know you and Alan Reed have had your problems, but he's a capable leader. And he's fair, when you're not boning his daughter."

"Yeah, I know." The younger man had the grace to blush a little. "He's not a bad guy, and he'll go with the flow. All he needs to do the right thing is a push in that general direction."

"Same can't be said of Sam Hopkins. He's not as dangerous as Hughes, but he's a sadistic bastard who's more interested in entertaining himself than taking care of anyone else."

"Levesque is all right," Julio offered. "That leaves Hopkins and my uncle."

"Hopkins and your uncle," Alec agreed. It would be so easy

to let Julio do the dirty work. Wash his hands of Cesar Mendoza and face Carmen with a clear conscience, safe in the knowledge that someone else would be fighting the bastard.

Easy. Cowardly. "Cesar's mine to challenge, Julio."

Julio's hands clenched into fists on the table. "I knew you were going to do that."

For so many reasons. "Your uncle is still in his prime. He's been preparing himself for a Conclave bid. You can be sure that means he's been training. And he's backed into a corner and he knows it."

"He's my uncle. It's *my* fight."

Alec wanted to hold back, blunt the truth. The words were horrible to think and even worse to say, but he had to. "He's your uncle. That might not stop him from killing you."

He saw the understanding reflected in Julio's eyes. "It wouldn't stop him, not in the slightest."

"You don't have the experience to fight him." Alec planted his fists on the table and leaned in. "Or if you think you do, why don't you give me a try, right now. See which of us is more prepared for this fight."

"Can *you* handle him?" Julio shot back. "Because you may not be thinking about it, but I'm more than a little worried about what'll happen to Carmen if our uncle tears out your throat."

Alec had been fighting one thing or another since he was old enough to stand. First at his parents' behest, as they gave him all the lessons they thought he'd need to take power. At eighteen, he'd run off and joined the army. Then years of mercenary work, more years of fighting other shifters. Challenges. Self-defense. Training—his own and training others.

It seemed like most of his life had been preparing him for this, for the one thing he'd always sworn he'd never do, but he could answer Julio honestly. "I'm not going to let your uncle tear my throat out. I can beat him."

Julio capitulated with a short nod. "Okay. Your fight. Win it so we can get down to business. I'll take care of Hopkins."

Instinct prompted caution. "I think we should keep you two a secret. Not give them any chance to steal our idea and start making alliances." Alec straightened and nodded to Julio.

"People won't be surprised if I challenge your uncle, not after this. And the whole council will have to show up to witness the fight."

Andrew leaned against the wall, his posture deceptively relaxed. "Then we'd better get the word out. About that much, at least."

The windowless room gave no hint about time, but it had to be approaching dawn now. Friday. The Conclave would spend the weekend calling in favors to cover up Cesar's mess and deciding on an appropriate punishment. Cesar himself would be tied up in defending himself.

"Monday," Alec said firmly. "We need a few days to get into place, make sure all of our people are protected. I'll issue the challenge Monday and, as the challenger, I'll get to set the time. A week from today, here in New Orleans."

His co-conspirators nodded in agreement, and Julio spoke up. "A week will give anyone who's interested a chance to get here. And *everyone* will be interested."

They sure as fuck would be. "Then let's give them something to spend the next twenty years talking about."

"Carmen!"

Someone had a hand on her shoulder, shaking her awake. Anger that felt like Kat pierced through sleep, and Carmen bolted straight up in her chair. "What is it? What happened?"

Kat's blue eyes were ice. Her fingers curled into fists as she straightened, and she spoke through clenched teeth. "Sera's here."

The rage licking at the edge of Carmen's consciousness doubled. "Is she all right?"

"No." Kat pivoted and stalked to the door. "You'll see what I mean."

Fuck. Carmen hurried to follow. After the things Franklin and Alec had said, not to mention the way Sera had acted on the phone, the possibilities were few—and very, very specific.

Kat led Carmen to one of the exam rooms, where a tired-looking young woman leaned against the wall. She had Franklin's hazel eyes and freckles and the same red hair, though hers hung in a long braid spilling over one shoulder.

She also had a black eye, the bruise spreading down across one pale cheek.

The fatigue hit Carmen first, followed by the fear and hopelessness. She shoved both aside and yanked the plastic off a stool before pulling it close to Sera. "Sit down for a second, sweetie."

"I'm fine." Such an obvious lie that Kat made an outraged noise, like a kettle about to boil over.

"Kat." Carmen steeled her voice as she situated herself between the other two women. "Can you give us a minute alone? Please?"

After a moment, Kat sighed and retreated, stopping just short of actually slamming the door behind her.

When she was gone, Sera tried for a smile. "It looks worse than it is. It's healing. It'll be gone in a day or two, I think."

As if that made it okay. Carmen probed Sera's cheekbone gently. "Did he hit you anywhere else?"

"No." The fear strengthened, undercut by an odd thread of satisfaction. "He hit first, but I hit harder. Actually, I beaned him with my KitchenAid."

"One of the little ones, or a big pro model?"

Sera choked on a hysterical little laugh. "The six-quart one. It was really nice. Guess he shouldn't have bought it for me, though, if he wanted to start beating me up in the kitchen."

"I don't think anything's broken." She stepped back. "I'm Carmen, by the way."

"Hi, Carmen." Sera touched her cheek and winced. "I don't want my dad to see this. I don't want him to worry while he's hurt."

"Hell, no." He'd climb out of bed and crawl if he had to, but he'd find Sera's husband and he'd kill him. "We might be able to heal the bruises, or maybe cover them with makeup if you want to see him this morning."

"Makeup, magic. Whatever it takes." Sera's hands dropped to her lap. "I don't know how badly I hurt Josh. I stole his truck and drove here, no license or anything. He'll set the human cops after me too. He knows I won't have bruises by the time they find me."

That, at least, was something Carmen could take care of. "If you'll let us take some pictures before we do anything else, we'll have a record. And Jackson and Alec can find out what happened to Josh." Maybe they could even find a way to dissuade him from causing future trouble for Sera.

"Okay." Her eyes fluttered shut. "This was the first time. Things have been bad for a while, but he'd never hurt me before. That's not how it works. He was stronger. He was supposed to keep me safe."

She whispered the words as if her heart was breaking, and Carmen wrapped her arms around her. "It's okay. You're all right now. You can be safe here."

"I'm sorry." Muffled words laced with stiff pride, though Sera didn't pull away. "I shouldn't be—it's stupid to cry over an asshole."

"The assholes are the ones who *make* you cry."

Sera nodded against Carmen's shoulder, her face still hidden. "Yeah. Yeah, they really are."

A knock shook the closed door. It opened a second later, and Julio stuck his head inside. "Carmen, Alec is about to go— Oh shit, I'm sorry."

Sera pulled back so fast she almost tilted off the stool. She lifted her hands to her cheeks to scrub away tears and winced when her hand bumped her bruised cheekbone. "Alec's here? God, he can't see me like this either."

"He won't. The last thing we need right now is for him to flip his shit. Julio, close the door."

He did, his gaze fixed on Sera's battered face. "What the hell...?"

Intense embarrassment filled the room, but Sera lifted her chin a little, almost a challenge, and pointedly ignored the question. "Kat didn't tell me what happened to my dad. Just said there was an explosion at the clinic."

Julio answered it out of what seemed like habit. "That's all we know right now. It was definitely some sort of incendiary device. There'll be an investigation."

"Maybe not such a formal one," Carmen interjected.

"No." He shook himself. "No, maybe not. But we'll find out what happened."

Some barely visible tension in Sera seemed to fade away. The defensive tilt of her chin lowered. The tight set of her shoulders relaxed a fraction. She tilted her head as she studied

Julio, quiet curiosity in her eyes. "I'm a coyote."

He stared back. "I'm aware of that."

A tiny furrow appeared between her eyebrows. "Most wolves aren't very friendly to me."

"I'm not most wolves, sweetheart." He glanced at Carmen. "Alec's about to head out to pick up some stuff. He wants to know if you need a change of clothes, anything."

He could head to her place and kill two birds with one stone. "Yeah, and Lily needs a few things too. Tell him I'll be there in a second."

"Sure." With one last look at Sera, he left.

"My brother," Carmen explained.

"Oh." Sera smiled a little. "Sucks for you. I'm pretty glad my parents didn't see fit to saddle me with an alpha bastard brother."

"Yeah? I guess I've got two now." Cryptic words, but explaining would take too much energy. "If you want to wait a while, I can find someone to fix up these bruises." Jackson, probably, though Carmen hoped he could keep it quiet, or she'd have to test just how well she could reach Alec through a haze of rage.

Sera's smile faded. "You need to go. I'll be okay. Kat's mad at me, but she'll get over it. She can help me out."

"She's not mad at you. She's scared for you. Terrified."

"She's mad, and she should be. She hated Josh." Sera laughed, a tired, broken little sound. "Guess she always knew."

She didn't need to be alone. She needed support, comfort—and Carmen didn't even have time to provide it, not with everything else going on. "I'm going to get my other brother. He can come in and hang out with you."

"It's okay." Sera reached out and folded her slender fingers around Carmen's. "I'm stronger than I look. I just want someone to fix my face so I can see my dad. If you tell me where to go or who to talk to... That spell caster Kat used to work for. Is he here?"

"Jackson. I'll find him right now."

"Thank you." Sera squeezed her hand before releasing it. "I think Kat's hovering outside the door. She's not very sneaky."

Carmen could feel her. "You're right, she's not." She passed her hand over Sera's head and took a deep breath. "Hang in there."

Then she turned to go, because there was so much left to do, and the last thing she could afford was to think too closely about Sera's pain. She had to stay strong and hold things together, at least until Franklin was well.

That was the best thing she could do for Sera anyway.

Chapter Nineteen

Franklin looked like hell, and Alec had never seen him happier.

The surgery had gone on for five nightmarish hours. Alec had spent them trying to keep a mostly grown-up and thoroughly hysterical Sera from crashing into the room where spell casters, shapeshifters and doctors were systematically breaking the bones in her father's legs. Even narcotics and Franklin's stone-faced stoicism couldn't keep him sedated. By the third hour, everyone in the warehouse was tensed against the next scream.

Agonizing, but fleeting. It might be weeks or months, but shapeshifter healing would repair the damage to Franklin's body. Sera and Lily had already repaired the damage to his heart. Bandaged and pale, Lily sat on one side of his bed, his hand pressed to her cheek as she watched him in silence. Sera hovered on the other side, her quiet murmur indecipherable over the quiet beeps of machinery.

Franklin had the two people who mattered most to him, safe and sound. He had half a dozen medical professionals on hand, ready to leap if the tiniest thing went wrong. He'd be fine.

And Alec was taking Carmen home for a few hours of uninterrupted sleep on a horizontal surface if he had to drag her there by the scruff of the neck.

She pushed through the door, her face and hands scrubbed and damp. "Okay, I'm ready. Let me check on them one more time."

Famous last words. "They're fine, Carmen. Franklin doesn't need anything else. And you're not the only doctor around anymore."

She stopped and rubbed her palms on the scrub bottoms she wore. "Right, I know. If I don't just leave, it'll be another hour or two. Let's go."

It seemed too easy, but Alec wasn't in the mood to try his luck. One hand at the small of Carmen's back urged her down the hallway, toward the cavernous main area.

They passed Kat and Miguel, curled up on one of the makeshift pallets and sound asleep, Kat's tiny little computer resting on the floor under her hand. Julio sat nearby in quiet conversation with Derek and Nicole. Alec didn't stop, not until they hit the side door and stepped out into the afternoon sun. "My truck's a couple blocks down. Gonna have to figure out better parking around here, that's for sure."

"One more thing on the list." Carmen leaned against him, letting him bolster her as they walked to his truck.

She remained silent as she climbed into the cab and buckled her safety belt. He'd already started the engine, put the truck in gear, and pulled out into the street when her hand crept across the seat and brushed his leg.

Driving with one hand was easy enough. He curled the other around her fingers, rubbing his thumb along her palm. "You did a damn good job, pulling that place together like you did. I couldn't have managed it."

"Most of the pieces were in place..." As the sleepy murmur died, Carmen's eyes snapped open. "And if you ever really considered making buttons of Wesley Dade's teeth, you should think twice."

The transition was so jarring he blinked. "Does Wesley Dade have something to do with this?"

She smiled as her eyes drifted shut again. "It doesn't matter. Just cut him some slack, okay?"

"Honey, you're punch-drunk. Get some sleep. It's a long drive back to my house."

"Mmm. Mine is closer."

Maybe, but only having her in his house—in his *bed*— would soothe the terror that had been gnawing at his gut since the first phone call about the clinic. "You care?"

"No." She squeezed his hand. "I like your house."

"I like you in my house." Which she probably knew better than he did. "We'll get there and sleep until this evening, okay?"

"Mmm," she said again, already tumbling into sleep.

She was so tired that she slept through the long drive back to his property, and the soft sound of her rhythmic breaths eased the tension rattling inside him a little more with every minute that ticked past. They'd have two days of comparative peace, and then—

Then the bottom would fall out of the world as he knew it.

No, that was unfair. There was nothing passive about the shakedown to come. He was kicking the bottom out with both feet and trusting there'd be somewhere to land. If not, a lot of people would get hurt. Small comfort that he'd be too dead to see it.

Carmen stirred as he turned down the long gravel drive that led to his house. "You with me, honey?"

"I'm here," she whispered, her voice low and thick. "I'll always be here."

His heart skipped a beat. "I know, darling. Hang on and I'll get you into a bed."

"I'm all right." She straightened and squinted against the sunlight slanting through the windshield. "It's a beautiful day."

"Nice enough." The grass on either side of the drive was starting to grow wild again. It'd be May before long, and if he didn't see about having it cut, his house would look like it was parked in the middle of a savanna. "You wanna lay out in the sun instead?"

"No. It's only that I didn't notice it until just now."

Hard to notice the weather when she'd been stuck inside a warehouse for the past eighteen hours. Alec eased the truck to a stop a few feet from his front porch and slid it into park. "If you can stand to eat before you pass out, I'll find something in the fridge."

"I'm not hungry." Her seat belt clicked as she released it, and she climbed out of the truck and stretched.

The sun turned her caramel skin golden. Even in ugly green scrubs and a T-shirt, with her hair in a sloppy knot and shadows under her eyes, she was the most gorgeous thing on two legs. The smile felt awkward curving his lips, though God knew it shouldn't by now. He'd been flashing it a lot since she'd wandered into his life.

It was a short walk to the porch, but he picked her up

225

anyway. "You scared a decade off of my life, and now you're going to let me smother you for an hour. You owe me."

Her head fell back with a groan of protest, though she slid her arms around his neck. "Even if I didn't mean to scare you?"

"Life's not fair. And neither am I."

She muffled a laugh against the side of his neck, though it quickly faded into a moan. "You may not be fair, but you smell good."

Having her lips nuzzled against his throat was asking for trouble. "Reach down and open the door for me, would you?"

She slid her hand over the wood, feeling for the knob without raising her head, and pressed an open-mouthed kiss to his skin as she pushed open the door.

He was hard before the damn thing hit the far wall, his dick straining against the zipper on his jeans. Walking was uncomfortable. Walking with Carmen licking him was fucking well impossible. "*Carmen.*"

Her lips skated over his jaw. "Alec."

The brand-new door Andrew had installed shuddered as he kicked it shut with more force than strictly necessary. In the next second, he had Carmen up against it, her long legs snug around his hips. "Don't think I'm not already fighting the urge to rip your damn clothes off and check every inch of you to make sure you're in one piece. If you don't cut it the hell out, I'll do it."

She released him long enough to strip her T-shirt over her head, leaving her in a white cotton bra. Then she cupped his face between her hands and smiled. "I'm in one piece. And I love you."

I love you too. But the words didn't come, because she'd shattered his control into pieces so fine they could blow away in the wind. He couldn't remember putting her down, but he didn't think he'd ever forget the triumph of tearing the scrub pants off her body, or the blind relief when he slid his hands down her thighs and calves and found smooth, unblemished skin.

"I'm all right." The murmured words didn't penetrate so much as the feeling, the overwhelming sense of peace that matched her gentle smile. "I'm not hurt."

The laces on her sneakers tangled under his fingers, and he snapped them with a frustrated jerk. Shoes, socks, they landed in the foyer in a haphazard circle, though one sneaker bounced down the stairs to the basement. Part of his brain marked its thudding progress as proof that time had slowed, because it seemed to take forever to skim her panties down her legs, but the shoe had barely settled on the cement floor below when he rose and turned his attention to her bra.

Simple. Gorgeous. Carmen. He fumbled with the fastening and bent the little metal hooks, but she didn't notice. She tore at his shirt and gasped when he touched her bare skin, arching away from the door with a shudder.

Gorgeous and his. A hand between her thighs proved it, and he pushed two fingers deep into the slick, gripping heat of her pussy. Wet and ready, *eager*, so hot for him that he moaned as he crushed his mouth to hers.

She cried out against his lips, her nails sharp on his shoulders, and her hips bucked as pleasure welled through the foyer, a hot weight pressing in on his skin. Her gift, let free, and the boundaries between them blurred. No *Alec* and *Carmen*, just *now* and *more*.

His hands found his belt. His fly. The zipper broke and he ripped the denim, but a second later his cock was in his hand. He thrust into her, driving deep as he lifted her against the door and snarled her name.

Carmen bit her lower lip and shuddered again, her eyes glazed and unfocused. "I feel you. Everything."

No way he'd last through one of her jaw-clenching orgasms with empathy wrapped around him tighter than the slick grip of her body. "Feel it all, sweetheart." He caught her hand and pinned it to the door next to her head, twining their fingers together as he ground deeper. "Feel every inch of me."

Her gaze sharpened as it met his, and the sheer adoration on her face thrilled every part of him. He clutched her thigh with his free hand and felt the bite of his fingers against her skin, felt the satisfaction she got from knowing he'd marked her. Intimacy beyond thought, beyond words or reason.

So he fell into it. Fell into her with every rough thrust, and she rewarded him with little spikes of ecstasy that shivered up his spine and whispered encouragement. She welcomed him, into her body and her heart. Open. Joyous.

His.

He buried his face against her throat and bit her, just a

tease, and Carmen sucked in a sharp breath. "*Yes—*" Throbbing pleasure tightened around them both. She was close, so close to the peak that she began to beg, whispers that quickly rose in volume as she shook.

Blood roared in his ears, pounding through him with the rhythm of their hearts. He thrust deeper, faster, chasing the perfect angle that would unravel that knot inside her and drive them both over.

And then he found it. Her head banged against the door, and her low, keening cry reached his ears a split second before the sweet rush of her orgasm hit him.

He came. Hard. Fast, out of control, riding her body's spasms until he was spent and she was trembling. Her fingers combed through the damp hair at his temple, and every heaving breath pushed her chest closer to his.

She spoke in a whisper. "I'm sorry I scared you."

For a second, he couldn't remember what in hell she was talking about. "I'm just glad you're okay. I need to keep you okay."

Her soft laugh tickled his cheek. "Take me to bed and hold me."

He could do that. He could do it damn near forever, which made the words easy. Right. "How about I take you to bed and love you?"

Carmen held him tighter. "Even better."

Carmen woke to darkness and a delicious ache in her muscles that flared and subsided as she stretched gingerly under the light sheet. Alec lay beside her, his features indistinguishable until her eyes adjusted to the scant moonlight filtering through the window.

He stirred, his face still relaxed in sleep, and her heart thumped. *Love.* She leaned close and kissed him, her lips to the corner of his mouth, marveling at the tenderness that rose. He was strong, undeniably so, but he needed her as much as she needed him.

He murmured something, a rasping rumble more noise than words, and rolled toward her. One arm fell heavily across her waist, and her conscience stung. How often during the last day had he insisted she catch whatever sleep she could manage? She should have done the same for him.

She settled against him and stroked his bearded jaw, trying to soothe him back to sleep.

"Won't work," he mumbled, but the corner of his mouth curved up. "But it feels good, so you can keep at it."

"I shouldn't have woken you," she whispered, "but I had to kiss you."

"Good reason." His hand landed on her hip, fingers spread wide.

Another muscle twinge made her groan. "Maybe we should have slept more and had less...sex." Sex, without a condom in sight. "Oh."

"Oh?" He still sounded sleepy. Oblivious. "You want less sex next time?"

She'd never been so mindless, so unthinking. "No," she murmured, "but maybe more birth control."

His hand tightened so fast she sucked in a sharp breath and grabbed his wrist. He released her with a muttered curse, then rolled onto his back. "Well. That answers that."

Carmen rubbed her hip absently. "Answers what?"

He reached over and covered her hand, his touch soft. Apologetic. "You're exactly the second person I've forgotten a condom with, and the first wasn't an empath. She could keep her head." He turned his head and gave her a rueful smile. "We might have to acknowledge that this could happen. A lot. Making babies is pretty much the ultimate instinctive drive."

"Honestly? I'm surprised we lasted this long." She kissed his shoulder with a soothing hum. "There's a regimen I've been on before, and I don't mind restarting it. It might be easier than trying to keep our heads."

"Do you know—?" His voice turned almost hesitant. Nervousness, and a purely masculine confusion. "You're a doctor. What are the chances—I mean, do you know if this is the right time for...?"

A quick calculation gave her an answer he'd likely be relieved to hear. "There's a possibility," she admitted, "but it's a slim one. It's a little late in my cycle for me to get pregnant."

"Oh." Uncertainty still twisted between them.

His ambivalence gave her pause. "Alec?"

He released his breath on a long sigh. "Sorry. Just...forgot it was possible to be anything other than overwhelmingly relieved about this shit. The last thing either of us needs is a kid to worry about, but..."

Part of him still wanted it, and she understood. They hadn't known each other long, but she *knew* him. It could take months or years to tease out all the threads of someone based on what they would honestly show or tell. But she'd seen inside Alec, the deepest parts he might not be able to articulate even if he wanted to share them with her.

She knew him, and she loved him. Everything between them was new, but she couldn't help but yearn for the chance to hold his child, to share that bond with him.

His nervousness spiked, and she gripped his hand. "I love children, and I definitely want to be a mother. If it takes a few years, that's fine, but if it happened earlier, I wouldn't cry." Carmen raised her head and met his gaze. "You'd be a good father."

Judging by the look in his eyes, her simple words had been a gift. He smiled and touched her cheek. "We can figure it out after we fix the world up a little, huh?"

"That sounds like it involves leaving this room." Something she didn't particularly want to do now that they'd forged a new intimacy.

"Need to get moving before too long anyway. Have to check with your brother and Kat, see if they got all the money moved around."

Julio would never allow himself to be distracted from a task. "If they had run into a problem, he would've called."

"Good. Suppose I'll have to get used to trusting him."

"Yes." He knew Andrew well already, had apparently taught him everything he knew about being a wolf. "I think Julio's relieved, in a way. It must be hard, knowing you could be doing more if you only had an idea of where to start."

Alec smiled. "I always knew where to start. I just didn't know how to keep going."

Now, he did. "You're really going to do this, aren't you?"

"I'm really going to do this." His hand drifted up her side, and he curled one finger in her hair. "This world the way it is... It's hopeless. It can be hard, it can be awful...but it doesn't get to be hopeless."

Her chest swelled with an emotion she knew he would feel, though she gave voice to it anyway. "I'm proud of you. It's not the easy path."

"Don't be proud of me yet. I'm counting on you walking that path with me."

She rolled to her side, took his hand and pressed it to her heart. "I love you. If you have to face something, *anything*, you won't do it alone."

His brown eyes stayed serious. "Do you really know what you're saying? This isn't like the human government. We don't spend four years dicking around and then worry about reelection. This is a lifetime job, and when it's not, it's because you're dead, or damn near."

Most of her family had held no dearer ambition for her. She'd avoided it, simply because she didn't believe in it, but things were different now. Alec was different. "I've lived my life focusing on the bad aspects of wolf society, and I probably still haven't seen the worst of it, but that doesn't matter. It doesn't change anything. Don't you see why?" She sat and tucked her hair behind her ears. "You take care of people. That's what you do, who you *are*, and I understand that. You can't walk away from it."

"And I won't walk away from you." He caught her hand and threaded their fingers together. "But you might want to walk away from this. You've known me two weeks. We're walking down one damn crazy path."

"I know you, and I love you." Echoing her own thoughts, though it occurred to her that he might not be as certain. "Do you need more time?"

"Not a minute." Quiet words, but no doubt shaped them, and none lingered in his heart. "I know love when I feel it, and I know how it feels to lose it. I'd marry you tomorrow, just so I wouldn't waste a second of having you be mine."

The declaration stole her breath. "It wouldn't change anything. I don't need rings or a ceremony to be yours."

"Yeah, but you're going to end up with both, you know." His thumb stroked over her bottom lip. "Still time to run. If I'm on the Conclave, it means big fancy weddings and half a dozen bridesmaids and, God help us all, my mother. My mother alone should send you screaming into the night."

Part of her *was* terrified of the responsibilities, the expectations. As much as Alec would have to play the political games, so would she have to deal with the social ones. "High tea with your mother doesn't scare me nearly as much as the thought of running away."

"Maybe *you* should join the Conclave," he murmured, dragging her down against him. "That woman scares the piss out of me."

"It should tell you how much I love you, then. I'm willing to make nice with your family." She stretched out over him, gliding her thumb absently over his collarbone. "What about you? Can you deal with mine?"

Foreboding slashed through the room, sharp and uncomfortable. "Most of them, yeah. Your uncle—can you deal with me dealing with him?"

Not an easy question to answer. She'd flown to Atlanta to be with her Aunt Teresa and her cousin Veronica the previous year when the Alpha's son-in-law challenged—and killed—Noah Coleman. It hadn't mattered that Noah was an angry, awful man who'd treated them both badly. He was still their family, and they had cried when he died.

Carmen met Alec's gaze. "If you can find a way to spare Cesar, I know you will. But don't do it for me. He crossed a line, and we all have to be prepared for the consequences of that, even if we had nothing to do with it."

"Then we'll deal. Both of us." He eased up, spilling her onto her back, and dropped a kiss to the corner of her mouth. "I wouldn't be doing this without you. Not because you had the idea, or because you wanted it." His lips pressed to the bare skin above her heart, soft and warm. "You believe in it. You let me feel it. You made me remember how good it is to believe."

A sad thing to forget. Her heart ached for him. "We'll remember," she told him softly. "And when things get hard, we'll remind each other."

"That's all I need, baby. You and me and a world of hope."

Chapter Twenty

The last time the Alpha had come to town, he'd held his meeting in Franklin's clinic. Neutral territory.

Neutral territory was gone. Blown to little fucking pieces, and the knowledge still grated. Alec wouldn't let Cesar Mendoza set a toe across the threshold of the makeshift clinic, so John Wesley Peyton had summoned them both to the Roosevelt, to one of the hotel's tastefully decorated suites, where they could mouth polite pleasantries before Alec made it clear that mediation wasn't an option.

Except when the door opened, Alec found himself facing the Alpha and no one else. "John."

"Alec. Come in." He stepped back, looking tired and rumpled and damn near worn out. "Mendoza isn't here yet."

John had always been older, but now he almost looked old. Alec crossed the threshold, then waited for the man to close the door and turn. "If you're hoping to talk me down, it's not going to work."

The Alpha's jaw clenched. "On the contrary, the mediation wasn't my idea. Cesar insisted, probably because he knows you're planning to rip his head off."

Funny how the guy willing to blow strangers up from a distance got oh-so-civilized when *his* neck was on the line. "He can keep his head, but I'm taking his council seat."

John snorted as he crossed to the small bar on the other side of the room. "If he'll relinquish it quietly and without bloodshed, I'll consider letting him live in exile."

Cesar wouldn't give in, and they both knew it. No point in belaboring it. "After I do that, I'm taking the Conclave seat."

The man choked on a sip of whiskey. "When you decide to get ambitious, you don't mess around, do you?"

"Not really. No point in getting in this game if I'm not gonna play for keeps, is there?"

"I suppose not." The Alpha gestured to the bar with an upraised brow and poured another drink at Alec's nod of assent. "If you want to survive, you'd better have a plan for dealing with Sam Hopkins and Drum Hughes. They'll be at your throat in a heartbeat."

John Peyton would probably sympathize with Alec's plan, but the Alpha might not have that luxury. Alec erred on the side of caution and nodded, answering the question without giving John words he'd have to pretend he hadn't heard. "By the end of the week, the Southeast council will be behind you."

An odd light sparked in John's eyes, but he let it go and changed the subject. "Cesar is bound to appeal to your sense of family, since you're involved with his niece."

"No."

"No, he won't, or no, appeal isn't an option?"

It felt like stepping off a cliff, and Alec didn't care. "My future wife isn't interested in seeing her uncle retain his council seat."

"No, I can't imagine she would be." John drained his whiskey and set the glass aside. "I can't say I'll be sorry to see Cesar taken down. No one deserves the trouble he's caused."

Alec let out a breath. "I'm in this, John. It's time for a change. Way past time."

"As it happens, I couldn't agree—" A knock on the door interrupted his words. "Well, here we go."

He opened the door to Cesar Mendoza, who stood there with bloodshot eyes and a too-pleasant smile. "Good to see you again, John."

"Cesar." The Alpha's dour expression didn't change as he stepped back. "We've been waiting for you."

Alec bared his teeth at Cesar. The man blanched, though his smile stayed frozen in place, and he held Alec's gaze for a moment before looking away.

"Sit," John ordered. "Both of you. Alec, you begin."

The suite had couches and chairs arranged around a low coffee table. Alec took a chair, one with its back to the wall, and waited until Cesar sank to a couch before sitting himself. "You violated neutral territory."

He didn't deny it. "No one was meant to be harmed—"

The Alpha cut in. "Your intentions matter less than the outcome, Cesar. You acted rashly. Don't justify it."

Irritation flashed in Cesar's eyes, though he covered it well, and his concession was stilted. "It was a grievous error in judgment."

"The latest," Alec ground out, already tired of the endless talking. "For that reason, in front of our Alpha, I'm challenging you, Cesar Mendoza. For your seat on the Southeast council and everything that comes with it."

The man tensed. "Really, is that necessary? Think of Carmen."

Alec's nails bit into his palm. "Like you were thinking of her when you blew up her boss and her best friend? Or like your brother was thinking of her when he damn near killed her with that fucking spell?"

Cesar floundered for a response. "I believe Diego knows what's best for his own child."

"Bullshit. *I'm* thinking of Carmen, so I'll give you a chance to back down. Yield, and let the Conclave decide what to do with you. That's your only way out."

His throat worked, and Alec could practically see him considering all the angles, trying to determine the best combination of likely risk versus potential reward, and weighing it all against his pride.

In the end, that pride won. His dark eyes went flinty, cold, and he sat straighter on the plush sofa. "If you want my seat, you'll have to take it. I accept your challenge."

Adrenaline surged. Alec's wolf flowed to the surface, so fast and vicious he was faintly surprised he didn't spill to the floor and sprout fur. How easy it would be to force the challenge now. Lay his enemy low, with the stink of fear in the air. It would solve the problem. Soothe his pride.

It wouldn't last. "Friday," he rasped, still fighting the call of the chase. "There's a place suitable for challenges on my property."

"As the challenged party, it's my right to choose the venue for—"

"I'm overruling your right to pick the place." The Alpha growled, and power spiked through the suite. "The bombing at Sinclaire's clinic is under investigation, Cesar. You've invited a scrutiny we can ill afford, put us all in danger. Be glad you're getting an honorable challenge at all."

John's words cowed him, that much was clear, but the man kept his head high. "Friday. May I be excused?"

"Get out."

Cesar all but fled, and John rubbed his hands over his face as the door closed behind him. "Christ, what a catastrophe."

Alec had been so busy cleaning up the mess, he hadn't had time to check in with the human investigation. "How bad is the exposure?"

"Nowhere near what it could have been. Right now, it's little more than vandalism. If the police knew Franklin was there or—God forbid—his girlfriend, the assistant District Attorney..." His weary sigh said it all. "We can't afford to act like petulant children when we don't get our way. We can't afford people like that on our ruling councils."

He sounded so tired, so defeated. Alec rose, took both of their glasses to the bar and reached for the whiskey. "They've been getting their own way for a long time. Maybe they can tell something's about to give."

"Is it?"

"Hasn't it already?" Alec brought the Alpha his glass. "Enrica Maglieri is the first woman to sit on the Conclave. A turned wolf of two years defeated a Conclave member in a fight. The Seer has a child and isn't living under their thumb anymore. The old guard has to be in a panic."

"The old guard, as you call it, will fight to the death to preserve what they see as theirs."

It was as clear a warning as Alec was likely to get, but nothing he didn't already know. He lifted his glass and smiled. "So let's fight."

A strange black Town Car was parked outside Alec's house when he and Carmen returned from the city. Carmen tensed when the driver's door opened and a vaguely familiar man stepped out. "Who the hell is that?"

Alec shifted the truck into park and gripped the steering wheel, his knuckles white. "That would be Alexander Jacobson, Junior. My father."

That meant the impeccably coiffed woman in the pink designer suit had to be his mother. She shaded her eyes against the slanting sunlight in an effort to see inside the cab of the truck and frowned.

Carmen laid her hand on Alec's knee and attempted a joke. "Hiding down on the floorboard isn't an option, is it?"

"I told you to run for the hills." Alec carefully lifted both hands from the wheel and flexed them. "If you want me to, I'll turn around and drive away. We can stay at your place. Or a hotel."

"No. We're not going to live that way, running from them until they give up and go away." She opened the truck door and stepped out. "Hello."

Alec's mother was a handsome woman, with flawless golden skin and darkly exotic eyes. She smiled at Carmen as she picked her way across the uneven gravel, mercenary interest darting ahead of her on a wave of tight anticipation. "You must be Carmen Mendoza. I'm Geraldine Parker Jacobson, Alexander's mother."

The roiling emotions turned her stomach, but Carmen managed a smile. "Alec's told me a lot about you."

"Oh, now I doubt that." Geraldine offered Carmen her hand. "It's all right, dear. I know my son."

The truck door slammed behind them, and Alec's boots crunched on the drive as he circled the truck. Carmen felt his solid heat at her back as she shook the older woman's hand, and she stepped closer as soon as she could, leaning into him. "Welcome to New Orleans."

Tension vibrated through Alec. "You could have called."

"I did," Geraldine replied serenely. She lifted one hand, a deceptively casual gesture that had Alec's father scrambling to her side. "Miss Mendoza, allow me to introduce my husband, Junior."

The older man held out a hand and flinched when Alec growled. Geraldine pinned her son with a cool look, but her rebuke was mild. "Manners, Alexander."

A tense situation, and it was up to Carmen to defuse it and

maintain a veneer of civility. "Come on inside," she invited. "I'll make some coffee, and we can visit for a little while."

"That sounds lovely." Geraldine turned, then glanced over her shoulder. "Alex, your father would like to have a few words with you. Perhaps you boys can follow us inside?"

A quick squeeze of Alec's hand, and Carmen released him. "I'll see you in a minute."

She led the woman up the porch steps and through the front door, trying to ignore the way Geraldine's gaze seemed to linger on the beat-up furniture and bare walls. "The kitchen is just through here."

"I see." Though disapproval flavored the words, so did sadness. "He hasn't made much of a home for himself, has he?"

For Alec, his house had been a place reserved for the times when he had nowhere else to go. "He hasn't had much of a reason to."

"I hope you give him one." The older woman folded her hands together and gave Carmen a serious look. "I know you're an empath. I won't pretend that I don't have ambitions for my son. I want to see him achieve his potential. I want to see him take the power he deserves. But I've never wanted him to be unhappy."

"And when those ambitions run counter to his happiness?"

"Sometimes they will. The strongest among us make sacrifices. We should, because we get absolute loyalty in return."

The loyalty they garnered was anything but absolute, and most of them were too much like Carmen's uncle—ready and eager to abuse what they *did* get. "If you're looking to me as an ally, I should tell you right now that I will never encourage Alec to do anything that goes against his conscience or his values. It's just not going to happen."

Geraldine smiled. "You're not weak-willed. That's good. I don't need an ally, but he will. I imagine sometimes you'll rather hate me, but I was born a Parker, just like the Alpha's late wife. My mother was an Ochoa. Leadership and power is in my blood, and in my son's."

It would be easy, maybe even satisfying in a petty way, to inform her that Alec wasn't interested in doing things the old way, that he didn't believe a good leader's abilities had to be intrinsically tied to his heritage. But there was no victory in it, nothing to be gained. Perhaps this woman had done the best she could, and perhaps power was simply the only thing that mattered to her.

It made no difference either way. Alec wouldn't be fighting to bring down people like his parents—doing so would result in little more than chaos. Change would come slowly, born of struggle and difficulty.

But change *would* come.

It allowed Carmen to return the woman's smile. "I can't think of anyone who would do a better job than your son."

"Then we *are* allies, whether you believe it or not. In that, at least." Her gaze drifted around the kitchen and dining room, a tiny wrinkle appearing on her otherwise perfect forehead. "You'll undoubtedly be busy with plans for the wedding, not to mention finding a place in New York. Perhaps you'll let me hire someone to take care of the house here. A Conclave member really should have a home fit for entertaining."

So many assumptions, it was difficult to know where to begin. Carmen took a deep breath and retrieved the coffee from the cupboard. "Actually, I'm going to handle that myself. But, if you have the time... I'll admit I could use some help with the wedding plans."

"I know just the person. I'll make a few calls. Take care of everything."

Allowing Geraldine control of one day out of a lifetime was palatable. Allowing her to decorate their home wasn't. "I understand we'll be expected to stage quite the party."

"For a Conclave member?" The woman's smile widened. "Oh, it will be the wedding of the decade."

On second thought, *palatable* might be too generous. Still, she and Alec could stand it, and they'd plan their own honeymoon, assuming they had time for one. Someplace quiet, peaceful, with no one but them for miles in any given direction.

Walker Gravois was tall, dark and arguably one of the most dangerous men in New Orleans. He'd have to be, to keep up with Zola, but the lion had a further edge, one Alec recognized all too well from a decade ago—the alertness of a man accustomed to fighting for his life.

They'd all need that edge soon enough.

Alec stood next to Walker in Zola's second-floor practice area, watching Andrew and Julio take swings at each other under Zola's watchful eye. Andrew was damn near half a foot taller than Julio, but Carmen's brother was built like a brick wall—solid muscle and unrelenting strength. Alec had seen him take more than one punch that would have laid anyone else in the room flat out, but Julio seemed capable of shaking off just about anything.

"Mendoza's a tank." Walker's lazy words still carried more than a hint of bayou accent. "But his head would be rolling right now if Andrew wasn't pulling his punches."

Because Andrew knew where to punch, and when. Instinct, training—something had clicked in the younger man's head, unleashing a formidable fighter. "This is half a year as a shapeshifter. Imagine how scary he'll be in another year or two."

"Don't really want to." Walker grinned. "One more reason to keep on his good side."

It helped with one of the nagging worries about what would come with the challenge tomorrow. "I'm glad I'm not sending him out to get his ass handed to him."

The lion sobered. "Still might not be an easy fight. I heard some stuff about Hughes. Real nasty shit."

"Never thought it would be easy. I just need to know Andrew has a chance."

"Oh, plenty, provided he can hold it together in an actual fight."

Julio ducked a swing and backed away with a snort. "We can hear the deconstruction. It's very uplifting."

Alec had no sympathy. "You'll hear a whole hell of a lot worse during an actual challenge. At least we want to see your punk asses make it through in one piece."

Andrew kept coming, and this time Julio landed a punch to his gut. It wasn't enough to stop him, but it gave him pause. Julio danced back, panting. "I think Callaghan's ready."

"What about you, Julio? *You* feel ready?"

"Why wouldn't I be? Y'all left me the easy one."

"Don't get cocky, kid." Alec took a step forward and snapped to get Andrew's attention. "Enough. You need to be fresh for tomorrow."

Andrew growled and spun away, flexing his shoulders, his breathing so deep and rhythmic it had to be a conscious effort to calm himself.

Zola slashed a disapproving look at Alec, moved to Andrew's side and murmured something too soft to hear. Then she raised her voice. "Julio, with me."

She disappeared down the stairs with the two of them, leaving Alec alone with Walker, who asked, "Got time for a serious question?"

He should have seen it coming. Anyone who had the slightest interest in the power structure of New Orleans had found a chance to speak to him over the past week, starting with his father's awkward attempts at reconciliation. No one knew if he was going to win, but they knew they'd better be prepared.

Walker was more straightforward than most, and Alec appreciated it. "Worried about the new world order and where the lions fit into it?"

"You hold my marker, mine *and* Zola's." Walker nodded slowly. "Just wondering if you plan to do anything with it once you snag this spot you're after."

Alec hadn't allowed himself to envision a world beyond Friday—not yet. "Whatever I do, we'll all figure it out together. The rest of the country may not be ready for it, but it's about time the wolves in New Orleans started playing friendly with everyone else."

"I'll hold you to that." He offered his hand. "Good luck."

Clasping the lion's hand, Alec could only hope he wouldn't need it.

Chapter Twenty-One

Carmen recognized the clearing behind Alec's house instantly. The place where he'd chased her, caught her.

Kissed her.

Now, people milled about, a dozen she knew and even more she didn't. All here to bear witness to a fight that could end in death.

More than one death. Alec stood a few feet away in a loose circle with Andrew and Julio, their voices a low murmur. On the other side of them, Kat stood by Miguel, her face pale and miserable.

As more people filtered into the clearing, Alec broke away from the other wolves and strode to Carmen's side. "How you holding up, sweetheart?"

She had her empathy locked down, everything and everyone shut out, even Alec. "I'm fine, I'm—" At this point, only a resolution would make her feel better. "Jorge Ochoa just accosted me and said he's always admired me. What is that all about?"

"Sucking up." Alec slid an arm around her waist and tugged her close. "It's good. It means he's sure I'm going to win."

Most of the gathered throng seemed to be, perhaps because they sensed Cesar only fought because he had no face-saving alternative. "Be careful. Promise me you will be."

"You know it." Heedless of the crowd, he leaned down and brushed his lips over her cheek. His voice lowered to a whisper. "I need you to do something. Something only you can do."

"Anything."

"When Andrew's fighting, keep an eye on Kat." His breath

barely stirred her hair, but his body was tense against hers. "Empathically. If something happens to him, even if he's just hurt... The last time she saw someone hurt him, she killed two men. Jackson can lock her down, but he needs to know if her empathy's about to go nova."

"I can ask her," she murmured. "I'm sure she'll want me to. She wouldn't want to risk hurting everyone."

"Don't mention—" He broke off, pulled back and smiled down at her. "Who am I kidding? You know how to handle it, and you have no idea what a relief that is."

"We're in this together." She caught sight of her father across the clearing and quickly averted her gaze. "Has anyone figured it out yet? The other challenges?"

"Not that I can tell." His smile faded. "And we shouldn't give them a chance. Everyone who matters is here. It's time."

Fear spiked, intense and unavoidable, but she knew her shields would hold it in. She stretched up to kiss his cheek. "You're ready."

"Because of you." He turned his head and caught her mouth in a hard, hungry kiss that promised it wouldn't be the last. "I'll be right back," he whispered against her lips, then turned and strode toward the center of the clearing.

Carmen released a breath on a shudder and ignored two people who looked like they might try to talk to her. Instead, she walked over and slid her hand into Kat's. "Can I stand with you?"

"Yes." Kat's fingers closed around hers, so tight and desperate Carmen's hand ached. Power prickled against her shields, the pressure of an empathic gift as angry as it was vast. Next to her, Kat shuddered. "I don't know what's worse. Watching, or not watching."

"Not watching." Imagination combined with ignorance, and the *waiting*... "Not watching would be worse."

"Maybe." Kat didn't sound convinced.

Quiet fell around them as Alec reached the middle of the rough circle of onlookers. He stood there for a moment, letting tension mount, then pivoted and found Andrew in the crowd.

Andrew stepped out into the circle. He spoke low, but his voice carried through the shocked hush. "I challenge Drummond Hughes for his seat on the Southeast council."

Shocked silence.

Kat's grip grew impossibly tighter, her breathing too quick.

Alec had pointed out Drummond Hughes to Carmen. He was a lean, sharp-looking man, made of hard angles and rough edges. Disdainful brown eyes narrowed as his gaze flicked over Andrew and jerked to the Alpha. "You dragged me here to face a farce of a challenge from a mongrel bastard who was human last year?"

John Peyton's blank expression didn't change. "Even new wolves are afforded the right of challenge, Hughes."

Hughes lifted a hand and jerked at his tie, but his gaze found Cesar's. "If you and your bitch niece planned this little misdirection hoping to catch me off guard, you're going to be fucking disappointed. I accept the challenge, but he doesn't deserve a clean fight as a wolf. I'll pound his human face in."

He peeled off his shirt, revealing a number of tattoos and scars scattered over his rangy form. He'd fought before, and hard, the kinds of fights that went down in littered alleys and underground clubs. The kind where people died bloody, horrible deaths.

Andrew tossed aside his own shirt and kicked off his shoes. "Yield or die," he said simply as he walked into the circle.

Frantic murmurs rose around the perimeter as Alec backed away, leaving the space to Hughes and Andrew. Kat's breath whistled out between her teeth, and her nails pricked Carmen's hand. Andrew's name left her lips on a heartbroken whisper that no one else would hear.

Hughes growled menacingly, and Andrew didn't blink. "Then we fight."

"We fight," Hughes agreed, stalking forward. He spat on the ground at Andrew's feet and muttered something too low for Carmen to catch, his face alight with fierce anticipation.

Andrew's hand shot up and closed around the man's throat. He punched him in the face once, twice, then a third time. Hughes hung, limp and already bloody, dangling from the steely grip. "Yield."

Silver flashed, so fast that only the glinting of the sun gave away the movement. Hughes had a switchblade in one hand, the other locked around Andrew's wrist, clutching as he drove the knife toward Andrew's side.

A quick headbutt startled Hughes enough to deflect the blow, and it sliced along Andrew's side instead of digging deep. Kat gasped and clutched at Carmen as Andrew knocked the knife away and drove his fist into his opponent's face one last time. The man dropped to the grass in a heap, unmoving.

Andrew turned to face the crowd, his gaze lingering on Kat. She stared back, her heart in her eyes and naked pain on her face.

A man Carmen didn't recognize rushed to kneel by Hughes, and his face was ashen as he looked up at John Peyton. "He's dead."

The Alpha stared at the fallen council member for a moment, then seemed to shake himself. "Andrew Callaghan. What belonged to Drummond Hughes is now yours, by right of tradition."

"I don't want his stuff," Andrew rasped. "Just the seat."

A ripple of reaction ran through the crowd. Before it settled, before anyone could speak, Julio stepped forward. "I challenge Sam Hopkins for his seat on the Southeast council."

Not silence, not this time. Outright pandemonium. Someone shouted a denial. Someone else cheered, a sound cut abruptly short when a middle-aged, slightly overweight man stepped out of a knot of suit-clad men to Carmen's right. "This is outrageous. We were summoned to witness a challenge, not be challenged ourselves. This is outright duplicity."

"Quiet!" The Alpha's roar cut through the outrage. "There's no law that prohibits this, nor are you guaranteed advance notice of a challenge. It stands. Now, will you answer it or forfeit?"

Hopkins sighed, as if tremendously put-upon. "I'll answer it, of course. We'll fight as wolves, if someone would clear the field."

Several younger wolves hurried to do so as Julio began stripping out of his clothes, but he hesitated as he caught Carmen's gaze. He looked grave, almost sad, and her heart thumped painfully.

She'd seen that look a hundred times before. Her mother had called it a Cassandra moment, when she'd had a prophetic vision or dream that spelled a doom she couldn't share because doing so was useless.

Julio. There was no time to speak. The Alpha had already confirmed the challenge, and no one could stop it now.

Alec appeared at Carmen's side, claiming the hand Kat wasn't holding. "I think your uncle's trying to convince himself that the challenge was a bluff," he murmured. "That he's getting out of this."

It didn't matter, not with that bleak look in Julio's eyes. "Something's wrong."

He stiffened at her side. "What do you feel?"

"It's hard to explain." Hopkins had stripped down already, and now he knelt, shifting forms so quickly it was all a shimmering blur of magic. As a wolf he cut a menacing figure, large and powerful and absolutely vicious.

"Your brother's survived plenty of challenges," Alec said, his voice steady. Unwavering. "He can do this."

Maybe she'd imagined it all, a product of her own nervousness and tension. "He can do this."

Julio bent low and shifted too, though Hopkins barely waited until the magic settled before pouncing with a snarl. They rolled through the grass, jaws snapping, and Hopkins landed his first blow, a rake of claws across Julio's snout. He yelped and bit, closing his teeth on the older wolf's leg.

More snarling. The wolves twisted over and over, moving so fast that sometimes she couldn't follow the fight at all. Julio was powerful, but Hopkins had cunning and experience. More than one feint turned into an attack, claws digging into Julio's body again and again. Shallow cuts, but they were slowing him down.

One strong rush knocked Julio off his paws, and only a last-minute wrench of his body kept Hopkins' teeth from sinking into his throat. They bit into his chest and shoulder instead, and Julio howled.

Closing her eyes wasn't an option. Closing her eyes would mean she couldn't watch what came next.

Julio struggled to stand. Hopkins aimed his next biting attack at Julio's other front leg, and he didn't even try to avoid it. Stunned, or maybe even going into shock—

A single loud roar, and Julio closed his massive jaws on the back of Hopkins' neck.

Hopkins howled in pain. He shook. He twisted. Julio's teeth

dug deeper, until even Carmen could smell the blood in the air. The older wolf hit the ground, back legs kicking frantically, his paws scrabbling at the dirt.

A loud growl echoed through the clearing, followed by a loud crack. Hopkins twitched and fell still, and Julio slowly released him and stumbled back. Carmen breathed a sob of relief when he didn't fall.

This time, the Alpha himself bent to check Hopkins, but stopped short at the sight of his glassy, lifeless eyes. "Julio Mendoza. What belonged to Sam Hopkins is now yours, by right of tradition."

All hell broke loose.

Through the planning and the schemes, it still came down to this—bloodstained dirt and violence.

Alec stood in the spot where Andrew had caved Hughes's face in and stared at the bloodied ground. Hughes had signed his own death warrant, not only through pride but cruelty. Alec had been close enough to hear the hissed challenge, the threat that had turned Andrew from merciful to murderous. *So which one of the pretty little bitches is yours? I'll take good care of her when you're dead.*

Ten seconds for Hughes to mutter the challenge, and half that time to die. Hopkins had lasted longer, but his blood also painted the clearing, metallic and sharp, sullying the place that had been his only a short time ago. His and Carmen's, where he'd stretched her out on the grass and let himself taste the sweetness of her mouth.

The first time. By God, it wouldn't be the last.

Chaos reigned around him, loud voices and shouts, people arguing or just talking to hear their own voices, as if any of them could make sense of what had just happened. A coup, a revolution—

Not the end.

Cesar met his gaze across the twenty yards that separated them. Hope had filled the man's face earlier, the need to believe that Hughes had been right, that Alec and Carmen had used a challenge to situate friends or family on the Southeast council. Even now, he looked uncertain.

Quietly, deliberately, Alec stripped his shirt over his head and let it fall. Cesar nodded, then glanced over to where Miguel and Carmen were taking stock of Julio's quickly healing wounds.

"Enough." Peyton didn't shout, but his command quieted the crowd all the same. "Do we have another challenge?"

"Mine." Alec hooked his thumbs in his belt and waited until Cesar looked back to him. "I picked the time. You pick the method. Do we fight as men or wolves?" *Or not at all?* A futile hope, but in the face of all the violence, all the blood, maybe Cesar would come to his senses.

Cesar began to unbutton his shirt. "We look each other in the face and fight as men."

Which meant Alec would have to stare into eyes too much like Carmen's and decide whether to end the man's life. Clever and cruel—a gambit Alec couldn't allow to succeed. "You refuse to yield?"

Another short nod. "I refuse."

Alec hated the senseless waste of it almost as much as he hated how his wolf yearned for it. He was furious at being denied, ready to rend Cesar limb from limb. Rage still lived in his heart, and his knuckles itched to slam into flesh. To utterly destroy his enemy.

He sought out Carmen in the crowd and held her gaze for a moment. She met his stare evenly, with resignation but also understanding. He'd tried, and that was all he could do.

I'm sorry. He couldn't say it with words, but they didn't need words. They never had.

The blow came from nowhere, a dirty punch that slammed into the side of Alec's head with a force that rattled his teeth. Someone in the crowd gasped, and Alec ignored the sudden murmurs as he recovered from the blow, resettling his weight and facing Cesar.

Fury etched the man's face, as if being forced to fight angered him. "Couldn't back down, could you, Jacobson?"

"No." Alec shifted his attention to Cesar's shoulders, watching for the minute clues that would telegraph the man's next move. "You should back down. You've got nothing to win. All of the assets you transferred to Carmen and her brothers are gone."

It ignited something wild in the other man's eyes. "Then I

have nothing to lose." He snarled and crouched, his teeth bared.

Figured the greedy bastard would miss the point. "Unless you back the fuck down, and we'll *give some of it back.*"

"Begging for scraps from a bastard like you? I'd rather die."

Pride. Stupid, reckless pride, and Alec was going to have to kill his lover's uncle because of it. "So be it."

Time slowed, and an eternity passed before Cesar rushed him with a roar. The first punch barreled toward Alec's abdomen, not too fast to dodge but so powerful that Alec could imagine how much it would hurt when he *didn't* manage to wrench his body out of the way. Cesar was built like his nephew—not Miguel's tall, lean form, but Julio's compact muscle.

Pain prickled up Alec's spine, the wolf clawing for the magic to burst free. The precious seconds needed to rein in the beast gave Cesar another opening, which he exploited with two quick, hard punches to the solar plexus.

Alec doubled over, a snarl escaping that wasn't even mostly human. Only rage and adrenaline straightened his body, and he slammed into Cesar, exploiting the older man's moment of self-congratulation. They both staggered back, Cesar's boot slipping in the bloodstained grass, and Alec managed a half-hearted punch to the man's gut before agony sliced through him again.

This time he could *feel* the fur just under his skin. If the wolf escaped, he'd lose. Cesar could put him down like a rabid beast and no one would think twice. A shapeshifter who couldn't hold the form in which he was supposed to fight didn't deserve the honor of victory.

Change, he silently begged as Cesar regained his footing. If Cesar changed, Alec could follow. Somehow he had to convince the man to do it, to let the animal free.

Somehow he had to stay alive long enough to do it, even with his wolf clawing him up from the inside out.

Cesar punched him in the throat and wheezed a laugh. "You're dying to get to teeth and claws, aren't you? Crazy bastard. I was there." He shoved Alec away and stepped back, to the outer edge of the circle. "I was there when you challenged your cousin. You're a fucking lunatic."

The words could have been lie or truth, Alec didn't know.

He couldn't remember who had witnessed the challenge, just the pounding rage as he killed his way through the purebred bastards who had thought any human who married a shapeshifter deserved to die.

His breath rattled out, sparking bright lights in the corner of his vision. He couldn't speak in anything louder than a whisper, but it was enough. "If you were there, that explains why you're scared to fight me as a wolf."

"Scared?" Cesar's eyes narrowed, and he kicked off his boots. "Crazy is crazy, man or wolf. Either way, I'll destroy you."

Stupid is stupid, man or wolf. Anticipation shuddered inside him, and Alec fumbled with his boots, tearing out the tongue of one and nearly ripping off the sole of the other. Barefoot, he could feel the blood drying on the grass, tacky and warm.

So much pain. So much rage. He'd tried everything he knew to stop it, to let Cesar yield. So much for a bloodless revolution. It had started in blood, and now it would end that way, with two wolves fighting to rip each other open.

He could only hope Carmen would still be able to look at him when it was over.

Cesar stripped off the rest of his clothes and hunched in the grass. The change flowed over him, leaving a snarling black wolf in his place. Alec let his pants fall and followed suit a moment later, pain and fear vanishing in the wild giddy rush of power and magic.

This was who he was. The strongest wolf. A predator.

He pounced, and Cesar met him full-on in the middle of the clearing with a crash of bone and hard muscle. Heavy and bulky, but still slow. With the wolf as his giddy ally, Alec was faster.

He landed the first bite, a vicious clash of teeth that should have closed around Cesar's throat but hit his shoulder instead. Alec clenched his jaw and hung on as Cesar twisted and clawed and finally wrenched free, tearing the flesh of his shoulder in the process.

No more mercy. No more chances to yield. Alec charged, ruthlessly pressing his advantage. He tasted blood and fur as he bit down again and again, driving Cesar across the slippery grass.

Cesar growled and stumbled, fell. There was no final surge,

no last-ditch attempt to drive Alec back. He struggled to rise and failed, his eyes wide and desperate. His sides heaved, and he kicked at the grass as blood welled from his wounds.

Kill kill kill.

Alec took one trembling step backwards. His rear paw slipped on a leaf, and his claws dug into the dirt.

Bite. Rend. Win.

Another step as the wild creature inside him howled protest. They were stronger. Better. They deserved triumph, and their enemy deserved death.

He lifted his nose. Scented the wind. So many smells, so many people. But *she* was there, so attuned to him that he thought he could pick her heartbeat out of the crowd. Racing. Scared.

She would understand the need for total victory. She might even forgive him.

Alec didn't want her forgiveness and understanding. He wanted her trust and pride.

If becoming a wolf had been easy, finding the shape of a man was a trial. The wolf was confused, edgy, but with their adversary brought low he was no longer frantic. Alec called magic and felt the change, maybe a few seconds slower than usual, but soon he knelt on the cool grass. Naked. Bloodied.

He wiped his face on the back of his arm and ignored the streaks of red as he rocked to his feet and turned to find one man in the crowd. Diego Mendoza. Carmen's father. Victory lurked in his eyes—the knowledge that he had a son on the council now. Diego had risked his youngest son's life and had nearly killed his daughter, all in a quest for power, and Cesar's death would bring that power one step closer to his grasp.

Alec had no intention of letting Diego win. "Come here and get your brother. If a doctor can hold him together, he'll live."

The victory melted into confusion. Diego started forward, then stopped.

A growl rose up, and Alec didn't check it. "*Now.*"

The command broke the man's paralysis. He rushed to his brother and picked him up, blood soaking into his shirt. His gaze found Carmen, then darted to Alec and away, and he carried Cesar off through the crowd.

"Diego." Not a shout, but it cut through the unnatural

stillness nonetheless. The man froze and looked back, and Alec felt his lips turn up in what must have been a chilling smile. "You and your brother have until midnight to get the fuck out of my state. You won't come back. You won't contact your children. If they want to talk to you, they'll call you. If you have a problem with that, you can challenge me now."

The last bit of triumph faded from Diego's expression, and his lips barely moved as he spoke. "Understood."

He left in silence. Alec bent and pulled on his jeans, though he didn't bother with his shirt or boots before glancing over to where Andrew stood. The man walked forward, heeding the silent summons. Julio followed, a little more slowly, though all but the worst of his wounds had already closed.

They stood beside him, and he turned to find the final two members of the Southeast council—Alan Reed and William Levesque. Reed stood with his younger brother, both immaculately dressed and wearing identical blank expressions, though Alan's jaw tightened whenever he looked at Julio.

Levesque, on the other hand, looked scared, his hands in tight fists, his eyes darting about the crowd, as if wondering who else Alec might pull from among it to challenge the only remaining council members. Good. That fear would keep them in line for the time being.

The final murmurs around them faded as Alec fixed his attention on Reed. Traditional words and forms didn't matter—there was nothing traditional about what he was about to do. "I lay claim to leadership of the Southeast council, and the right to sit on the Conclave as its representative. You can challenge me for that right, if you'd like, but Andrew Callaghan and Julio Mendoza stand behind me."

Judging from their expressions, the men had already made the connection—anyone who cared to go against one of them would have to face all three. It wouldn't hold the challenges at bay forever, maybe not even for long, but today...

No one spoke up. No one dared.

Alec slanted a look at John Peyton. "Well?"

"Are we done?" The Alpha surveyed those gathered, but silence reigned, and he pulled himself up to his full, considerable height. "I hope everyone here will listen and heed my words. The next time anyone has grandiose ideas of the wealth and power to be garnered through our leadership, remember one thing. *Leadership*. If you can't or won't set a positive example for those you aim to lead...stay the fuck out of it."

It was better than Alec had hoped. It was damn near validation, and everyone standing there knew it. Word would spread—to the other councils, to the men who had considered vying for a spot on them. To turned wolves like Andrew, who had never in the history of their people managed to have a voice without having that voice taken away.

The culminating achievement of Alec's life, most would say, and he might even agree. But he didn't want his parents' proud smiles or the satisfaction of seeing respect in the eyes of strong leaders. He didn't want the wariness in the gazes of those who knew their own closets held too many skeletons, or even the relief and happiness that filled the faces of his friends.

He looked to Carmen, who stood still and pale, her cheeks wet with tears. When his eyes met hers, she broke away from the onlookers and ran to him.

He hurried to meet her, unwilling to touch her with blood under his bare feet. Her body barreled into his and he closed both arms, savoring her warmth. Soft and alive, she was his. His muse, his life, his lover.

His.

The crowd didn't matter. Alec buried his face in her hair and whispered, soft and rasping. "Let me feel it."

She dragged in a rough breath, and her emotions enveloped him. Fading sadness and fear, eclipsed by relief and pride and a need so sharp it almost cut.

The air left his lungs in a ragged sigh, and tension unraveled as he held her. Needed her. Loved her. This was what made it worth it, what would keep making it worth it while they fought their way up an impossible hill. The little bits of life that were nothing but sweetness and light.

Shapeshifter society had been dark for too long. Together they could turn up the sun.

Chapter Twenty-Two

Alec watched the dust cloud from the final unwanted visitor disappear down his driveway and let out a quiet breath. "So," he said to Andrew, who stood at his side, "how's it feel to go down in history?"

"Pretty damn surreal." The young wolf kicked at a piece of gravel. "Thought they'd never leave."

It had taken them three hours to extricate themselves from sycophantic new admirers and faux-sycophantic enemies hoping to spot a weakness. Julio handled it with practiced ease, though his straightforward bluntness had blanched more than a few prissy faces. Alec was used to having the well-bred wolves stare at him as if he had two heads. Andrew, though...

Well, he'd get used to it too. He'd have to. "It helps that they expect you to be as ass-backwards and uncivilized as I am. My reputation can precede both of us."

"Yeah." Andrew squinted at him in the dying light. "So, it's our job to take care of shit that goes down around here."

"Yeah. We can do it different. Make alliances with other people. Psychics, the lions, the spell casters."

The younger man nodded. "I want to look for the guy who attacked Kat. They still haven't found him, right?"

One of a hundred loose ends Alec wouldn't have time to deal with now. "No. I can probably get you the surveillance footage from his escape, and any files Jackson has. I'm sure he can help you out."

Andrew shoved his hands in his pockets. "What about you and Carmen? Headed to New York soon?"

"We'll have to spend some time there. Maybe a lot of time." Alec's gaze drifted to the other side of the drive, where Carmen stood with Julio, Miguel—and Kat. Though her hand was curled tight around Miguel's, Kat's gaze kept darting to Andrew with a furtive desperation Alec recognized—she was reassuring herself he was still in one piece.

He wanted to say something, but even he learned a lesson if you hit him with it enough times. Andrew would talk about Kat's safety, but he wouldn't talk about Kat. Alec changed the subject. "You and Julio will need to run the day-to-day stuff here. But we'll have a few months to settle in. Get the lay of the—"

"I've got to go," Andrew cut in with a rasp. When Alec looked up, he found Andrew turning away from Kat and Miguel and their joined hands. "Tell Kat that I—fuck."

Six months ago, Andrew had stood in this same driveway as a newly made wolf, every instinct focused on Kat. He'd needed her so hard he'd hurt her, uncertain in his strength and the demands of his body. Sometimes Alec thought that each second the man had spent training since had been a desperate attempt to find control, to convince himself a fragile human woman would be safe in his arms.

Six months might not be enough. Six *years* might not be enough. Alec knew all too well how terrifying it could be to ride that edge of control and wonder if letting go would hurt the person you loved.

Carmen's quiet empathy had given him peace from that fear, but there was nothing quiet about the power in Kat. Too easy to envision a thousand ways she and Andrew could hurt each other—*kill* each other. No easy answers there, and nothing he could say to comfort Andrew.

He still tried, because magic hung in the air and, for the first time in years, Alec wanted to believe in happy endings again. "Life cycles around, Andrew. Sometimes we get second chances. Maybe yours will be with her, or with someone you haven't met yet. But trust me. It can be just as good the second time around."

The declaration startled a grin out of Andrew, a broad smile that made him look, for just a moment, as laid-back and carefree as he'd been as a human. "You're a hopeless fucking romantic." He clapped Alec on the shoulder and dug his keys out of his pocket. "Congratulations."

Alec returned the smile. "Go get some rest. Sleep late tomorrow—it's the last chance you'll get for a really long time."

Andrew started to his car, and Alec turned toward Carmen again, but stopped when Jackson ambled down the porch steps. He lifted a hand, and the wizard shook his head with a laugh. "How's it feel to be the big cheese around here?"

"Always have been, man." Alec jerked his head toward the path around the house. "Walk with me?"

"Only if 'leave the gun, take the cannoli' isn't going to be part of the conversation."

Jackson seemed pretty fucking pleased with the world, though Alec supposed he'd been like that for a while. "Nah, had my fill of politics and violence for the night. I was thinking we should talk about the business."

"Uh-huh. You leaving your name on the window for show, or did you have something else in mind?"

"We were always helping people, a few at a time. Supernaturals knew they could come to our office to find me. I was thinking maybe we could take that to the next level. Do more." He smiled. "C'mon, Jackson. You know you wanna save the world with us."

Jackson pretended to consider it. "Can saving the world wait 'til I get back from Vegas?"

His partner had joked about drive-through Las Vegas weddings so often Alec didn't have to ask. He wasn't surprised by the spike of happiness—Jackson deserved the love he'd found with Mackenzie—but it was oddly relaxing not to feel the usual accompanying jealousy. "About time. You better be damned ashamed if I end up hitched before you do."

"No way. It'll take a year to plan the kind of to-do y'all have to make." Jackson glanced up at the darkening sky. "I'm engaged, you're engaged, and no one's dead. Seems like a good night for a party."

"You'd know all about it." Alec clapped his friend on the shoulder. "Why don't you go get things started? I'll be along in a few minutes."

Jackson retreated into the house, and Alec sighed and glanced back to where Carmen still talked to her brothers. All he wanted in the world was a few uninterrupted moments with her. A chance to celebrate in private.

Maybe this was his first test as the leader of their region—smile and play host when he really wanted to chase his lover through the woods and take her where he caught her. The urge had been with him since the fight, but looking at her now, in the uncertain twilight with the wind stirring her hair and her eyes alight with pleasure...

Christ, he needed her.

He always would, and maybe that was the best part of all.

The house bustled with celebration. Music spilled out of the open doors and windows into the night, following Carmen as she slipped off the back porch and went in search of Alec.

Cicadas sang through the deepening darkness as she walked through the back yard. He wouldn't return to the clearing, not so soon after the fights that had stained the ground that afternoon, and the barn was dark.

She followed her intuition more than anything, and it led her down a path she only vaguely remembered. It wasn't until she heard the lapping of water that she felt him—Alec, deep in thought. Pensive.

Wondering.

Moonlight glinted off the lake's marshy surface as she walked up to stand beside him. "Jackson and Mac went for pizza."

His fingers curled around her hand. "With the way things are carrying on in there, I hope they took a moving van to bring it back in."

"I hope they don't get too much. Five minutes after they left, Walker and his brother showed up in a catering van. They're boiling shrimp in your kitchen as we speak."

A chuckle spilled free. "Every victory party needs a voodoo chef. John makes some damn good food, you know."

"So I've heard." She leaned her head on his shoulder. "What are you thinking about?"

"You." One arm looped around her waist, and he tugged her to his chest and turned around slowly, away from the lake. "Right there. That's where it happened."

Her cheeks heated. "Where I ran like an idiot and fell asleep on you?"

"Where an empath up to her ears in feral instinct looked at me and saw safety."

It was exactly what had happened, the only reason she'd ever allowed herself the luxury of rest that day. "What should I have seen?"

"A bastard. A stranger. A killer."

"Nope." She stroked his arm soothingly. "You tricked everyone else, but there's no fooling someone who can see inside you."

"And understand what she sees." His chin came to rest on her head. "Everything's going to change now. It's good. It's been a long time coming. But God almighty, Carmen...what if I'm not up to this?"

"Up to what? Making sure that all the people in your care, under your authority, have the opportunity to live their lives as best they can? That they have help when they need it, and someone to make them stop if they step over the line or hurt others?"

"No." A whisper, fading into the night. "What if I'm not up to figuring out all the ways the world needs to change?"

There had to be things she didn't even know about yet, but she knew where to begin. "The need, Alec. There have to be people out there who need your help, even if they think they can't ask for it, or they don't know how. Start with that. Then, the injustice. Every time someone expects special treatment or a different set of rules because of money or their family name."

"We could spend the next decade on that." He kissed her temple and then her cheek, his arms tightening around her waist. "Franklin finally told me where the money's coming from, and Dade said there's more if we need it. Enough to establish clinics throughout the Southeast. I was hoping you'd organize that, since I don't know where to start."

"I have a few ideas." Carmen spun in his arms and looked up at him. "You can do this, honey. Just think of all the reasons you didn't want to have anything to do with it in the first place. You can change them now."

"*We* can change them now." A full moon hung heavy overhead, reflecting the white glint of his teeth as he grinned down at her. "I'm going to marry the hell out of you, Carmen

Mendoza. You're not getting away. You're mine."

The perfect time to lower her walls and let him back in so he could feel her delight at his words. "Good. If you marry me, I won't have to chase after you."

His amusement curled around her, followed by his pleasure at the touch of her empathy. "I thought we had it pretty well established that I'm the one chasing you, no matter where you run."

"Mmm, that's what I let you think. You chased me until I caught you." She stretched up until her lips brushed his. "Sneaky, right?"

"Mmm, sneaky. And bullshit." A soft growl, and he nipped her lower lip. "Don't pretend you don't love getting caught."

She loved everything, every part of being with him. Words failed her, but that was okay. She nuzzled her face to his and let him feel it instead, bypassing her clumsy tongue altogether.

For once he had the words, and he whispered them against her lips. "Love you. Love every damn bit of you."

Contentment flooded her, a curious peace edged with excitement. "Your house is full of people. How am I supposed to drag you to bed right now?"

"Who needs a bed?" Teeth scraped her earlobe, a sharp bite as dark promise wrapped around her. "I'll give you a head start this time."

Anticipation and arousal curled through her, smoke from a building fire. "That's wicked."

"That's nothing." He released her and took a step back. "Wicked is what happens when I catch you."

"*If* you catch me," she countered, her mind already whirling with the sensual possibilities.

"I'll always catch you." Quiet. Sure.

The rest of Carmen's life stretched before her, a continuous wave of good and bad, joyous and sorrowful, just like everyone else's. This was what would make it perfect—unwavering devotion.

Love.

She turned and ran for the barn with a laugh. Every quick stride echoed her heartbeat, singing through her blood along with the joy they shared. Alec would catch her, and she would show him the moon.

The night, the *world*, was theirs, and all that mattered was the two of them.

About the Author

How do you make a Moira Rogers? Take a former forensic science and nursing student obsessed with paranormal romance and add a computer programmer with a passion for gritty urban fantasy. To learn more about this romance-writing, crime-fighting duo, visit their webpage at www.moirarogers.com, or drop them an email at moira@moirarogers.com. (Disclaimer: crime-fighting abilities may appear only in the aforementioned fevered imaginations.)

He's the last man she should ever want.
She's the last woman he can ever have.

Crossroads
© 2010 Moira Rogers
Southern Arcana, Book 2

Coming from a family with psychic gifts, Derek Gabriel was aware of but separate from the dangers of the supernatural world, until a rogue wolf shifter stripped away his humanity. The change he barely survived didn't drive him insane, but the cultural bias against him as an inferior transformed wolf might. And it doesn't help that he's fallen for the daughter of the most powerful wolf in the country.

Almost from the moment she was born, Nicole Peyton started planning her escape from the strict confines of elite shapeshifter society, an old-fashioned world where women are valued only for their bloodlines and bank accounts. In New Orleans she has a bar she loves, friends in decidedly low places, and a smoldering sensual tension with an incredibly attractive and deliciously unsuitable man.

Their forbidden longing erupts into unbridled need—until Nick's sister burns into town with a strike team hard on her heels. Saving her means Nick has to play by the Conclave's rules...and give up the man she is growing to love.

Unless Derek does something completely crazy—issue a challenge that could shake the foundations of their world.

Warning: This book contains forbidden lust, strip poker, instinct-driven sex in odd places, devious shapeshifters, and love and loss in a world of paranormal politics and supernatural schemes.

Available now in ebook and print from Samhain Publishing.

HOT STUFF

Discover Samhain!

THE HOTTEST NEW PUBLISHER ON THE PLANET

Romance, fantasy, mystery, thriller, mainstream and more—Samhain has more selection, hotter authors, and everything's available in ebook.

Pick your favorite, sit back, and enjoy the ride! Hot stuff indeed.

SAMHAIN
PUBLISHING

WWW.SAMHAINPUBLISHING.COM

CPSIA information can be obtained at www.ICGtesting.com
Printed in the USA
LVOW042112120712

289829LV00003BA/35/P